FIC MARS

DATE DUE

NOV 05 2016			
2-22-17 ILL			
9-11-17 ILL			
			PRINTED IN U.S.A.

OATH OF OFFICE

(A LUKE STONE THRILLER—BOOK 2)

JACK MARS

ISBN: 978-1-63291-619-8

BOOKS BY JACK MARS

LUKE STONE THRILLER SERIES

ANY MEANS NECESSARY (Book #1)
OATH OF OFFICE (Book #2)
SITUATION ROOM (Book #3)

CHAPTER ONE

Luke Stone's entire body trembled. He looked at his right hand, his gun hand. He watched it shake as it rested on his thigh. He couldn't get it to stop.

He felt nauseated, sick enough to vomit. The sun was moving west, and the brightness of it made him dizzy.

Go time was in thirteen minutes.

He sat in the driver's seat of a black Mercedes M Series SUV, staring down the block at the house where his family might be. His wife, Rebecca, and his son, Gunner. His mind wanted to conjure images of them, but he wouldn't allow it. They could be somewhere else. They could be dead. Their bodies could be chained to cinderblocks with heavy shipping chains, and rotting at the bottom of Chesapeake Bay. For a split second, he saw Rebecca's hair moving like seaweed, back and forth with the current, deep underwater.

He shook his head to clear it.

Becca and Gunner had been abducted last night by agents working for the men who had taken down the United States government. It was a coup d'état, and its planners had taken Stone's family as a bargaining chip, hoping to stop him from toppling the new government in turn.

It hadn't worked.

"That's the place," Ed Newsam said.

"Is it?" Stone said. He looked at his partner in the passenger seat. "You know that?"

Ed Newsam was big, black, and rippling muscle. He looked like a linebacker in the NFL. There was no softness to him anywhere. He wore a close-cropped beard and a flat-top haircut. His massive arms were dark with tattoos.

Ed had killed six men yesterday. He had been strafed by machine gun fire. A flak vest had saved his life, but a stray bullet had found his pelvis. Cracked it. Ed's wheelchair was in the back of the car. Neither Ed nor Luke had slept in two days.

Ed looked at the tablet computer in his hand. He shrugged.

"That's definitely the house. If they're in there or not, I don't know. I guess we're about to find out."

The house was an old three-bedroom beach house, a little bit rambling, three blocks from the Atlantic Ocean. It fronted the bay and had a small dock. You could pull a thirty-foot boat right up behind it, walk ten feet of dock, climb a few steps, and enter the house. Night was a good time to do this.

The CIA had used the place as a safe house for decades. In the summer, Dewey Beach was so crowded with vacationers and college-age party types, the spooks could sneak Osama bin Laden in there and no one would notice.

"When the hit comes, they don't want us in on it," Ed said. "We don't even have an assignment. You know that, right?"

Luke nodded. "I know."

The FBI was the lead agency on this raid, along with a Delaware state police SWAT team that had come down from Wilmington. They had been quietly amassing in the neighborhood for the past hour.

Luke had seen these things unfold a hundred times. A Verizon FIOS van was parked down at the end of the block. That had to be FBI. A fishing boat was anchored about a hundred yards out in the bay. Also feds. In a few minutes, at 4 p.m., that boat would make a sudden run right at the safe house dock.

At the same instant, an armored truck from SWAT would come roaring down this street. Another would come down the street one block over, in case anyone tried to make an escape through the backyards. They were going to hit hard and fast, and they would leave no wiggle room at all.

Luke and Ed were not invited. Why would they be? The cops and the feds were going to run this thing by the book. The book said Luke had no objectivity. It was his family in there. If he went in, he would lose his head. He would put himself, his family, the other officers, and the entire operation at risk. He shouldn't even be on this street right now. He shouldn't be anywhere near here. That's what the book said.

But Luke knew the type of men inside that house. He probably knew them better than the FBI or SWAT. They were desperate right now. They had gone all-in on a government overthrow, and the plot had failed. They were looking down the barrel at treason, kidnapping, and murder charges. Three hundred people had died in the coup attempt, and counting, including the President of the United States. The White House was destroyed. It was radioactive. It might be years before it was rebuilt.

Luke had been with the new President last night and this morning. She was not in the mood for mercy. The law was on the books: treason was punishable by death. Hanging. Firing squad. The country might go old-school for a little while, and if so, men like the ones inside that house were going to get the brunt of it.

All the same, they wouldn't panic. These were not common criminals. They were highly skilled and trained men, men who had seen combat, and who had won out against heavy odds. Surrender was not part of their vocabulary. They were very, very clever, and they would be hard to dislodge. A paint-by-numbers SWAT team raid wasn't going to be good enough.

If Luke's wife and child were in there, and if the men inside managed to fight off the first attack... Luke refused to think about it.

It wasn't an option.

"What are you going to do?" Ed said.

Luke stared out the window at the blue sky. "What would you do, if you were me?"

Ed didn't miss a beat. "I'd go in hard as I could. Kill every single man I saw."

Luke nodded. "Me too."

*

The man was a ghost.

He stood in an upstairs bedroom at the back of the old beach house, staring at his prisoners. A woman and a little boy, tucked away in a room with no windows. They sat side by side in folding chairs, their hands cuffed behind them, their ankles cuffed together. They wore black hoods over their heads so they couldn't see. The man had left them without gags in their mouths, so the woman could speak quietly to her son and keep him calm.

"Rebecca," the man said, "we might have some excitement here in a little while. If we do, I want you and Gunner to stay quiet. You're not to scream or call out. If you do, I'll have to come in here and kill you both. Is that understood?"

"Yes," she said.

"Gunner?"

Beneath his hood, the boy made a sort of croaking noise.

"He's too frightened to speak," the woman said.

"That's good," the man said. "He should be afraid. He's a smart boy. And a smart boy won't do anything stupid, will he?"

3

The woman didn't answer. Satisfied, the man nodded to himself.

Once, the man had a name. Then, over time, he had ten names. Now he didn't bother with names. He introduced himself as "Brown," if such niceties were necessary. Mr. Brown. He liked it. It made him think of dead things. Dead leaves in fall. Barren, burned out woods, months after a fire had destroyed everything.

Brown was forty-five years old. He was big, and he was still strong. He was an elite soldier, and he kept himself that way. He had learned to withstand pain and exhaustion many years ago in Navy SEAL School. He had learned how to kill, and not be killed, in a dozen hot spots around the world. He had learned how to torture at the School of the Americas. He had put what he learned into practice in Guatemala and El Salvador, and later, at Bagram Air Force Base and Guantanamo Bay.

Brown didn't work for the CIA anymore. He didn't know who he worked for and he didn't care. He was a freelancer, and he got paid by the job.

The money, and it was a lot of money, came in cash. Canvas bags full of brand new hundred-dollar bills left in the trunk of a rental sedan at Reagan National Airport. A leather briefcase with half a million dollars in random tens, twenties, and fifties from Series 1974 and 1977 waiting in a locker at a gym in suburban Baltimore. They were old bills, but they had never been touched before, and they were as good as any General Grant minted in 2013.

Two days ago, Brown got a message to come to this house. It was his house until further notice, and his job to run it. If anyone showed up, he was in charge. Okay. Brown was good at many things, and one of them was being the boss.

Yesterday morning, somebody blew up the White House. The President and Vice President escaped to the bunker at Mount Weather, with about half the civilian government. Last night, somebody blew up Mount Weather with all the kiddies still inside. A couple hours later, a new President took the stage, the former Vice President. Nice.

A total flip, from liberals running the show to conservatives, and it all happened in the course of one day. Naturally, the public needed someone to blame, and the new masters pointed their fingers at Iran.

Brown waited up to see what happened next.

Late in the night, four guys pulled up to the back dock in a motorboat. The guys brought this woman and child. The prisoners

4

belonged to someone named Luke Stone. Apparently, people thought Stone might turn into a problem. This morning, it became clear just how much of a problem he was.

When the smoke cleared, the whole overthrow had gone belly up in a matter of hours. And there was Luke Stone, standing astride the rubble.

But Brown still had Stone's wife and kid, and he had no idea what to do with them. Communications were down, to say the least. He probably should have killed them and abandoned the house, but instead he waited for orders that never came. Now, there was a Verizon FIOS van out in front of the house, and a nondescript flying deck fishing boat maybe a hundred meters out on the water.

Did they think he was that dumb? Jesus. He could see them coming a mile away.

He stepped into the hallway. Two men stood there. Both of them mid-thirties, crazy hair and long beards—lifetime special operators. Brown knew the look. He also knew the look in their eyes. It wasn't fear.

It was excitement.

"What's the problem?" Brown said.

"In case you didn't notice, we're about to get hit."

Brown nodded. "I know."

"I can't go to jail," Beard #1 said.

Beard #2 nodded. "I can't either."

Brown was with them. Even before this happened, if the FBI found out his real identity, he was looking at multiple life sentences. Now? Forget it. It might take months for them to identify him, and in the meantime he would sit in a county jail somewhere, surrounded by low-rent hoodlums. And the way things were right now, he couldn't bank on an angel to step in and make it all go away.

Still, he felt calm. "This place is harder than it looks."

"Yeah, but there's no way out," Beard #1 said.

True enough.

"So we hold them off, and see if we can negotiate something. We've got hostages." Brown didn't believe it as soon as the words were out of his mouth. Negotiate what, safe passage? Safe passage to where?

"They're not going to negotiate with us," Beard #1 said. "They'll tell us lies until a sniper gets a clear shot."

"Okay," Brown said. "So what do you guys want to do?"

"Fight," Beard #2 said. "And if we get rolled back, I want to come up here and put a bullet in the heads of our guests before I get one myself."

Brown nodded. He'd been in a lot of tight spots before, and he had always found a way out. There might still be a way out of this one. He thought so, but he didn't tell *them* that. Only so many rats could make it off a sinking ship.

"Fair enough," he said. "That's what we'll do. Now take up your positions."

*

Luke shrugged into his heavy tactical vest. The weight settled onto him. He fastened the vest's waistband, taking a little of the weight off his shoulders. His cargo pants were lined with lightweight Dragon Skin armor. On the ground at his feet was a combat helmet with an aftermarket facemask attached.

He and Ed stood behind the open rear door of the Mercedes. The smoked window of the rear door hid them somewhat from the windows of the house. Ed leaned against the car for support. Luke pulled Ed's wheelchair out, opened it, and placed it on the ground.

"Great," Ed said and shook his head. "I got my chariot, and I'm ready for battle." A sigh escaped from him.

"Here's the deal," Luke said. "You and I are not playing around. When SWAT goes in, they'll probably put guns on the porch door that faces the dock, and swing a hammer on that backyard door. I don't think it's going to work. My guess is the backyard door is double steel and doesn't budge, and the porch is going to be a firestorm. We've got ghosts in there, and they're not going to have the doors covered? Come on. I think our guys are going to get pushed back. Hopefully nobody gets hit."

"Amen," Ed said.

"I'm going to walk up behind the initial action. With this." Luke lifted an Uzi submachine gun out of the trunk.

"And this." He pulled out a Remington 870 pump shotgun.

He felt the heft of both guns. They were heavy. The weight was reassuring.

"If the cops get in and secure the place, great. If they can't get in, we don't have any time to waste. The Uzi's got Russian-made overpressure armor-piercing rounds. They should punch through most body armor the bad guys could be wearing. I've got half a dozen magazines fully loaded, just in case I need them. If I end up in a hallway fight, I'll go to the shotgun. Then I'm going to be shredding legs, arms, necks, and heads."

"Yeah, but how do you plan on getting inside?" Ed said. "If the cops aren't in, how do you get in?"

Luke reached into the SUV and pulled out an M79 grenade launcher. It looked like a big sawed-off shotgun with a wooden stock. He handed it to Ed.

"You're going to get me in."

Ed took the gun in his large hands. "Beautiful."

Luke reached in and grabbed two boxes of M406 grenades, four to a box.

"I want you to move up the block behind the parked cars on the other side of the street. Just before I get there, rip me open a nice hole right through the wall. Those guys are going to be focused on the doors, expecting the cops to try to do a knock-down. We're going to put a grenade right in their laps instead."

"Nice," Ed said.

"After the first one hits, give them one more for good luck. Then get yourself down and out of harm's way."

Ed ran his hand along the grenade launcher's barrel. "You think it's safe to do it this way? I mean… that's your people in there."

Luke stared at the house. "I don't know. But in most cases I've seen, the prisoner room is either upstairs or in the basement. We're on the beach and the water table is too high for a basement. So I'll guess that if they're in this house, they're upstairs, in that far right corner, the one with no windows."

He checked his watch. 4:01 p.m.

Right on cue, a blue armored car came roaring around the corner. Luke and Ed watched it pass. It was a Lenco BearCat with steel armor, gunports, spotlights, and all the trimmings.

Luke felt the tickle of something in his chest. It was fear. It was dread. He had spent the past twenty-four hours pretending that he had no emotion about the fact that hired killers were holding his wife and son. Every so often, his real feelings about it threatened to break through. But he stomped them back down again.

There was no room for feelings right now.

He looked down at Ed. Ed sat in his wheelchair, grenade launcher on his lap. Ed's face was hard. His eyes were cold steel. Ed was a man who lived his values, Luke knew. Those values included loyalty, honor, courage, and the application of overwhelming force on the side of what was good, and right. Ed was not a monster. But at this moment, he may as well be.

"You ready?" Luke said.

Ed face's barely changed. "I was born ready, white man. The question is are you ready?"

Luke loaded up his guns. He picked up his helmet. "I'm ready."

He slipped the smooth black helmet over his head, and Ed did the same with his. Luke pulled his visor down. "Intercoms on," he said.

"On," Ed said. It sounded like Ed was inside Luke's own head. "I hear you loud and clear. Now let's do this." Ed started to roll away across the street.

"Ed!" Luke said to the man's back. "I need a big hole in that wall. Something I can walk through."

Ed raised a hand and kept going. A moment later he was behind the line of parked cars across the street, and out of sight.

Luke left the trunk door up. He crouched behind it. He patted all his weapons. He had an Uzi, a shotgun, a handgun, and two knives, if it came to that. He took a deep breath and looked up at the blue sky. He and God were not exactly on speaking terms. It would help if one day they could get on the same page about a few things. If Luke had ever needed God, he needed Him now.

A fat, white, slow-moving cloud floated across the horizon.

"Please," Luke said to the cloud.

A moment later, the shooting started.

CHAPTER TWO

Brown stood in the small control room just off the kitchen.

On the table behind him sat an M16 rifle and a Beretta nine-millimeter semi-automatic, both fully loaded. There were three hand grenades and a ventilator mask. There was also a black Motorola walkie-talkie.

A bank of six small closed-circuit TV screens was mounted on the wall above the table. The images came to him in black and white. Each screen gave Brown a real-time feed from cameras planted at strategic points around the house.

From here, he could see the outside of the sliding glass doors as well as the top of the ramp to the boat dock; the dock itself and the approach to it from the water; the outside of the double-reinforced steel door on the side of the house; the foyer on the inside of that door; the upstairs hallway and its street-facing window; and last but not least, the windowless interrogation room upstairs where Luke Stone's wife and son sat quietly strapped to their chairs, hoods covering their heads.

There was no way to take this house by surprise. With the keyboard on the desk, he took manual control of the camera on the dock. He raised the camera just a hair until the fishing boat out on the bay was centered, then he zoomed in. He spotted three flak-jacketed cops outside on the gunwales. They were pulling anchor. In a minute, that boat was going to come zooming in here.

Brown switched to the back porch view. He turned that camera to face the side of the house. He could just get the front grille of the cable van across the street. No matter. He had a man at the upstairs window with the van in his gun sights.

Brown sighed. He supposed the right thing to do would be to raise these cops on the radio and tell them he knew what they were doing. He could bring the woman and boy downstairs, and stand them up right in front of the sliding glass door so everybody could see what was on offer.

Rather than start with a firefight and bloodbath, he could skip straight to fruitless negotiations. He might even spare a few lives that way.

He smiled to himself. But that would spoil all the fun, wouldn't it?

He checked the foyer view. He had three men downstairs, the two Beards and a man he thought of as the Australian. One man

9

covered the steel door, and two men covered the rear sliding glass door. That glass door and the porch outside of it were the main vulnerabilities. But there was no reason the cops would ever get that far.

He reached behind him and picked up the walkie-talkie.

"Mr. Smith?" he said to the man crouched near the open upstairs window.

"Mr. Brown?" came a sarcastic voice. Smith was young enough that he still thought aliases were funny. On the TV screen, Smith gave a wave of his hand.

"What's the van doing?"

"It's rocking and rolling. Looks like they're having an orgy in there."

"Okay. Keep your eyes open. Do not… I repeat… Do not let anyone reach the porch. I don't need to hear from you. You have authorization to engage. Copy?"

"I copy that," Smith said. "Fire at will, baby."

"Good man," Brown said. "Maybe I'll see you in hell."

Just then, the sound of a heavy vehicle came in from the street. Brown ducked low. He crawled into the kitchen and crouched by the window. Outside, an armored car pulled up in front of the house. The heavy back door clunked open, and big men in body armor began to pile out.

A second passed. Two seconds. Three. Eight men had gathered on the street.

Smith opened up from the skies above.

Duh-duh-duh-duh-duh-duh.

The power of the gunshots made the floorboards vibrate.

Two of the cops hit the ground instantly. Others ducked back inside the truck, or behind it. Behind the armored car, three men burst out of the cable TV van. Smith lit them up. One of them, caught by a rain of bullets, did a crazy dance in the street.

"Excellent, Mr. Smith," Brown said into the Motorola.

One of the police had gotten halfway across the street before he was shot. Now he was crawling toward the near sidewalk, maybe hoping to reach the shrubbery in front of the house. He wore body armor. He was probably hit where the gaps were, but he might still be a threat.

"You've got one on the ground still coming! I want him out of the game."

Almost immediately, a hail of bullets struck the man, making his body twitch and shudder. Brown saw the kill shot in slow motion. It hit the man in the gap at the back of his neck, between the top of his torso armor and the bottom of his helmet. A spray cloud of blood filled the air and the man went completely still.

"Nice shooting, Mr. Smith. Lovely shooting. Now keep them all locked down."

Brown slipped back into the command room. The fishing boat was pulling up. Before it even reached the dock, a team of black-jacketed and helmeted men began to jump across.

"Masks on downstairs!" Brown said. "Incoming through that sliding door. Prepare to return fire."

"Affirmative," someone said.

The invaders took up positions on the dock. They carried heavy armored ballistic shields and got low behind them. A man popped up and raised a tear gas gun. Brown reached for his own mask and watched the projectile fly toward the house. It hit the glass door and punched through into the main room.

A different man popped up and fired another canister. Then a third man fired yet another. All the tear gas canisters burst through the glass and into the house. The glass door was gone. On Brown's screen, the area near the foyer began to fill with smoke.

"Status downstairs?" Brown said. A few seconds passed.

"Status!"

"No worries, matey," the Australian said. "A little smoke, so what? We've got our masks on."

"Fire when ready," Brown said.

He watched as the men at the sliding door opened fire toward the dock. The invaders were pinned down out there. They couldn't get up from behind their ballistic shields. And Brown's men had stacks of ammunition ready.

"Good shooting, boys," he said into the walkie-talkie. "Be sure to sink their boat while you're at it."

Brown smirked to himself. They could hold out here for days.

*

It was a rout. There were men down all over the place.

Luke walked toward the house, scanning carefully. The worst of the shooting was coming from a man in the upstairs window. He was making Swiss cheese out of these cops. Luke was close to the

11

side of the house. From his angle he didn't have a shot, but the man also probably couldn't see him.

As Luke watched, the bad guy finished a downed cop with a kill shot to the back of the neck.

"Ed, how's your look on that upstairs shooter?"

"I can put one right down his throat. Pretty sure he doesn't see me over here."

Luke nodded. "Let's do that first. It's getting messy out here."

"You sure you want that?" Ed said.

Luke studied the upstairs. The windowless room was on the far side of the house from the sniper's nest.

"I'm still banking they're in that room with no windows," he said.

Please.

"Just say the word," Ed said.

"Go."

Luke heard the distinctive hollow report of the grenade launcher.

Doonk!

A missile flew from behind the line of cars across the street. It had no arc—just a sharp flat line zooming up on a diagonal. It hit right where the window was. A split second passed, then:

BANG.

The side of the house blew outward, chunks of wood, glass, steel, and fiberglass. The gun in the window went silent.

"Nice, Ed. Real nice. Now give me that hole in the wall."

"What do you say?" Ed said.

"Pretty please."

Luke raced around and ducked behind a car.

Doonk!

Another flat line zoomed by, four feet above the ground. It hit the side of the house like a car crash, and punched a gaping wound through the wall. A fireball erupted inside, spitting smoke and debris.

Luke nearly jumped up.

"Hold on," Ed said. "One more on its way."

Ed fired again, and this one went deep into the house. Red and orange flared through the hole. The ground trembled. Okay. It was time to go.

Luke climbed to his feet and started running.

The first explosion was above his head. The entire house shook from it. Brown glanced at the upstairs hallway on his screen.

The far end of it was gone. The spot where Smith had been stationed was no longer there. There was just a ragged hole where the window and Mr. Smith used to be.

"Mr. Smith?" Brown said. "Mr. Smith, are you there?"

No answer.

"Anybody see where that came from?"

"You're the eyes, Yank," came a voice.

They had trouble.

A few seconds later, a rocket hit the front of the house. The shockwave knocked Brown off his feet. The walls were collapsing. The kitchen ceiling suddenly caved in. Brown lay on the floor among falling junk. This had gone the opposite of what he expected. Cops rammed down doors—they didn't fire rockets through walls.

Another rocket hit, this one deep inside the house. Brown covered his head. Everything shook. The whole house could come down.

A moment passed. Someone was screaming now. Otherwise, it was quiet. Brown jumped up and ran for the stairs. On the way out of the room, he grabbed his handgun and one grenade.

He passed through the main room. It was carnage, a slaughterhouse. The room was on fire. One of the Beards was dead. More than dead—blown to shredded pieces all over the place. The Australian had panicked and taken his mask off. His face was covered in dark blood, but Brown couldn't tell where he was hit.

"I can't see!" the man screamed. "I can't see!"

His eyes were wide open.

A man in body armor and helmet stepped calmly through the shattered wall. He quieted the Australian with an ugly blat of automatic gunfire. The Australian's head popped apart like a cherry tomato. He stood without a head for a second or two, and then dropped bonelessly to the floor.

The second Beard lay on the ground near the back door, the double-steel reinforced door which Brown had been so delighted about just a few moments ago. The cops were never going to get through that door. Beard #2 was cut up from the explosion, but still in the fight. He dragged himself to the wall, propped himself upright, and reached for the gun strapped at his shoulder.

The intruder shot Beard #2 in the face at point-blank range. Blood and bone and gray matter splattered against the wall.

Brown turned and stormed up the stairs.

*

The air was thick with smoke, but Luke saw the man bolt for the stairs. He glanced around the room. Everyone else was dead.

Satisfied, he took the stairs at a run. His own breathing sounded loud in his ears.

He was vulnerable here. The stairs were so narrow it would be the perfect time for someone to spray gunfire down on him. No one did.

At the top, the air was clearer than below. To his left was the shattered window and wall where the sniper had taken position. The sniper's legs were on the floor. His tan work boots pointed in opposite directions. The rest of him was gone.

Luke went right. Instinctively, he ran to the room at the far end of the hall. He dropped his Uzi in the hallway. He took the pump shotgun off his shoulder and dropped that, too. He slid his Glock from its holster.

He turned left and into the room.

Becca and Gunner sat tied to two folding chairs. Their arms were pulled behind their backs. Their hair was wild, as if some funny person had just mussed it with his hand. Indeed, a man stood behind them. He dropped two black hoods to the floor and placed the muzzle of his gun to the back of Becca's head. He crouched very low, putting Becca in front of him as a human shield.

Becca's eyes were very wide. Gunner's were tightly closed. He was weeping uncontrollably. His entire body shook with silent sobs. He had wet his pants.

Was it worth it?

To see them like this, helpless, in terror, had it been worth it? Luke had helped stop a coup d'état the night before. He had saved the new President from almost certain death, but was it worth this?

"Luke?" Becca said, as if she didn't recognize him.

Of course she didn't. He pulled his helmet off.

"Luke," she said. She gasped, maybe in relief. He didn't know. People made sounds in extreme moments. They didn't always mean anything.

Luke raised his gun, sighting it directly between Becca's and Gunner's heads. The man was good. He wasn't giving Luke anything to hit. But Luke left the gun pointed there anyway. He watched patiently. The man wouldn't always be good. No one was good forever.

Luke felt nothing right now, nothing but... dead... calm.

He did not feel relief flooding his system. This wasn't over yet.

"Luke *Stone*?" the man said. He grunted. "Amazing. You're everywhere at once these past couple of days. Is it really you?"

Luke could picture the man's face from the moment before he ducked behind Becca. He had a thick scar across his left cheek. He had a flat-top haircut. He had the sharp features of someone who had spent his life in the military.

"Who wants to know?" Luke said.

"They call me Brown."

Luke nodded. A name that wasn't a name. The name of a ghost. "Well, Brown, how do you want to do this?"

Below them, Luke could hear the police storming the house.

"What options do you see?" Brown said.

Luke stood without moving, his gun waiting for that shot to appear. "I see two options. You can either die right this minute or, if you're lucky, in prison a long time from now."

"Or I could blow your lovely wife's brains all over you."

Luke didn't answer. He just pointed that gun. His arm wasn't tired. It would never get tired. But the cops were coming upstairs in a minute, and that was going to change the equation.

"And you'll be dead one second later."

"True," Brown said. "Or I could do this."

His free hand dropped a grenade into Becca's lap.

As Brown dashed away, Luke dropped the gun and dove for it. In one series of motions, he picked up the grenade, flipped it toward the back wall of the room, collapsed the two chairs, and pushed both Becca and Gunner to the ground.

Becca screamed.

Luke gathered them together, rough with it, no time for gentleness. He pushed them closer and closer, mounted them, blanketed them with his body, and with his armor. He tried to make them disappear.

For a split second, nothing happened. Maybe it was a ruse. The grenade was a fake, and now the man called Brown would have the drop on him. He would kill them all.

BOOOOOM!

The explosion came, deafening in the close confines of the room. Luke gathered them closer. The floor shook. Shards of metal sprayed him. He ducked his head low. Bare flesh on his neck was torn away. He covered them and held them.

A moment passed. His little family trembled beneath him, frozen in shock and fear, but alive.

Now it was time to kill that bastard. Luke's Glock lay on the floor beside him. He grabbed it and jumped to his feet. He turned.

A huge ragged hole had been blown through the back of the room. Through it, Luke could see daylight and blue sky. He could see the dark green water of the bay. And he could see the man called Brown was gone.

Luke approached the hole from an angle, using the remnants of the wall to shield himself. The edges were a shredded mix of wood, broken drywall, and ripped up fiberglass insulation. He expected to see a body on the ground, possibly in several bloody pieces. No. There was no body.

For a split second, Luke thought he saw a splash. A man might have dived into the bay and disappeared. Luke blinked to clear his eyes, then looked again. He wasn't sure.

Either way, the man called Brown was gone.

CHAPTER THREE

9:03 p.m.
Bethesda Navy Medical Center – Bethesda, Maryland

The light of the laptop computer flickered in the semi-darkness of the private hospital room. Luke sat slumped in an uncomfortable armchair, staring at the screen, a pair of white ear buds extending from the computer to his ears.

He was almost breathless with gratitude and relief. His chest hurt from gasping for air the past four or five hours. He sometimes thought about crying, but he hadn't done so yet. Maybe later.

There were two beds in the room. Luke had pulled some strings, and now Becca and Gunner lay in the beds, sleeping deeply. They were under sedation, but it didn't matter. Neither of them had slept a wink between the time they were abducted and the moment when Luke stormed the safe house.

They had spent eighteen hours in sheer terror. Now they were out cold. And they were going to be out for a good long while.

Neither one of them had been hurt. True, they were going to carry emotional scars from this, but physically, they were fine. The bad guys did not harm the merchandise. Maybe Don Morris's hand had been in there somewhere, protecting them.

He gave a brief thought to Don. Now that events had played out, it seemed right to do so. Don had been Luke's greatest mentor. Since the time Luke joined Delta Force at twenty-seven years old, until early this morning, twelve years later, Don had been a constant presence in Luke's life. When Don first created the FBI Special Response Team, he had made a place for Luke. More than that—he had recruited Luke, wined him, dined him, and stole him away from Delta.

But Don had turned at some point, and Luke never saw it coming. Don had been among the conspirators who had tried to topple the government. One day, Luke might understand Don's reasoning for all this, but not today.

On the computer screen in front of him, a live stream played from the packed media room of what they were calling "the New White House." The room had at most a hundred seats. It had a gradual slope, upward from the front, as though it doubled as a movie theater. Every seat was taken. Every space along the back wall was taken. Dense throngs of people stood in the wings on both sides of the stage.

Images of the house itself briefly appeared on the screen. It was the beautiful, turreted and gabled Queen Anne–style 1850s mansion on the grounds of the Naval Observatory in Washington, DC. And it was indeed white, for the most part.

Luke knew something about it. For decades, it had been the official residence of the Vice President of the United States. Now, and for the foreseeable future, it was the home and office of the President.

The screen cut back to the media room. As Luke watched, the President herself came to the podium: Susan Hopkins, the former Vice President, who had taken the oath of office this very morning. This was her first address to the American people as President. She wore a dark blue suit, her blonde hair in a bob. The suit seemed bulky, which meant she was wearing bulletproof material beneath it.

Her eyes were somehow both stern and soft—her media people had probably coached her to look angry, brave, and hopeful all at once. A top-flight makeup artist had covered the burns on her face. Unless you knew where to look, you wouldn't even see them. Susan, as she had been her entire life, was the most beautiful woman in the room.

Her resume thus far was impressive. It included teenage supermodel, young wife of a technology billionaire, mom, United States Senator from California, Vice President, and now, suddenly, President. The former President, Thomas Hayes, had died in a fiery underground inferno, and Susan herself was lucky to be alive.

Luke had saved her life yesterday, twice.

He undid the mute feature on his computer.

She was surrounded by bulletproof glass panels. Ten Secret Service agents stood on the stage with her. The crowd of reporters in the room was giving her a standing ovation. The TV announcers were speaking in hushed tones. The camera panned, finding Susan's husband, Pierre, and their two daughters.

Back to the President: she was holding her hands up, asking for quiet. Despite herself, she broke into a bright smile. The crowd erupted again. That was the Susan Hopkins they knew: the enthusiastic, gung-ho queen of daytime talk shows, of ribbon-cutting ceremonies and political rallies. Now her small hands made fists and she raised them high above her head, almost like a referee indicating a touchdown. The audience was loud and grew louder.

The camera panned. Hardened Washington, DC, and national journalists, one of the most jaded groups of people known to man, stood with moist eyes. Some of them were openly weeping. Luke caught a brief glimpse of Ed Newsam in a dark pin-striped suit, leaning on crutches. Luke had been invited as well, but he preferred to be here in this hospital room. He wouldn't consider being anywhere else.

Susan came to the microphone. The audience quieted, just enough so she could be heard. She put her hands on the podium, as if steadying herself.

"We're still here," she said, her voice shaking.

Now the crowd exploded.

"And you know what? We're not going anywhere!"

Deafening noise came through the ear buds. Luke turned the sound down.

"I want…" Susan said, and then stopped again. She waited. The cheering went on and on. Still she waited. She stepped back from the microphone, smiled, and said something to the very tall Secret Service man standing next to her. Luke knew him a little. His name was Charles Berg. He had also saved her life yesterday. Over an eighteen-hour span, Susan's life had been on the line almost nonstop.

When the crowd noise died somewhat, Susan stepped back to the podium.

"Before we talk, I want you to do something with me," she said. "Will you? I want to sing 'God Bless America.' It's always been one of my favorite songs." Her voice cracked. "And I want to sing it tonight. Will you sing it with me?"

The crowd roared its assent.

Then she did it. All by herself, in a small, untrained voice, she did it. There was no celebrity singer there with her. There were no world-class musicians accompanying her. She sang, just her, in front of a room full of people, and with hundreds of millions of people watching worldwide.

"'God bless America,'" she began. She sounded like a little girl. "'Land that I love.'"

It was like watching someone walk out onto a high wire between buildings. It was an act of faith. Luke's throat felt tight.

The crowd did not leave her out there by herself. Instantly, they began to flood in. Better, stronger voices joined her. And she led them.

Outside the darkened room, somewhere down the hall in the quiet of an after-hours hospital, people on duty began to sing.

In the bed next to Luke, Becca stirred. Her eyes opened and she gasped. Her head darted left and right. She seemed ready to spring out of the bed. She saw Luke there, but her eyes showed no recognition.

Luke took out his ear buds. "Becca," he said.

"Luke?"

"Yes."

"Can you hold me?"

"Yes."

He closed the cover to the laptop. He slid into the bed next to her. Her body was warm. He gazed at her face, as beautiful as any supermodel's. She pressed herself tight against him. He held her in his strong arms. He held her so close, it was almost as if he wanted to become her.

This was better than watching the President.

Down the hall, and everywhere in the country, in bars, in restaurants, in homes, and in cars, the people sang.

CHAPTER FOUR

June 7th
8:51 p.m.
Galveston National Laboratory, campus of the University of Texas Medical Branch – Galveston, Texas

"Working late again, Aabha?" a voice said from Heaven.

The exotic, black-haired woman was almost ethereal in her beauty. Indeed, her name was a Hindi word for beautiful.

She was startled by the voice, and her body jerked involuntarily. She stood, wearing a white airtight containment suit, deep inside the Biosafety Level 4 facility at the Galveston National Laboratory. The suit which protected her also made her look almost like an astronaut on the moon. She always hated wearing the suit. She felt trapped inside of it. But it was what her job demanded.

Her suit was attached to a yellow hose which descended from the ceiling. The hose continually pumped clean air from outside the facility into the containment suit. Even if the suit ruptured, the positive pressure from the hose ensured that none of the laboratory air could get inside.

BSL-4 labs were the highest security laboratories in the world. Inside them, scientists studied deadly, highly infectious organisms that posed a severe threat to public health and safety. Right now, in her blue-gloved hand, Aabha held a sealed vial of the most dangerous virus known to man.

"You know me," she said. Her suit had a microphone that would carry her voice to the guard watching her on closed circuit television. "I'm a night owl."

"I know it. I've seen you here a lot later than this."

She pictured the man watching over her. Tom was his name. He was overweight, middle-aged, she thought divorced. Just her and him, alone inside this big empty building at night, and he had very little to do but look at her. It would give her the creeps if she thought about it too much.

She had just removed the vial from the freezer. Moving carefully, she approached the biosafety cabinet, where under normal circumstances, she would open the vial and study its contents.

Tonight wasn't normal circumstances. Tonight was the culmination of years of preparation. Tonight was what Americans called the Big Game.

Her co-workers at the lab, including Tom the night watchman, thought the beautiful young woman's name was Aabha Rushdie.

It wasn't.

They thought she had been born into a wealthy family in the great city of Delhi, in northern India, and that her family had moved to London when she was a young girl. It was laughable. Nothing like that had ever happened to her.

They thought she had obtained a Ph.D. in microbiology and extensive BSL-4 training from King's College, London. This wasn't true either, but it might as well be. She knew as much about handling bacteria and viruses as any Ph.D. candidate, if not more.

The vial she held contained a freeze-dried sample of the Ebola virus, which had wreaked such havoc in Africa in recent years. If it were just an Ebola virus sample taken from a monkey, or a bat, or even a human victim... that alone would make it very, very dangerous to handle. But there was much more to the story.

Aabha glanced at the digital clock on the wall. 8:54 p.m. One minute to go. She need only delay for a very short time longer.

"Tom?" she said.

"Yes?" came the voice.

"Did you watch the President on the TV last night?"

"I did."

Aabha smiled. "What did you think?"

"Think? Well, I think we got problems."

"Really? I like her very much. I think she is a great lady. In my country..."

The lights in the laboratory went out. It happened without any warning—no flickering, no beeping, nothing at all. For several seconds, Aabha stood in absolute darkness. The sound of convection fans and electrical equipment that was a constant background hum in the lab slowed to a halt. Then there was total silence.

Aabha put what she hoped was just the right note of alarm in her voice.

"Tom? Tom!"

"Okay, Aabha, it's okay. Hold on. I'm trying to get my... What's going on in there? My cameras are down."

"I don't know. I'm just..."

A bank of yellow emergency lights came on, and the fans started up again. The low light turned the empty lab into an eerie, shadowy world. Everything was dim, except for the bright red EXIT lights which shone in the semi-dark.

"Wow," she said. "That was scary. For a minute there, my air hose stopped working. But it's back on now."

"I don't know what happened," Tom said. "We're on reserve power all over the building. We have full-power backup generators that should have kicked on, but they didn't. I don't think this has ever happened before. I still don't have my cameras. Are you okay? Can you find your way out?"

"I'm okay," she said. "A little scared, but okay. The exit lights are on. Can I just follow them?"

"You can. But you need to follow all safety protocols, even in the dark. Chemical shower for the suit, regular shower for you—all of it. Otherwise, if you feel like you can't follow protocol, we need to wait until I can send someone in there, or until we get the power back up."

Her voice shook a tiny amount. "Tom, my air hose went off. If it goes off again... Let's just say I don't want to be in here without my air hose. I can follow the protocols in my sleep. But I need to get out of here."

"That's fine. All procedures to the letter, though. I trust you. But I don't have any lights. It looks like it's going to be dark everywhere, the whole way out. The airlock was off for a minute, but it just came back on. It's probably best if we get you out of there. Once you're through the airlock, you shouldn't have any problems. Let me know when you're through, okay? I want to shut it down again to conserve power."

"I will," she said.

She moved slowly through the darkness toward the exit door to the airlock, the vial of Ebola still cupped in her gloved right hand. It would take twenty or thirty minutes to follow all procedures on her way out. That wasn't going to happen. She planned to cut corners from here on out. This would be the fastest lab exit they had ever seen.

Tom was still talking to her. "Also, please make sure you secure all materials and equipment before you exit. We wouldn't want anything dangerous floating around."

She opened the first door and slid through. Just before it closed, she heard his voice for the last time.

"Aabha?" he said.

Aabha drove the BMW Z4 convertible with the top down.

It was a warm night, and she wanted to feel the wind in her hair. It was her last night in Galveston. It was her last night as Aabha. She had accomplished her mission, and after five long years undercover, this part of her life was over.

It was an amazing feeling, to cast off an identity as though it were a suit of clothes. It was freedom, it was exhilaration. She felt like she could be the protagonist in a television advertisement.

She had grown tired of studious, serious Aabha a long time ago. Who would she become next? It was a delicious question.

The drive to the marina was brief, just a few miles. She pulled off the highway and down the ramp to the parking lot. She took her overnight bag and her purse out of the trunk and left the keys in the glove compartment. In an hour a woman she had never seen, but who had similar features to Aabha, would get in and drive it away. The car would be two hundred miles away by the morning.

This made her a touch sad because she had loved this car so much.

But what was a car? Nothing more than many individual parts, welded and screwed and fastened together. An abstraction, really.

She walked on high heels through the marina. Her shoes clacked on the tiled ground. She passed the swimming pool, closed at this time of night, but lit up from below by an unearthly blue light. The thatched roofs of the little picnic sun shelters rustled in the breeze. She walked down a ramp to the first dock.

From here, she could see the great boat lighting up the night out on the water, well beyond the farthest reach of a Byzantine maze of interconnected docks. The boat, a 250-foot oceangoing yacht, was far too large to bring in close to the marina. It was a floating hotel, complete with disco, pool and hot tub, workout room, and its own four-person helicopter and helipad. It was a mobile castle, fit for a modern king.

Here at the dock, a small motorboat waited for her. A man offered his hand and helped her cross from the dock to the gunwale and then down into the cockpit. She sat in the back as the man untied and pushed off, and the driver put the boat in gear.

Approaching the yacht in the speedboat was like piloting a tiny space capsule to dock with the most gigantic star destroyer in the universe. They didn't even dock. The speedboat pulled behind the yacht, and another man helped her climb a five-rung ladder to the deck. This man was Ismail, the notorious *assistant.*

"Do you have the agent?" he said when she had climbed on board.

She smirked. "Hi, Aabha, how are you?" she said. "Nice to see you. I'm glad you escaped unscathed."

He made a motion with his hand as if a wheel were turning. *Let's go, let's go.* "Hi, Aabha. Whatever you just said. Do you have the agent?"

She reached into her purse and pulled out the vial full of Ebola virus. For a split second, she had a funny urge to toss it into the ocean. She held it up for his inspection instead. He stared at it.

"That tiny container," he said. "Incredible."

"I gave five years of my life for this container," Aabha said.

Ismail smiled. "Yes, but a hundred years from now, people will still sing songs of the heroic girl called Aabha."

He held his hand out as if Aabha were going to put the vial in his palm.

"I'll give it to him," she said.

Ismail shrugged. "As you wish."

She climbed a flight of green-lit stairs and entered the main cabin through a glass door. The giant cabin had a long bar against one wall, several tables along the walls, and a dance floor in the middle. Her boss used the room for entertaining. Aabha had been in this room when it was like a club in Berlin—standing room only, music pumping so loud the walls seemed to pulsate with it, lights strobing, bodies pressed together on the dance floor. Now the room was silent and empty.

She moved along a red carpeted hallway with half a dozen staterooms on either side, and then she climbed another flight of stairs. At the top of the stairs was another hall. She was deep inside the boat now, moving deeper. Most guests never came this far. She reached the end of this hall and knocked on the wide double doors she found there.

"Come in," a man's voice said.

She opened the left-hand door and went in. The room never ceased to amaze her. It was the master bedroom, located directly below the pilot house. Across the room from her, a curved, floor to ceiling, 180-degree window gave a view of what the boat was approaching, as well as much of what was to its right and left. Often, these views were of wide-open ocean.

On the left side of the room was a sitting area with a large sectional sofa formed into a party pit. There were also two easy chairs, a four-seat dining table, and a huge flat panel television on the wall, with a long sound bar mounted just below it. A tall, glass-faced liquor case stood near the wall in the corner.

To her right was the custom-built double-king-sized bed, complete with mirror mounted on the ceiling above it. The owner of this boat enjoyed his entertaining, and the bed could easily accommodate four people, sometimes five.

Standing in front of the bed was the owner himself. He wore a pair of white silk drawstring pants, a pair of sandals on his feet, and nothing else. He was tall and dark. He was perhaps forty years old, his hair peppered with gray, and his short beard just starting to turn white. He was very handsome, with deep brown eyes.

His body was lean, muscular, and perfectly proportioned in an inverted triangle—broad shoulders and chest tapering down to six-pack abs and a narrow waist, with well-muscled legs below. On his left pectoral was a tattoo of a giant black horse, an Arabian charger. The man owned a string of chargers, and he took them as his personal symbol. They were strong, virile, regal, as he was.

He appeared fit, healthy, and well-rested, in the way of a vastly wealthy man with easy access to skilled personal trainers, the best foods, and doctors ready to administer the precise hormone treatments to defeat the aging process. He was, in a word, beautiful.

"Aabha, my lovely, lovely girl. Who will you be after tonight?"

"Omar," she said. "I brought you a gift."

He smiled. "I never doubted you. Not for one moment."

He beckoned to her, and she went to him. She handed him the vial, but he placed it on the table next to the bed almost without looking at it.

"Later," he said. "We can think about that later."

He pulled her close to him. She moved into his strong embrace. She pressed her face to his neck and got his scent, the subtle smell of his cologne out in front, and the deeper, earthier smell of him. He was not a clean freak, this man. He wanted you to smell him. She found it exciting, his smell. She found everything about him exciting.

He turned and pressed her, face down, onto the bed. She went willingly, eagerly. In a moment, she writhed as his hands removed her clothes and roamed her body. His deep voice murmured to her, words that might normally shock her, but here, in this room, made her groan with animal pleasure.

*

When Omar awoke, he was alone.

That was good. The girl knew his preferences. While sleeping, he did not like to be disturbed by the jarring movements and noises of others. Sleep was rest. It was not a wrestling match.

The boat was moving. They had left Galveston, exactly on schedule, and were heading across the Gulf of Mexico toward Florida. Sometime tomorrow, they would anchor near Tampa, and the little vial Aabha had brought him would go ashore.

He reached over to the table and picked up the vial. Just a small vial, made of thick, hardened plastic, and blocked at the top with a bright red stopper. The contents were unremarkable. They looked like little more than a pile of dust.

Even so…

It took his breath away! To hold this power, the power of life and death. And not just the power of life and death over one person—the power to kill many, many people. The power to destroy an entire population. The power to hold nations hostage. The power of total war. The power of revenge.

He closed his eyes and breathed deeply from his diaphragm, seeking calm. It had been a risk for him to come to Galveston personally, and an unnecessary one at that. But he had wanted to be there in the moment when such a weapon passed into his possession. He wanted to hold the weapon, and feel the power in his own hand.

He placed the vial back on the table, pulled on his pants, and rolled out of bed. He shrugged into a Manchester United soccer jersey and went out onto the deck. He found her there, sitting back in a lounge chair and gazing out at the night, the stars, and the vast dark water around them.

A bodyguard stood quietly near the door.

Omar gestured to the man, and the man moved to the railing.

"Aabha," Omar said. She turned to him, and he could see how sleepy she was.

She smiled, and he smiled as well. "You've done a wonderful thing," he said. "I'm very proud of you. Perhaps it's time for you to sleep."

27

She nodded. "I'm so tired."

Omar bent down and their lips met. He kissed her deeply, savoring the taste of her, and the memory of the curves of her body, her movements, and her sounds.

"For you, my darling, rest is much deserved."

Omar glanced at the bodyguard. He was a tall, strong man. The guard removed a plastic bag from his jacket pocket, moved in behind her, and in one deft move slipped the bag over her head and pulled it tight.

Instantly, her body became electric. She reached back, trying to scratch and pummel him. Her feet kicked her up out of the chair. She struggled, but it was impossible. The man was far too strong. His wrists and forearms were taut, rippling with veins and muscle doing their work.

Through the translucent bag, her face became a mask of terror and desperation, her eyes round saucers. Her mouth was a huge O, a full moon, gasping for air and finding none. She sucked in thin plastic instead of oxygen.

Her body tensed and became rigid. It was like she was a wood carving of a woman, her body sloping, bending slightly backwards at the middle. Gradually, she began to settle down. She weakened, subsided, and then stopped entirely. The guard allowed her to sink slowly back into her chair. He sank with her, guiding her. Now that she was dead, he treated her with tenderness.

The man took a deep breath and looked up at Omar.

"What shall I do with her?"

Omar stared out at the dark night.

It was a shame to kill such a good girl as Aabha, but she was tainted. Sometime soon, perhaps as early as tomorrow morning, the Americans would learn that the virus was missing. Soon after that, they would discover that Aabha was the last person in the laboratory, and was there when the lights went out.

They would come to realize that the power failure was the result of an underground cable being deliberately cut, and the failure of the backup generators was the result of careful sabotage conducted several weeks ago. They would make a desperate search for Aabha, a no-holds-barred search, and they must never find her.

"Get some help from Abdul. He has empty buckets and some fast-drying cement in the equipment locker down by the engine room. Take her there. Weight her with a bucket of cement around her feet and calves, and drop her into the deepest part of the ocean.

A thousand feet deep or more, please. The data is readily available, is it not?"

The man nodded. "Yes sir."

"Perfect. Afterwards have all my sheets, pillows, and blankets laundered. We must be thorough and destroy all evidence. On the very unlikely chance that the Americans raid this ship, I don't want the girl's DNA anywhere near me."

The man nodded. "Of course."

"Very good," Omar said.

He left his bodyguard with the corpse and went back into the master bedroom. It was time to take a hot bath.

CHAPTER FIVE

June 10th
11:15 a.m.
Queen Anne's County, Maryland – Eastern Shore of
Chesapeake Bay

"Well, maybe we should just sell the house," Luke said.

He was talking about their old waterfront country house, twenty minutes up the road from where they were now. Luke and Becca had rented a different, much more spacious and modern house for the next two weeks. Luke liked this new house better, but they were here only because Becca wouldn't go back to their place.

He understood her reluctance. Of course he did. Four nights ago, both Becca and Gunner had been abducted from that house. Luke hadn't been there to protect them. They could have been killed. Anything could have happened.

He glanced out the big, bright kitchen window. Gunner was outside in jeans and a T-shirt playing some imaginary game, the way nine-year-old kids sometimes did. In a few minutes, Gunner and Luke were going to take the skiff out and go fishing.

The sight of his son gave Luke a pang of terror.

What if Gunner had been killed? What if both of them had simply disappeared, never to be found again? What if two years from now, Gunner didn't play imaginary games anymore? It was all a jumble in Luke's mind.

Yes, it was horrible. Yes, it should never have happened. But there were larger issues here. Luke and Ed Newsam and a small handful of people had taken down a violent coup attempt, and had reinstalled what was left of the democratically elected government of the United States. It was possible that they had saved American democracy itself.

That was nice, but Becca didn't seem interested in larger issues right now.

She sat at the kitchen table in a blue robe, drinking her second cup of coffee. "Easy for you to say. That house has been in my family for a hundred years."

Rebecca's hair was long, flowing down her shoulders. Her eyes were blue, framed in thick eyelashes. To Luke, her pretty face looked thin and drawn. He felt sick about that. He felt sick about the whole thing, but he couldn't think of something he could say that would make this better.

A tear rolled down Becca's cheek. "My garden is over there, Luke."

"I know."

"I can't work in my garden because I'm afraid. I'm afraid of my own house, a house I've been going to since I was born."

Luke said nothing.

"And Mr. and Mrs. Thompson... they're dead. You know that, don't you? Those men killed them." She looked at Luke sharply. Her eyes were hot and mad. Becca had a tendency to grow angry with him, sometimes over very small matters. He forgot to do the dishes, or take the garbage outside. When she did, she would get a look in her eyes similar to the one she had now. Luke thought of it as the Blame Look. And for Luke, right now the Blame Look was too much.

In his mind, he caught a brief image of their neighbors, Mr. and Mrs. Thompson. If Hollywood were to cast a kindly older couple who lived next door, the Thompsons would be it. He liked the Thompsons, and he would never have intended for their lives to end like that. But a lot of people died that day.

"Becca, I didn't kill the Thompsons. Okay? I'm sorry they're dead, and I'm sorry you and Gunner were taken—I will be sorry for that the rest of my life and I will do everything I can to make it up to both of you. But I didn't do it. I didn't kill the Thompsons. I didn't send people to abduct you. You seem to be blurring these things in your mind, and I won't have it."

He paused. It was a good time to stop talking, but he didn't stop. His words came out in a torrent.

"All I did was fight my way through a blizzard of gunfire and bombs. People were trying to kill me all day and all night. I got shot, I got blown up, I got run off the road. And I saved the President of the United States, your President, from almost certain death. That's what I did."

He breathed heavily, as if he had just sprinted a mile.

He regretted everything. That was the truth. It hurt him to think that the work he did had ever caused her pain, it hurt more than she would ever know. He had left the job last year for that very reason, but then he had been called back for one night—one night that turned into a night, a day, and another impossibly long night. A night during which he thought he had lost his family forever.

Becca no longer trusted him. He could see that much. His presence frightened her. He was the cause of what had happened. He was reckless, he was fanatical, and he was going to get her, and their only son, killed.

Tears streamed silently down her face. A long minute passed.

"Does it even matter?" she said.

"Does what matter?"

"Does it matter who the President is? If Gunner and I were dead, would you really care who was President?"

"But you're alive," he said. "You're not dead. You're alive and well. There's a big difference."

"Okay," she said. "We're alive." It was agreement that wasn't agreement.

"I want to tell you something," Luke said. "I'm retiring. I'm not going to do it anymore. I might have to take a few meetings in the coming days, but I'm not going on any more assignments. I did my part. Now it's over."

She shook her head, but just slightly. It was as if she didn't even have the energy to move. "You've said that before."

"Yes. But this time I mean it."

*

"You want to always keep the boat on an even keel."

"Okay," Gunner said.

He and his dad loaded the boat with gear. Gunner wore jeans, a T-shirt, and a big floppy fishing hat to keep the sun off his face. He also had a pair of Oakley sunglasses his dad had given him because they looked cool. His dad wore the same exact pair.

The T-shirt was okay—it was from *28 Days Later*, which was a pretty awesome zombie movie with English people in it. The problem with the shirt was it didn't have any actual zombies on it. It was just a red biohazard symbol against a black background. He guessed that made sense. The zombies in the movie weren't really the undead. They were people who got infected with a virus.

"Slide that cooler athwartships," his dad said.

His dad had all these crazy words he used whenever they went fishing. It made Gunner laugh sometimes. "Athwartships!" he shouted. "Aye, aye, Captain."

His dad motioned with his hand to show the placement he wanted; across the middle, sideways, not near the back rail where

Gunner had originally stowed it. Gunner slid the big blue cooler into place.

They stood, facing one another. His dad gave him a funny look from behind his sunglasses. "How are you doing, son?"

Gunner hesitated. He knew they were worried about him. He had heard them whispering his name in the night. But he was okay. He really was. He had been afraid, and he was still a little bit afraid now. He had even cried a lot, which was okay. You were supposed to cry sometimes. You weren't supposed to hold it in.

"Gunner?"

Well, he might as well talk about it.

"Dad, you kill people sometimes, don't you?"

His dad nodded. "Sometimes I do, yeah. It's part of my job. But I only kill bad guys."

"How can you tell the difference?"

"Sometimes it's hard to tell. And sometimes it's easy. Bad guys will hurt people who are weaker than them, or innocent people who are just minding their own business. My job is to stop them from doing that."

"Like the men who killed the President?"

His dad nodded.

"Did you kill them?"

"I killed some of them, yes."

"And the men who took Mom and me? You killed them, too, didn't you?"

"I did, yeah."

"I'm glad you did that, Dad."

"I am too, monster. They were the exact kind of men who are good to kill."

"Are you the best killer in the world?"

His dad shook his head and smiled. "I don't know, buddy. I don't think they keep tabs on who the best killers are. It's not really like a sport. There's no world champion of killing. In any case, I'm retiring from the whole thing. I want to spend more time with you and Mom."

Gunner thought about it. He had seen a news show about his dad on TV the day before. It was really just a short segment, but it was his dad's picture and name, and video of his dad when he was younger and in the Army. Luke Stone, Delta Force operator. Luke Stone, FBI Special Response Team. Luke Stone and his team had saved the United States government.

"I'm proud of you, Dad. Even if you never got to be world champion."

His dad laughed. He gestured toward the dock. "Okay, are we ready?"

Gunner nodded.

"We'll head way out, drop anchor, see if we can find a few stripers feeding on the dropping tide."

Gunner nodded. They pulled away from the dock and moved slowly through the No Wake zone. He braced himself as the boat picked up speed.

Gunner scanned the horizon ahead of them. He was the spotter, and he had to keep his eyes sharp and his head on a swivel, as his dad liked to say. They had been out together fishing three times earlier in the spring, but they hadn't caught anything. When you went fishing and you didn't catch anything, Dad called that being "on the snide." Right now, they were on the snide big time.

In a few moments, Gunner spotted some splashes in the middle distance off the starboard quarter. Some white terns were diving, dropping like bombs into the water.

"Hey, look!"

His dad nodded and smiled.

"Stripers?"

Dad shook his head. "Bluefish." Then he said, "Hold on."

He gunned the engine and soon they were skimming, skittering, still picking up speed, as the boat got up on plane with Gunner nearly thrown backwards. A minute later, they eased up to the thrashing whitewater, the boat came off plane, and they settled back into the swells.

Gunner grabbed the two long fishing rods with the single hooks. He handed one to his dad and then cast his line without waiting. Almost instantly, he felt a tug, a heavy pull. A wild liveliness came into the rod now, vibrating with life. Some unseen force nearly yanked the rod out of his hands. The line snapped and went slack. The bluefish had broken him off. He turned to tell his dad, but the old man was hooked up now too, his rod bent double.

Gunner grabbed a net and got ready. The bluefish—silver and blue and green and white and very, very angry, was hoisted from the water and into the cockpit.

"Nice fish."

"A slump breaker!"

The bluefish flopped on deck, caught in the green mesh of the hand net.

"Will we keep him?"

"No. He gets us off the snide, but we're here for stripers. Blues are exciting, but striped bass are bigger and they're better on the grill, too."

They released the fish—Gunner watched as his dad seized the still-jerking, snapping bluefish, and removed the hook, his fingers just inches from those hungry teeth. His dad dropped the fish over the side, where with a quick tail whip, it headed for the deep.

No sooner had the fish disappeared than his dad's phone started to ring. His dad smiled and looked at the phone. Then he put it aside. It buzzed and buzzed. After a while, it stopped. Ten seconds passed before it started ringing again.

"Aren't you going to answer it?" Gunner said.

His dad shook his head. "No. In fact, I'm going to turn my phone off."

Gunner felt a surge of fear in his stomach. "Dad, you have to answer it. What if it's an emergency? What if the bad guys are taking over again?"

His dad stared at Gunner for a long second. The phone stopped buzzing. Then it started again. He answered it.

"Stone," he said.

He paused and his face darkened. "Hi, Richard. Yes, Susan's chief-of-staff. Sure. I've heard of you. Well, listen. You know I'm taking some time off, right? I haven't even decided if I'm still on the Special Response Team, or whatever it's called now. Yes, I understand, but there's always something urgent. No one ever calls me at home and tells me it isn't urgent. Okay... okay. If the President is serious that she wants a meeting, then she can call me personally. She knows where to reach me. Okay? Thanks."

When his dad hung up, Gunner watched him. He didn't look like he was having as much fun as just a minute ago. Gunner knew that if the President called, his dad would quickly pack his bags and go somewhere. Another mission, maybe more bad guys to kill. And he would leave Gunner and his mom home alone again.

"Dad, is the President going to call you?"

His dad ruffled Gunner's hair. "Monster, I sure hope not. Now what do you say? Let's go get some stripers."

*

35

Hours later, the President still hadn't called.

Luke and Gunner had caught three nice stripers, and Luke showed Gunner how to gut, clean, and filet them. It was old ground, but repetition was how you learned. Becca even got into the act, bringing a bottle of wine out to the patio and setting a cheese and cracker plate on the outdoor table.

Luke was just firing up the grill when the phone rang.

He looked at his family. They had frozen on the first ring. He and Becca made eye contact. He couldn't read what was in her eyes anymore. Whatever it was, it was not supportive approval. He answered the phone.

A deep voice, a man: "Agent Stone?"

"Yes."

"Please hold for the President of the United States."

He stood numb, listening to blank air.

The phone clicked and she came on. "Luke?"

"Susan."

His mind flashed back to an image of her, leading the entire country, and much of the world, in singing "God Bless America." It was an amazing moment, but that's all it was, a moment. And it was the kind of thing politicians were good at. It was practically a parlor trick.

"Luke, we've got a crisis on our hands."

"Susan, we always have a crisis on our hands."

"Right now, I am up to my ass in alligators."

Nice. He hadn't heard that one in a while.

"We're going to have a meeting. Here at the house. I need you there."

"When is the meeting?"

She didn't hesitate. "In an hour."

"Susan, with traffic, I'm two hours away. That's on a good day. Right now, half the roads are still closed."

"You won't be sitting in traffic. There's a helicopter on the way to you now. It'll be there in fourteen minutes."

Luke looked at his family again. Becca had poured herself a glass of wine and sat faced away from him, staring toward the late afternoon sun sinking toward the water. Gunner stared down at the fish on the grill.

"Okay," Luke said into the phone.

CHAPTER SIX

6:45 p.m.
United States Naval Observatory – Washington, DC

"Agent Stone, I'm Richard Monk, the President's chief-of-staff. We talked on the phone today."

Luke had come off the Naval Observatory helipad five minutes before. He shook hands with a tall, fit-looking guy, maybe late-thirties, probably right around Luke's age. The man wore a blue dress shirt with sleeves rolled up his forearms. His tie hung askew. His upper body was scientifically muscular, like in an ad for *Men's Health.* He worked hard and he played hard—that's what Richard Monk's look told anyone who would listen.

They walked the marble hallway of the New White House toward wide double doors down at the end. "We've adapted our old conference room into a situation room," Monk said. "It's a work in progress, but we're going to get there."

"You're lucky to be alive, aren't you?" Luke said.

The mask of confidence on the man's face faltered, only for a second. He nodded. "The Vice... Well, she was the Vice President at the time. The President and I and a bunch of staff were on a West Coast swing when President Hayes summoned her back East. It was very sudden. I stayed behind in Seattle with a few people to tie up some loose ends. When Mount Weather happened..."

He shook his head. "It's too horrible. But yes, that could have been me, too."

Luke nodded. Workers were still pulling bodies out of Mount Weather days after the disaster. Three hundred so far, and counting. Among them were the former Secretary of State, the former Secretary of Education, the former Secretary of the Interior, the head of NASA, and dozens of United States Representatives and Senators.

The firefighters had only put out the central underground fire yesterday.

"What is the crisis that Susan called me out here for?" Luke said.

Monk gestured toward the end of the hall. "Uh, President Hopkins is there in the conference room, along with some key staff. I think I'm going to let them tell you what's going on."

They passed through the double doors and into the room. More than a dozen people were already seated at a large oval table. Susan Hopkins, President of the United States, sat at the far side of the room from the door. She was small, almost unassuming, surrounded by large men. Two Secret Service agents stood on either side of her. Three more stood in various corners of the room.

A nervous-looking man stood at the head of the table. He was tall, balding, a little paunchy, wearing glasses and an ill-fitting suit. Luke sized him up in about two seconds. This was not his normal venue, and he believed himself to be in deep trouble. He looked like a man who was currently being grilled from all sides.

Susan stood. "Everyone, before we begin, I want to introduce you to Agent Luke Stone, formerly of the FBI Special Response Team. He saved my life a few days ago, and he was instrumental in saving the Republic as we know it. That is not an exaggeration. I'm not sure I've ever before met an operative as skilled, as knowledgeable, and as fearless in the face of adversity. It's a credit to our nation, our Armed Forces, and our intelligence community that we identify and train men and women like Agent Stone."

Now everyone stood and applauded. To Luke's ears, the applause sounded stilted and formal. These people *had to* applaud. The President wanted them to. He raised a hand, trying to make it stop. The situation was absurd.

"Hi," he said when the clapping ended. "Sorry I'm late."

Luke sat in an empty chair. The man standing in the front stared directly at him. Now Luke couldn't tell what was in the man's eyes. Hope? Maybe. He looked like a desperate quarterback about to launch a Hail Mary pass in Luke's direction.

"Luke," Susan said. "This is Dr. Wesley Drinan, Director of the Galveston National Laboratory at the University of Texas Medical Branch. He is briefing us on a possible security breach at the Biosafety Level 4 lab there."

"Ah," Luke said. "All right."

"Agent Stone, are you familiar with Biosafety Level 4 laboratories?"

"Uh, Luke is fine. I'm familiar with the term. Maybe you can bring me all the way up to speed, however."

Drinan nodded. "Of course. I'll give you the thirty-second elevator pitch. BSL-4 labs are the highest level of security when dealing with biological agents. BSL-4 is the level required for work with dangerous and exotic viruses and bacteria that pose a high risk of laboratory infections, as well as those which cause severe to fatal disease in humans. These are diseases for which vaccines or other treatments aren't currently available. In general, I'm talking about Ebola, Marburg, and some of the emerging hemorrhagic viruses that we're just discovering in deep jungle regions of Africa and South America. Sometimes we also handle newly mutated influenza viruses until we understand their transmission mechanisms, infection rates, mortality rates, and so on."

"Okay," Luke said. "I get it. And something was stolen?"

"We don't know. Something is missing. But we don't know what happened to it."

Luke didn't speak. He simply nodded at the man to keep him talking.

"We had a power failure two nights ago. That in itself is rare. Rarer still is that our backup generators didn't immediately kick on. The design of the facility is that in the event of an outage, there should be a seamless shift from main power to backup power. It didn't happen. Instead, the facility went to emergency reserves, which is a low-power state that only keeps essential systems running."

"What sort of non-essential systems went down?" Luke said.

Drinan shrugged. "The things you can imagine. Lights. Computers. Camera systems."

"Security cameras?"

"Yes."

"Inside the facility?"

"Yes."

"Was there anyone inside?"

The man nodded. "There were two people inside at the time. One was a security guard named Thomas Eder. He's worked at the facility for fifteen years. He was at the guard station and not inside the containment facility. We've interviewed him, as have the police and the Texas Bureau of Investigation. He's being cooperative."

"Who else?"

"Uh, there was a scientist inside the containment facility. Her name is Aabha Rushdie. She's from India. She is a beautiful person and a very good scientist. She studied in London, has gone through multiple BSL-4 trainings, and has all the required security clearances. She's been with us for three years and I've worked directly with her on many occasions."

"Okay…" Luke said.

"When the power went down, she temporarily lost flow in her air hose. This is a potentially dangerous situation. She was also cast into total darkness. She became afraid, and it seems that Thomas Eder may have allowed her to exit the facility without following all the required safety protocols."

Luke smiled. This seemed like an easy one. "And then something was missing?"

Drinan hesitated. "The following day, an inventory discovered that a vial of a very specific Ebola virus had gone missing."

"Has anyone spoken with the Rushdie woman?"

Drinan shook his head. "She's also gone missing. Yesterday, her car was found by a rancher on an isolated property in the hill country fifty miles west of Austin. The state police suggest that cars abandoned like that are often a sign of foul play. She's not at her apartment. We've tried to contact her family in London, with no luck."

"Would she have any reason to steal the Ebola virus?"

"No. It's impossible to believe. I've wrestled with this for two days. The Aabha I know is not someone who... I can't even say it. She just isn't that way. I don't understand what's going on. I'm afraid she might have been kidnapped or fallen into the hands of criminals. I'm at a loss for words."

"We haven't even reached the worst part," Susan Hopkins said abruptly. "Dr. Drinan, can you tell Agent Stone about the virus itself, please?"

The good doctor nodded. He looked at Stone.

"The Ebola is weaponized. It's similar to Ebola found in nature, like the Ebola that killed ten thousand people during the West African outbreak, only worse. It's more virulent, more fast acting, can be transmitted more easily, and has a higher fatality rate. It is a very dangerous substance. We need to either get it back, destroy it, or determine to our satisfaction that it was already destroyed."

Luke turned to Susan.

"We want you to go down there," she said. "See what you can find out."

Those were the exact words Luke didn't want to hear. Over the phone, she had invited him to a meeting. But she had brought him here to give him a mission.

"I wonder," he said, "if we can talk about this in private?"

40

"Can we get you anything?" Richard Monk said. "Coffee?"

"Sure, I'll have a cup of coffee," Luke said.

He wouldn't mind drinking some coffee right now, but mostly he accepted the offer because he thought that would make Monk leave the room. Wrong. Monk simply picked up a phone and ordered some from the kitchen downstairs.

Luke, Monk, and Susan were in an upstairs sitting room near the family living quarters. Luke knew that Susan's family didn't live here. When she was Vice President, he hadn't paid much attention to her, but he had somehow gotten the idea that she and her husband were estranged.

Luke sat back in a comfortable easy chair. "Susan, before we start, I want to tell you something. I've decided to retire, effective immediately. I'm telling you before I tell anyone else, so you can find someone else to head the SRT."

Susan didn't speak.

"Stone," Monk said, "you might as well know now. The Special Response Team is on the chopping block. It's finished. Don Morris was involved in the coup, right from the beginning. He is at least partially responsible for one of the worst atrocities to ever take place on American soil. And he created the Special Response Team. I'm sure you can understand that security, and especially the President's security, is the most important thing on our radar right now. It's not just SRT. We are investigating suspect sub-agencies within CIA, NSA, and the Pentagon, among others. We need to root out the conspirators, so nothing like this can ever happen again."

"I understand your concerns," Luke said.

And he did. The government was fragile right now, maybe as fragile as it had ever been. The Congress was mostly wiped out and a retired supermodel had been elevated to the Presidency. The United States had been shown to have feet of clay, and if there were any coup plotters still around, there was no reason why they shouldn't make another grab for power.

"If you're going to eliminate the SRT anyway, then this is a perfect time for me to leave." The more he said things like this, the more real it became to him.

It was time to put his family back together. It was time to recreate that idyllic place in his mind where he, Becca, and Gunner could be alone, away from these concerns, where even if the worst happened, it wouldn't matter all that much.

Heck, maybe he should just go home and ask Becca if she wanted to move to Costa Rica. Gunner could grow up bilingual. They could live on the beach somewhere. Becca could have an exotic garden. Luke could go surfing a couple of times a week. The west coast of Costa Rica had some of the best swells in the Americas.

Susan spoke for the first time. "It's a horrible time for you to leave. The timing couldn't be worse. Your country needs you."

He looked at her. "You know what, Susan? That's not really true. You think that because I'm the guy you happened to see in action. There are a million guys like me. There are guys more capable than me, more experienced, more level-headed. You don't seem to know this, but some people think I'm a loose cannon."

"Luke, you can't leave me here," she said. "We are teetering on the verge of disaster. I've been stuck into a role I was not... I wasn't expecting this. I don't know who to trust. I don't know who is good and who is bad. I'm half-expecting to turn a corner and catch a bullet in the head. I need my people around me. People I can put all my faith in."

"I'm one of your people?"

She looked him directly in the eyes. "You saved my life."

Richard Monk broke into the conversation. "Stone, what you don't know is the Ebola is replicable. That wasn't covered in the meeting. Wesley Drinan told us in confidence that it's possible people with the right equipment and knowledge could make more of it. The last thing we need is an unknown group of people running around with weaponized Ebola virus, trying to stockpile it."

Luke looked at Susan again.

"Take this job," Susan said. "Figure out what happened to the missing woman. Find the missing Ebola. When you come back, if you really want to retire, I will never ask you to do another thing. We started something together a few nights ago. Do this one last thing for me, and I'm ready to say the job is finished."

Her eyes never left his. She was a typical politician in many ways. When she reached for you, she found you. It was hard to say no to her.

He sighed. "I can leave in the morning."

Susan shook her head. "We've already got a plane waiting for you."

Luke's eyes widened, surprised. He took a long breath.

"OK," he finally said. "But first I need to get some people from the Special Response Team together. I'm thinking of Ed Newsam, Mark Swann, and Trudy Wellington. Newsam's on injury leave right now, but I'm pretty sure he'll come back if I ask him."

A look passed between Susan and Monk.

"We've already contacted Newsam and Swann," Monk said. "They've both agreed, and both are en route to the airport. I'm afraid that Trudy Wellington won't be possible."

Luke frowned. "She won't do it?"

Monk stared down at a yellow legal pad in his hands. He made a quick note to himself. He didn't bother to look up. "We don't know because we didn't contact her. Unfortunately, using Wellington is out of the question."

Luke turned to Susan.

"Susan?"

Now Monk looked up. He scanned back and forth between Luke and Susan. He spoke again before Susan said a word.

"Wellington is dirty. She was Don Morris's mistress. There's just no way she can be part of this. She's not even going to be employed by the FBI a month from now, and she may well be up on treason charges by then."

"She told me she didn't know anything," Luke said.

"And you believe her?"

Luke didn't even bother answering that question. He didn't know the answer. "I want her," he said simply.

"Or?"

"I left my son staring at a striped bass on the grill tonight, a striper that we caught together. I could start my retirement from all this right now. I kind of enjoyed being a college professor. I'm looking forward to getting back to it. And I'm looking forward to watching my son grow up."

Luke stared at Monk and Susan. They stared back at him.

"So?" he said. "What do you think?"

CHAPTER SEVEN

June 11th
2:15 a.m.
Ybor City, Tampa, Florida

It was dangerous work.

So dangerous that he did not like to go out to the laboratory floor at all.

"Yes, yes," he said into the telephone. "We have four people on right now. We will have six when the shift turns over. By tonight? It's possible. I don't want to promise too much. Call me around ten a.m., and I will have a better idea."

He listened for a moment. "Well, I would say a van would be big enough. That size can easily pull back to the loading dock. These things are smaller than the eye can see. Even trillions of them don't take up that much space. If we had to do it, we might be able to fit it all in the trunk of a car. But if so, I would suggest two cars. One to go on the road, and one to go to the airport."

He hung up the phone. The man's code name was Adam. The first man, because he was the first man hired for this job. He fully understood the risks, even if the others did not. He alone knew the entire scope of the project.

He watched the floor of the small warehouse through the big office window. They were working around the clock in three shifts. The people in there now, three men and a woman, wore white laboratory gowns, goggles, ventilator masks, rubber gloves, and booties on their feet.

The workers had been selected for their ability to do simple microbiology. Their job was to grow and multiply a virus using the food medium Adam supplied, then freeze-dry the samples for later transport and aerosol transmission. It was tedious work, but not difficult. Any laboratory assistant or second year biochemistry student could do it.

The twenty-four-hour schedule meant that the stockpiles of freeze-dried virus were growing very quickly. Adam gave a report to his employers every six or eight hours, and they always expressed their pleasure with the pace. In the past day, their pleasure had begun to give way to delight. The work would soon be complete, perhaps as early as today.

Adam smiled at that. His employers were well-pleased, and they were paying him very, very well.

He sipped coffee from a Styrofoam cup and continued to watch the workers. He had lost count of the amount of coffee he had consumed in the past few days. It was a lot. The days were beginning to blur together. When he became exhausted, he would lie down on the cot in his office and sleep for a little while. He wore the same protective gear as the workers out in the lab. He hadn't taken it off now in two and a half days.

Adam had done his best to build a makeshift laboratory in the rented warehouse. He had done his best to protect the workers and himself. They had protective clothing to wear. There was a room in which to discard the clothing after each shift, and there were showers for the workers to wash off any residue afterward.

But there were also funding and time constraints to consider. The schedule was fast, and of course there was the question of secrecy. He knew the protections were not up to the standards of the American Centers for Disease Control—if he'd had a million dollars and six months to build this place, it still wouldn't be enough.

In the end, he had built the lab in less than two weeks. It was located in a rugged district of old, low-slung warehouses, deep inside a neighborhood that had long been a center of Cuban and other immigration to the United States.

No one would look at the place twice. There was no sign on the building, and it was elbow-to-elbow with a dozen similar buildings. The lease was paid for the next six months, even though they only needed the facility for a very short time. It had its own small parking lot, and the workers came and went like warehouse and factory workers everywhere—in eight-hour intervals.

The workers were well-paid in cash, and few of them spoke any English. The workers knew what to do with the virus, but they didn't know exactly what they were handling or why. A police raid was unlikely.

Still, it made him nervous to be so close to the virus. He would be relieved to finish this part of the job, receive his final payment, and then evacuate this place as if he had never been here. After that, he would take a flight to the west coast. For Adam, there were two parts to this job. One here, and one... somewhere else.

And the first part would be done soon.

Today? Yes, perhaps even as early as today.

He would leave the country for a while, he had decided. After all of this was over, he would take a nice long holiday. The south coast of France sounded nice to him right now. With the money he was making, he could go anywhere he liked.

It was simple. A van, or a car, or perhaps two cars would pull into the yard. Adam would close the gates so nobody on the street could see what was happening. His workers would take a few moments loading the materials into the vehicles. He would make sure they were careful, so maybe the whole thing would require twenty minutes.

Adam smiled to himself. Soon after the loading was done, he would be on a plane to the west coast. Soon after that, the nightmare would begin. And there was nothing anyone could do to stop it.

CHAPTER EIGHT

5:40 a.m.
The Skies Over West Virginia

The six-seat Learjet shrieked across the early morning sky. The jet was dark blue with the Secret Service seal on the side. Behind it, a sliver of the rising sun just poked above the clouds.

Luke and his team used the front four passenger seats as their meeting area. They stowed their luggage, and their gear, in the seats at the back.

He had the team back together. In the seat next to him sat big Ed Newsam, in khaki cargo pants and a long-sleeved T-shirt. He had a pair of crutches tucked to the side of his seat, just under the window.

Across from Luke and to the left, facing him, was Mark Swann. He was tall and thin, with sandy hair and glasses. He stretched his long legs out into the aisle. He wore an old pair of ripped jeans and a pair of red Chuck Taylor sneakers. He had been liberated from duty as a pedophile decoy, and he looked like he couldn't be much more pleased than he was.

Directly across from Luke sat Trudy Wellington. She had curly brown hair, was slim and attractive in a green sweater and slacks. She wore big round glasses on her face. She was very pretty, but the glasses made her look almost like an owl.

Luke felt okay, not great. He had called Becca before they left. The conversation hadn't gone well. It had barely gone at all.

"Where are you going?" she said.

"Texas. Galveston. There's been a security breach at a lab there."

"The BSL-4 lab?" she said. Becca was herself a cancer researcher. She had been working on a cure for melanoma for some years. She was part of a team, based at several different research institutions, that had been having some success killing melanoma cells by injecting the herpes virus into them.

Luke nodded. "That's right. The BSL-4 lab."

"It's dangerous," she said. "You realize that, I'm sure."

He nearly laughed. "Sweetheart, they don't call me in when it's safe."

Her voice was cold. "Well, please be careful. We love you, you know."

47

We love you.

It was an odd way to say it, as if she and Gunner as a team loved him, but not necessarily as individuals.

"I know," he said. "I love you both very much."

There was silence over the line.

"Becca?"

"Luke, I can't guarantee we're going to be here when you get back."

Now, aboard the plane, he shook his head to clear it. It was part of the job. He had to compartmentalize. He was having family problems, yes. He didn't know how to fix them. But he also couldn't bring them with him to Galveston. They would distract him from what he was doing, and that could be dangerous, for himself and everyone involved. His focus on the matter at hand had to be total.

He glanced out the window. The jet streaked across the sky, moving fast. Below them, white clouds skidded by. He took a deep breath.

"All right, Trudy," he said. "What do you have for us?"

Trudy held up her computer tablet for everyone's inspection. She positively beamed. "They gave me my old tablet back. Thanks, boss."

He shook his head and smiled just a touch. "Luke is fine. Now give it to us. Please."

"I'm going to assume no prior knowledge."

Luke nodded. "Fair enough."

"Okay. We are on our way to the Galveston National Laboratory, in Galveston, Texas. It is one of only four known Biosafety Level 4 facilities in the United States. These are the highest security microbiology research facilities, with the most extensive safety protocols for workers. These facilities deal with some of the most lethal and infectious viruses and bacteria known to science."

Swann raised a hand from out of his slump. "You say one of four known facilities. Are there unknown facilities?"

Trudy shrugged. "Certain life sciences corporations, especially ones that are closely held, could have BSL-4 facilities without the government knowing about it. Yeah. It's possible."

Swann nodded.

"The thing that's different about this facility in Galveston is the other three BSL-4 facilities are located on highly secure

48

government installations. Galveston is the only one on an academic campus, a fact which was repeatedly raised as a security concern before the facility first opened in 2006."

"What did they do about it?" Ed Newsam said.

Trudy smiled again. "They promised they'd be extra careful."

"Terrific," Ed said.

"Let's get to the meat of it," Luke said.

Trudy nodded. "Okay. Three nights ago, a power failure occurred."

Luke drifted just a bit as Trudy went through the material the lab director covered with Susan and her staff the night before. The night guard, the woman, the vial of Ebola. He heard these things, but he was barely listening.

An image of Becca and Gunner on the patio as he was leaving flashed in his mind. He tried to squash it, but it lingered on. For a long second, all he saw was Gunner staring down dejectedly at a striped bass on the grill.

"It sure sounds like sabotage," Newsam said.

"It most likely was," Trudy said. "The system was built for redundancy, and not only did the primary power source fail, the redundancy also failed. That just doesn't happen very often unless someone helps it happen."

"What do we know about the woman who was inside at the time?" Luke said. "What is her name? Anything new on her?"

"I did some looking into her. Aabha Rushdie, twenty-nine years old. She's still missing. She has an exemplary record as a junior scientist. Doctorate in Microbiology. Highest honors at King's College, London. Advanced training in BSL-3 and BSL-4 protocols, including certification to work solo in the lab, which is not a place everyone reaches.

"She's been at Galveston for three years, and has worked on a number of important programs, including the weapons program we're concerned with."

"Okay," Swann said. "This is a weapons program?"

Trudy raised a hand. "I'll get to that in a minute. Let me finish with Aabha. The most interesting thing about her is she died in 1990."

Everyone stared at Trudy.

"Aabha Rushdie died in a car crash in Delhi, India, when she was four years old. Her parents moved to London soon after. Later, they divorced and Aabha's mother moved back to India. Her father died of a heart attack seven years ago. And five years ago, Aabha suddenly came back to life, with a life story, schools attended, jobs, and glowing recommendations from college professors in India, all just in time to study for her doctorate in England."

"She's a ghost," Luke said.

"It would seem so."

"But why is she Indian?"

Trudy glanced at her notes. "There are about a billion people in India, but no is really sure of the total figure. The country is far behind the Western world in computerizing birth and death records. There's widespread corruption in the civil services there, so it's pretty straightforward to buy the identity of someone who is dead. India is a major global source of fake people."

"Yeah," Swann said, "but then you have to hire an Indian ghost."

Trudy raised a finger. "Not necessarily. To Westerners, there's very little difference in the appearance of people from northern India, where Delhi is, and people from Pakistan, which is right nearby. In fact, to Indians and Pakistanis themselves there isn't much difference. So I'm going to go out on a limb here and guess that Aabha Rushdie is actually a Pakistani, and most likely a Muslim. She might be an agent of the intelligence services there, or worse, a member of a conservative Sunni or Wahhabi sect."

Ed Newsam audibly groaned.

Luke's heart did a lazy belly flop somewhere inside his chest. Of all the analysts he had worked with, Trudy's intel was always at the highest level. Her scenario-spinning ability might well be the best of the bunch. If she was correct in this case, then a Sunni from Pakistan had just stolen a vial of Ebola virus.

Good morning. Rise and shine.

He looked around at the four of them. His eyes landed on Trudy.

"Give us all of it," he said.

"Okay, here comes the worst part," Trudy said.

"It gets worse?" Swann said. "I thought we just heard the worst part. How does it get any worse than that?"

"First, the heads of the Galveston facility spent the first forty-eight hours after they realized a theft had occurred covering it up. Well, I don't want to say they covered it up. They did their own internal investigation, which bore no fruit at all. They sent people to look for Aabha Rushdie, although she was probably already long gone. They could not initially believe that Aabha had stolen a virus. The people I talked to late last night still can't believe it. Everyone there loved her, apparently, though no one knew much about her."

"You mean, like they didn't know she's been dead for twenty-five years?" Swann said.

Trudy went on. "So they interviewed all of the lab technicians, to see if anyone had taken the vial by accident. No one confessed, and there was no reason to suspect anyone. They checked their inventory records, and of course, the vial had been inventoried as secured just a few hours before the lights went out."

"Why do you suppose they delayed?"

"That's the second thing, and probably the worst part of all of this. The vial taken isn't just the Ebola virus. It's a weaponized version of the Ebola virus. Three years ago, the lab received a large grant from the United States Centers for Disease Control, and match funding from the National Institutes of Health, and the Department of Homeland Security. The funding was to find ways to modify the virus, making it even more virulent than it already was—increasing the ease with which it could be transmitted from person to person, the speed with which the Ebola disease would onset, and the percentage of infected people the virus would kill."

"Why the hell would they do that?" Swann said.

"The idea was to weaponize the virus before any terrorists could, then study its properties, identify its vulnerabilities, and find ways to cure people who might one day become infected by it. The lab scientists succeeded with the first part of this task—weaponization—beyond anyone's wildest dreams. Using a gene therapy technique known as insertion, the researchers were able to create a number of mutations to the original Ebola virus.

"The new virus can be introduced into a population through an aerosol spray. Once infected, a person will become contagious within an hour, and will show onset of symptoms within at most two to three hours. In other words, an infected person could begin to infect others *before* symptoms of the disease appear.

"This is important. It's a radical departure from the virus in its natural state. The progression of Ebola in human populations is normally stopped when victims are quarantined in a hospital before, or very soon after, they become contagious. To stop this virus, an entire geographic area, sick people and healthy people, would have to be quarantined together. You wouldn't know right away who had the virus and who didn't. That means road closures, checkpoints, and barricades."

"Martial law," Ed Newsam said.

"Exactly. And even worse, this virus can pass from person to person through tiny droplets in the air, and the illness usually presents with a violent cough. So no exposure to blood, vomit, or excrement is necessary, another radical departure from the original."

"Anything else?" Luke said. He felt like he had already heard enough.

"Yes. The absolute worst part, as far as I'm concerned. The virus is highly virulent and very deadly. The lethality of the hemorrhagic illness it brings on is estimated at about ninety-four percent without medical intervention. This is the rate at which it killed off a colony of three hundred rhesus monkeys at a secure research facility in San Antonio two months ago. The virus was deliberately introduced into the colony, and within forty-eight hours, two hundred eighty-two of the monkeys were dead. More than half died within the first six hours. Of the eighteen who survived, three never contracted the illness, and fifteen recovered on their own over the next few weeks.

"The disease presents a nightmare scenario in which organs fail, blood vessels collapse, and the victim becomes completely debilitated and basically bleeds out, often in spectacular fashion. We're talking about blood from the mouth, the ears, the eyes, the anus, and vagina, basically any bodily orifice, sometimes including the pores of the skin."

Swann raised his hands. "Okay. You said ninety-four percent died without medical intervention. What would the kill rate be if there was a medical intervention?"

Trudy shook her head. "No one knows. The virus is so contagious, so fast-acting, and so lethal that medical intervention may not be possible. As far as we know, nearly every unprotected person who comes into contact with the virus will become sick. The only effective way to stop an outbreak might be to quarantine a population until the disease runs its course."

"With the people trapped inside the quarantine zone left to die?" Ed Newsam said.

"Yes, in most cases. And it's a horrible death."

A long moment passed. Luke shook his head. This was a far cry from the tone the facility director had used with the President the evening before. The guy had clearly been trying to downplay the severity of the breach, even with the President of the United States in the room.

Luke looked up from his thoughts. Everyone on the plane was staring at him.

"We have to get that vial back," he said.

CHAPTER NINE

"We're too far behind," Trudy said.

Her voice trembled the slightest amount. She said it abruptly, with no prompting from anyone. Trudy had become uncharacteristically quiet on the second half of the flight down here. While Swann and Newsam traded tall tales, she had sat with her head against the window, typing notes into her tablet.

Now, Luke watched her. She and Swann were unpacking laptop computers and setting them up on a long table. Luke's team was in an old classroom. The room was on the seventh floor, on the other side of the building from the BSL-4 lab, and down at the end of a long hallway. It was quiet up here. There was nobody around.

This was their operations center. The room looked like it hadn't been used in years.

Luke ran a finger along the windowsill. It was coated with a fine layer of dust. The lab heads wanted to seem like they were cooperating, but this was less than robust cooperation. Luke got the feeling they were tucked away back here because no one wanted them snooping around the facility. Well, it wasn't going to matter what the lab people wanted.

He glanced out the window at the sunny, sticky South Texas morning.

"Tell me," he said.

She didn't even look at him. "I've been running numbers and scenarios. The situation is very, very bad, worse than I even thought at first. This crime took place four days ago. It might as well have been a year."

"I'm listening," he said.

"Well, there's no reason to assume the vial is still in the hands of the person who stole it. In fact, I'd say the chances are ninety-nine percent that it isn't. It probably passed hands, and got on an airplane the same night it was stolen, or very early the next morning. So we're looking at a possible operations radius that includes the entire world. The vial could be anywhere on Earth by now."

Luke hadn't allowed himself to think about it in that way. He wasn't ready to search the whole world. At this moment, he was more concerned about Trudy than the Ebola. He had seen a lot of breakdowns in his time as a soldier and an operative, and Trudy was beginning to look like a candidate for one. He couldn't say he blamed her. It had been a hell of a past week.

The government had nearly been toppled, and people were wondering what she knew, and when. Don Morris, her boss until very recently, and the man with whom she'd been having an affair, was in federal prison as a co-conspirator. She was under a lot of stress. Everyone had their breaking point.

"Okay," he said. "We're going to take this one step at a time. We're still crawling right now."

She shook her head. "You don't get it. The Ebola is already weaponized. All that's required now is to multiply it, which is a pretty straightforward affair. College students could do it. You could set up a lab, in Syria say, or in the tribal areas of Pakistan, or in northern Nigeria, outside the reach of any law or state. If you make enough of the stuff, then we're talking about the potential for multiple attacks, again and again, with one of the most dangerous substances known to man."

Luke thought about what she was saying for a long moment. "Wouldn't it take a lot of money and expertise to build a lab like that? I mean, look at this place." He gestured ironically at the empty, low-tech classroom. "It must have cost a billion dollars."

She shook her head emphatically. "It doesn't matter what we spend on facilities. This is the United States. You can do the same thing only faster, and on the cheap, especially if the people handling the virus are true believers. You're not concerned with safety. You're building to the barest minimum standards. You don't care if your people get sick. Also, this theft was obviously planned months, if not years, in advance. They could have built the lab two years ago, waiting for this day."

Luke felt that familiar sick feeling in the pit of his stomach. It was an old friend by now. Trudy was right. Of course she was. They were far behind. He would call the President today and tell her they needed more resources. Hell, they needed a gigantic manhunt. They needed Navy SEAL and Delta Force operators banging down doors and busting through walls.

And that would come. But first he needed to steer this conversation back onto a productive course. There were things they could do, right here and right now, and they needed to start doing them. The thief wasn't so far ahead that they couldn't catch up.

"The first thing we need to do is figure out where the woman went," he said to the room. "Can we do that?"

Trudy shook her head. "Let's just say the possibilities are unlimited. I mean, it's the ultimate needle in a haystack."

"Why?" Luke said. He knew why, but he needed to hear it. It would help him clarify his own thoughts.

Trudy shrugged. "She could have gone anywhere, by any means. She could be recovering from facial surgery by now, with a dye job, and a whole new identity. She had too many options available for us to calculate. First off, she disappeared in Texas, a state with thirty million people, and a dozen major highways. We're not far from Houston, where there are two major airports. Then there's San Antonio, Austin, and Dallas, all major hubs of transportation. Not to mention she could have gone right out of Galveston, by air or by sea."

Ed Newsam grunted. He leaned against a blank white wall, his crutches next to him. "If I'm carrying precious cargo, no way I'm flying out with regular folks at a public airport. Too risky. One chance in a hundred they spot a little vial like that during the security check, but what if they do? You went to all that trouble to steal the prize, only to lose it the next day at the airport? Unh-uh."

"Sure," Trudy said. "But that's assuming she didn't drive her car out to the West Texas hill country. What if she did? What if she drove out into the middle of nowhere, away from any traffic or security cameras, and someone picked her up? Then what?"

"All right," Luke said.

He raised a hand as if to say STOP. Even so, he liked where this was going. His people were thinking, their minds were sparking off each other, reaching out across time and space, making connections. This was how they were going to track down that woman.

"Let's dial this back to the beginning," he said. "Don't assume anything, right? This is a secure facility. That means there are video cameras in the parking lot. Maybe they were working that night, maybe they weren't. But there's also going to be traffic cams on the roads leading over to the highway, and security cameras on entryways to businesses, in alleyways, and in parking lots. She's going to be picked up as a peripheral image on a lot of footage."

"True enough," Trudy said.

"So we start from the moment she left the grounds. We have that time, right?"

Trudy nodded. "We have the security guard's testimony. Also, if it wasn't down, the electronic key system will have data on her ID passing out of the building."

"Perfect," Luke said. "What was she driving again?"

Trudy glanced at her tablet. "A blue BMW Z4 convertible. Texas plates."

"Great. It's a distinctive car. It doesn't look like everything else. Find that car on camera, then follow it out from here in an ever-expanding arc. See where she went. Did she stop anywhere? If you think about it, it's not really a needle in a haystack. We know what time she left, and from where. We're right on the coast—we know she didn't drive south into the Gulf of Mexico, and there really aren't many places to go west or east. That's going to narrow the amount of surveillance footage we need."

"This is also a sensitive area," Swann said. He had three laptops lined up across the table. He opened them each in turn. In his left hand he held a loop of yellow cabling.

"You've got a ton of shipping here, you've got oil refineries, you've got this biological facility, and it's all on this little strip of land. It wouldn't surprise me if there are satellites watching this peninsula twenty-four hours a day. Our satellites, Russian satellites, Saudi satellites, Iranians, Israelis, Chinese, various corporate and black satellites. I'll bet you five dollars there's plenty of interest in what goes on here."

"Can you access that stuff?" Luke said.

Swann smiled.

"Okay," Luke said. "If you can get four-day-old satellite data off of corporate or Chinese servers, you're the man."

"I am the man," Swann said. "Watching you, watching me, that's the game we're all playing."

Luke nodded. "Good. My bet is that Ed is right. She didn't go out of a major airport. Too much scrutiny. So pay particular attention for gaps in the video footage. Try to sync it with the satellite data. Does she disappear from video for a while? If so, where is she? Is she near a small private airport, or even an old airfield? Is she near a marina? There's nothing but open ocean here. She could have gone out by boat."

"What if she pulled into the parking lot of a little league field and just handed the vial to someone?" Trudy said.

"We try to pinpoint that moment. If Swann can get satellite data, maybe we see the two cars parked side by side. Then we have two cars to follow. Listen, I'm not saying it's easy. I'm just saying it's necessary. If there's too much information to sift through, hire it out like we've done before. I don't care. Personally, I think she stops somewhere, and if so, I want to see her do it."

"And if she didn't?"

"If she didn't stop, then we follow her as far as we can out to the hill country. We at least try to confirm that she really did jump in her car and drive two or three hundred miles with a vial of weaponized Ebola in her glove box. I don't think she did, but I'm open to being wrong about it."

A young man in a white lab coat and glasses stood in the open doorway. He appeared there all of a sudden, as if he had come carefully down the hallway without making a sound. He cleared his throat.

"Agent Stone? The director is ready to see you, sir."

Luke looked at Trudy and Swann.

"Are we a go?"

They nodded. "We're a go," Swann said.

"Then go, kids, go. Get me that BMW. Once we have that, we have a beachhead. We'll fight for territory from there. In the meantime, Ed and I are going downstairs to work over this director."

CHAPTER TEN

"I need to go inside the lab," Luke said.

The balding man with the pronounced paunch shook his head just slightly. He leaned back in his chair. He was Wesley Drinan, Ph.D., Director of the Galveston National Laboratory. He wore a long white lab coat, instead of the suit from the day before. The coat had various stains on it. He had a pair of safety goggles on a cord draped around his neck. Drinan had returned to his natural environment.

Even so, he did not seem relaxed. He seemed sick. His face was red and a fine sheen of sweat gave a glossy look to his forehead. His eyes were bloodshot and tired. His skin was off-white, like a color you might paint the finished basement.

Doing a quick round-trip to Washington to answer questions from the President didn't seem to agree with him.

"Mr. Stone, I'm afraid that's impossible," Drinan said. "You don't have the training required to go in there. In any event, the lab is closed until we conclude our investigation."

Luke and Ed were sitting in Drinan's office, across the desk from him. The office was large and sunny, with a huge brown desk near one wall. There were two windows behind the desk that looked out on the green lawns and concrete walkways of the campus.

Sitting catty-corner to the desk was Drinan's deputy director, a slightly round middle-aged woman with red hair and red glasses to match. Luke hadn't even bothered to catch her name. His focus was Drinan.

Luke had taken a dislike to Director Drinan. If Trudy was right, then Drinan had downplayed the severity of this situation in front of the President and her team yesterday. Luke didn't like that. He didn't like Drinan's officious, self-important personality. Right now, he was looking for something he could like about Wesley Drinan, and he wasn't finding anything.

"You can call me Agent Stone," Luke said. "And the truth is your girl Aabha didn't have the training to go in there either. But that didn't seem to stop her."

Drinan shook his head again, more emphatically this time. "On the contrary. Aabha Rushdie was..." Drinan caught himself speaking about her in the past tense. "Aabha is an accomplished young scientist. She was a remarkable student, and as a professional, she has mastered every facet of..."

"Aabha Rushdie died in 1990," Ed Newsam said.

Ed was slumped deep into his chair in his typical laconic style, his crutches leaning alongside his body. In contrast to the director, Ed seemed very relaxed. He seemed almost ready to take a nap. He shrugged, as if to soften the harsh abruptness of his statement.

"So I've been told," Ed added.

Drinan looked from Ed, to Luke, then to his deputy director. If anything, his face became a darker shade of red. He turned back to Luke.

"What does your..."

"Partner," Luke said.

"What does your partner mean by that?"

Luke shrugged. "We have access to the best intel available. You know how your job is to study and safeguard diseases? Our job is to conduct investigations. We do a very good job. The woman who worked here, and who called herself Aabha Rushdie, was a fake. She was a plant of some kind. A spy, if you like. She may have been working for Pakistani intelligence. That would be the best-case scenario. It's kind of a long shot, but it's the one we're hoping for. She may also have been working for Sunni Muslim extremists. Unfortunately for everyone, that's much more likely. If that was indeed the case, then by now, a violent terrorist organization probably has their hands on your weaponized Ebola virus."

Drinan stared at Luke, his mouth hanging open a small amount.

"The real Aabha Rushdie was a little girl who died in a car crash in India in 1990. The woman you knew was using Aabha Rushdie as a cover story."

As Luke watched, Drinan's face darkened to a dangerous shade of red, a red bordering on purple. He looked like a bottle of cheap wine. Luke was no doctor, but Drinan sure looked like a man with a stroke in his future.

For the past five minutes or so, Luke had watched how the overhead light reflected off Drinan's gold wedding band. Occasionally, the stubby fingers of Drinan's right hand would find the ring and give it a little twist around his ring finger. The ring was on Drinan's mind, whether he knew it or not.

"Aabha was your mistress," Luke said. He didn't know he was thinking it until the words were out of his mouth. All the same, it wasn't a question. Aabha did whatever was necessary to penetrate this facility completely. Of course she did. Her handlers wouldn't have it any other way. You don't insert an operative into a situation like this and go halfsies with it.

Next to Drinan, the deputy director gasped. Her mouth hung open. She turned and stared at Drinan.

"Wesley?" she said.

Luke raised a hand to quiet her. He directed his words to Drinan. "You've been worried about Aabha these past few days. Your blood pressure is sky high. You're not sleeping because you've been terrified for her safety. You're also afraid of being found out. These are the reasons you've downplayed the seriousness of this breach, and conducted this bogus internal investigation. You were buying time while looking for Aabha. You were hoping this whole thing was a mistake."

Drinan hung his head. A long moment passed. When Drinan finally spoke, his voice was small.

"Yes."

Luke nodded. The whole picture came together for him with an almost audible CLANG. "Her access to the BSL-4 lab and the materials in the lab was quite a bit accelerated, wasn't it? And that happened as a result of her relationship with you."

The man nodded. He mumbled something under his breath.

"I'm sorry," Luke said. "I didn't hear you."

Drinan nearly shouted. "Yes!"

Suddenly, the deputy director rose from her seat, turned, and stalked out of the room. She slammed the door behind her. The sound of her heels echoed down the hallway.

"Mmm, mmm, mmm," Ed said. "Maybe there were two affairs going on."

There was a moment of quiet.

"You're in a lot of trouble," Luke told Drinan. "What it boils down to is you traded access to a high-security lab for sexual favors. These are grounds for immediate dismissal, of course. You have a wedding ring on, so I'll assume you're also headed for a rough patch there. More important, you've committed half a dozen felonies that I can think of right off the top of my head. You're looking at years in jail even if we get that vial back this afternoon. Last but not least, as a byproduct of your incredibly selfish and unprofessional behavior, you've put countless civilian populations, and possibly the entire world, at risk."

Ed barely stirred from his slouch. "I hope she was worth all that."

Drinan began to cry now, his head hanging almost to his knees.

"What am I going to do?" he said.

"Well," Luke said, "for starters, you're going to grant me access to that lab."

*

Luke's breath sounded loud in his ears.

He wore a blue jumpsuit inside the white containment suit. Inside of his suit, no part of his skin touched the air of the laboratory. An orange hose ran from his suit to the ceiling, pumping air into the suit. He knew the design. The air wasn't so he could breathe. It was to create positive pressure, driving air into the lab and away from him. Theoretically, no virus molecules could enter the suit as long as the hose was pumping.

He was the only one in the lab. To the uninitiated, it looked like a pretty normal microbiology lab. Clean metal surfaces, spotless floor, glass cabinets, and stools for studying samples. But Luke knew it was much more than that.

He had studied the map of the lab before coming in here. Standing here was like being inside a submarine—a submarine parked deep inside a giant vault. The entire facility was surrounded by double HEPA filters, catching 99.99 percent of even the tiniest airborne particles before they entered the air of the vault. Airborne virus particles were far too big to make it through the filters.

Luke had passed through a buffer hallway, several locked doors, and finally an airlock to get in here. It was a complex, highly technical arrangement, with numerous built-in redundancies. There were video cameras and security protocols at every turn.

And none of it had worked. When push came to shove, a beautiful woman simply walked out of the facility with the virus in her hand.

"Luke?" Ed's voice was everywhere at once.

"Yeah, man."

"How's it going in there?"

"It's okay. I'm just getting acclimated."

"You almost ready?"

"Yeah. Just give me another minute."

Ed was up in the security room, watching through a camera. He was up there with the guard, Tom Eder, who had let Aabha walk out of here. Eder was already on record that he had a crush on Aabha, and enjoyed watching her through the security cameras.

She must be quite a creature, that Aabha. A creature of the night. According to Eder, she was often here until midnight or later.

"Okay, Tom," Luke said. "What would I do?"

"Okay," Eder's voice said. "You would walk to that cabinet in front of you, enter your personal four-digit security code, and remove the material you want to work with."

"Every person in the lab has their own code?" Luke said.

"Yes. It makes inventory easier. The system time stamps when a person went into the cabinet. If something turns up missing, we know who the last person inside the cabinet was."

Luke nodded. All the more reason to know right away that Aabha had taken the virus. All the more reason to hang Wesley Drinan out to dry.

"For today, we've given you a twenty-four-hour dummy pass code. It's 9999."

Luke went to the cabinet, slowly punched in the code with his thick-gloved finger. The light on the keypad went from red to green, and Luke opened the door. There were dozens of vials in the cabinet, each sitting in a round slot. It was impossible for him to tell what was what. He took any vial, palmed it, then shut the cabinet.

"Okay, Luke," Tom said, "now you would turn to your left and walk toward the biosafety cabinet there, as if you were going to study the contents of the vial. That's when the lights will go off. Are you ready?"

"I'm ready."

The lights went out. For a long moment, Luke stood in absolute darkness. There were no windows in this lab. When the lights went off, all light went out of the room. He couldn't see anything.

"Don't turn the lights on yet," he said. "Give me another minute."

He stared into the black. His eyes didn't adjust to the low light. There was no light to adjust to. It did something funny to his balance, being in darkness so total. He took a deep breath and held it. The air pumping into his hose slowed to a stop. The fans in the room slowed to a stop. In a moment, there was no sound.

He pictured what it was like for the woman called Aabha. She has the Ebola vial in her hand. She is going to leave with it. She knows Tom has a crush on her. She knows she can manipulate him easily. Manipulation is her stock-in-trade.

Is she nervous? Is she excited? Is she such a cold-blooded pro that she doesn't feel anything?

Where is she going when she leaves here? Why is she doing this?

Where is she now?

Luke didn't consider himself psychic. He didn't know if he even believed in psychics. But he did believe that human intuition, the subconscious, could solve problems the waking mind could not. There were links to the larger world, and to other people, deep inside the mind.

In his mind, he searched for Aabha. A beautiful woman in an expensive sports car. A woman with no past. A woman with no future.

He saw her driving in the night. She was very confident. She felt she could navigate this shadow world, this black world of lies. But she was wrong. Once she stole the Ebola, she became nothing more than a loose end. Her handlers had no reason to let her live, and every reason to kill her.

Luke reached for her in the darkness, but she wasn't there. He nodded to himself. He couldn't know it, and yet he knew it anyway.

Aabha was dead.

The lights came on suddenly. Not the low-level emergency lights and the EXIT signs like they had agreed upon—all the overhead lights. The brightness briefly staggered him. His hose came back on, once again delivering air to his containment suit.

"What's going on?" he said. "I thought we were going to make this the way it was that night."

Ed's voice: "Luke, we need to cut this thing short. I just got a call from Trudy upstairs. She and Swann think they might have found Aabha."

CHAPTER ELEVEN

12:45 p.m.
United States Naval Observatory – Washington, DC

"You were very lucky," the doctor said.

His name was Otto Jazayeri, and he had flown up from Jupiter Island, Florida, this morning to give his opinion on the new President's facial burns. He was overweight, bald, with thick glasses. He reminded Susan of a sitting Buddha in a blue suit and tie. He wore a scope over his right eye, which made the eye seem enormous, like a cow's eye. He flicked off the light on the apparatus and placed the scope on the table.

They sat together in the upstairs reception room. Susan had banished the Secret Service from the room. She knew that three of them waited just outside the door. The Secret Service was hesitant to allow her out of their sight, but they relaxed the rules here at home. In the past forty-eight hours, all of the windows in the house had been reinforced with an extra layer of bulletproof glass.

Susan's daughter Michaela sat on the floor nearby, leafing through a *US Weekly* magazine. Michaela was one of the eleven-year-old twins, growing up without a mom. Lauren lounged on the sofa on the other side of the room, her ears covered by fancy headphones, her mind absorbed by whatever was happening on her iPhone. They were beautiful, beautiful girls. Long brown hair, blue eyes—in another few years they could probably begin their careers as models. Of course, Pierre wouldn't hear of it.

He stood by the floor-to-ceiling window, gazing out at the grounds, his arms folded behind him. This was Pierre being pensive, quiet, possibly depressed. In Susan's experience, he was one of the most exuberant and expressive people on Earth. He had a mind that never stopped.

"What's the story?" Susan said.

She spoke normally, in a controlled manner. Inside, she felt like she was cracking apart. Her face had been burned! It seemed so stupid, so vain, in a time when hundreds of people had been murdered, people she had known and respected, people she had hated, the best and the worst all torched together... and Susan sat here with her stomach in knots, worried about her face.

She blinked and for a split second, she could see the flames erupting through the doorway to the Mount Weather media room, a fireball coming down the hall. She could feel the big Secret Service man tackling her again, her head hitting the floor. She could almost remember dreaming in darkness as hundreds of people were incinerated thirty yards away.

She could get her face fixed, she supposed. But who was going to fix her mind?

The doctor pursed his lips. He had a vague accent that Susan couldn't place. He had probably been in the United States a long time.

"The first doctors who saw you did a decent job, and diagnosed you more or less correctly. You have second-degree burns across the right side of your face, your neck, and on your right hand. Most of the burn surface is superficial and will heal on its own. I'm going to prescribe you a certain antibiotic ointment, which will protect you against infection. You should apply this several times a day. In two weeks, you will notice marked improvement and fading of the red discoloration."

Susan released her breath. "I can't tell you what a relief that is."

The man raised a hand. "I'm not finished. I was referring to most of the burn surface. But a small portion of your burns are what we call partial deep burns. In those instances, almost the entire skin-producing architecture has been damaged. With this type of burn, the healing process is slower and may extend beyond fourteen days. If the healing process stops, we will be looking at the potential for permanent scarring. In such a case, it's best to excise the burn and cover the area with a skin graft. You have a beautiful face, as you know, and very well preserved skin for a woman your age. In my opinion, it will be worth undergoing surgery to save your appearance."

"You're saying you want to operate?" Pierre said from the window.

"I'm saying I want to wait ten days or two weeks, see how the healing is progressing, and if I'm not satisfied, then I will want to operate."

"Is there a recovery period?" Susan said.

The doctor nodded. His head movement was barely perceptible. "There is a tolerable recovery period, during which your face will be bandaged, and will not be exposed to light or air."

66

"I'm in the public eye a lot."

"I know. I was thinking that it would add an element of interest. People will watch to see how your healing is progressing."

Pierre turned around. Suddenly he was the billionaire businessman. It was a side of himself that he rarely showed anymore.

"Otto, are you out of your mind? That's about the dumbest thing I've heard in all my days. This isn't a reality TV show. Susan is the President of the United States." He lowered his voice so the girls wouldn't hear him. "She was nearly killed less than a week ago. We don't need any more elements of interest around here."

The doctor was unmoved. He addressed Susan. "My flight is at four p.m., so I should be going. I will leave you to discuss this with your husband. I can return in another week. We'll move forward however you prefer."

When the doctor left, Pierre moved close to her. She studied his pale blue eyes and the lines that had formed on his face.

"You don't seem yourself," he said.

She shrugged. "How would you seem, if you were me?"

He smiled. "I'd be in a straitjacket by now, curled up in a ball in the corner of a rubber room."

She laughed, and for a moment, things were good.

He gestured with his head toward the bathroom. She followed him in there to get a moment away from the girls. The bathroom was large, modern, sterile, out of place within the 1850s style of the house itself. It was a bathroom for visitors.

"Are you okay?" Pierre said.

Susan didn't even have to think about it. She glanced around the room for a second, wondering how many microphones there were in here. Oh well. She had to speak sometime. She had to tell someone what was real. Pierre was one of the few people on Earth she completely trusted.

"No. I'm not okay. I'm barely holding myself together."

Suddenly, the tears were about to come. She held them back for the moment, but they were like flood waters, rising and rising. Pierre stepped close and took her in his arms. She melted into him, and it felt so good, almost like it once did.

"They want to kill me, Petey. I can't stand it. I'm so afraid."

"I know," he said. He held her. Her body started to shake.

"Luke Stone... the day after the attacks... he went to the house where his wife and son were held. He murdered four men like it was nothing. Two of the men were identified today. They were both former CIA agents. These are the type of men who tried to kill me? Why? How can I stop them?"

Pierre just held her.

She couldn't breathe. "My face is all burned. God, my face! They're going to kill me. I know it. I can never be safe again. Oh my God."

The tears came now. In a moment, they were more than tears. Her body was wracked by sobs. Her legs felt weak. She clung to him, wishing he could protect her, knowing that he couldn't. His money, his prestige, it wasn't enough.

She pushed herself against him. Her mouth opened wide in a silent scream. His neck was wet with her tears.

"Please," she said. "Please make them stop."

He held her while she cried. After a while, he began to rock her like a baby. "It's okay," he whispered to her. "It's okay. You're okay."

After a long while, she began to feel better. She leaned her head against his chest and took a deep breath.

"I want to tell you something," he said. "I'm going back to California. I'm taking the girls, and I want you to come with me. We can leave as soon as tomorrow. We can leave tonight, if we really want. We'll hole up at the Malibu house with a hundred armed guards. Eventually, the killers will forget all about you."

"How can I go to California?" she said. "I'm the President of the United States."

He pulled away just slightly and looked directly into her eyes. The boy she had married was gone. The laughing, carefree man-child who created vast fortunes with his mind—where did he go? Also gone.

It was bad. Pierre wasn't built for this life. He had been pampered since his earliest days. He had never grown up. His parents—a brain surgeon and a daughter of the French nobility—had given him whatever exotic toys he wanted. He had never stopped playing with toys. He was badly out of his element.

Susan could see it in those beautiful pale blue eyes. Pierre was afraid, maybe more afraid than she was.

"Quit," he said simply. "You don't owe these people anything. You've said it to me yourself. You never wanted to be President. Why get killed for something you didn't even want? Just walk away from the whole thing. I'm sure they can find someone else who would love to be in your shoes right now. Let that person die for nothing."

It was tempting, the things he was saying. But it was also wrong, so far wrong that she almost couldn't imagine where it was coming from. She looked away for a second, then back into his eyes. Her paranoid self, the one who had survived the Mount Weather disaster, the one who had been strafed by machine gun fire while riding in an armored car, could almost believe that Pierre had somehow been replaced by an imposter.

But no. It was him. He wanted out from this, and he wanted her out with him.

"I can't do that," she said. "I do owe them. The American people voted for me, they hired me for this job."

"They hired you to be Vice President."

She nodded. "Right. And to replace the President if he died. So I'm it. The country is in crisis, one of the worst in American history, and I owe them my leadership. I owe them the best I can do, such as it is."

As she spoke, she felt a certain strength and confidence coming back. She was tough, tougher than Pierre would ever be. She knew that about herself. She had grown up fast as a teenager in the shark-infested waters of elite fashion modeling. She had fought and won the bruising political battles necessary to become a U.S. Senator from California, and then Vice President. Somehow, she would fight her way through this.

"I'm sorry to hear you say that," Pierre said.

Susan smiled then, just a touch. "I'm not."

A knock came at the bathroom door, startling them both.

"Yes?" she said. She glanced in the mirror. Her makeup had smeared. Her mascara had run down from the corners of her eyes. She looked a little like a circus clown.

"Madame President?"

Susan recognized the voice of a young aide named Anne.

"Yes. I'm in here with my husband."

"Yes, ma'am. I was sent to get you. An Al Qaeda affiliate has just released a new video on the internet. Your security advisors want you to see it."

Susan sighed. Terrorist organizations released videos on a daily basis. Suicide bombers preparing for their missions, prisoners being executed, religious figureheads making proclamations... It made for dreary watching. And it was probably the least of their worries right now.

"What is the video about?"

Anne's voice sounded small and girlish from the other side of the thick wooden door. Still, Susan wasn't about to open the door looking like this. "Uh, they are threatening to... uh... destroy the United States."

"And our people consider this a credible threat?"

"Yes."

Susan looked at Pierre. He shook his head.

"Tell them I'll be there in ten minutes."

*

"Who are we looking at?" Susan said.

There was a still photo on the video screen. It showed a brown-skinned man with a long black beard, speckled with white. He wore glasses, a white turban on his head, and a black robe. He was very thin.

"The man's name is Abu Saddiq Mohammed," said Kurt Kimball, Susan's new National Security Advisor. He had been in the job two days. Three days ago, he had been working for the Rand Corporation, writing briefs on international hotspots and terrorism threats. Kurt was tall with broad shoulders, and as bald as a cue ball.

Twenty people sat at the conference table and lined the walls in the new Situation Room. The Room, as the staffers were starting to call it, was taking shape on the fly. It had been in almost constant use since Susan had taken the oath of office. People were taking their meals in here. There were threats emerging everywhere you looked.

Kimball went on. "Saddiq Mohammed was born sometime in the mid-1950s among a tribe of border-crossing desert nomads in the southern Arabian peninsula. He probably has no formal education. He went to Afghanistan to join the mujahideen fighting against the Russians, perhaps as early as 1979 or 1980. As you know, that loose confederacy of fighters coalesced over time into various factions, including Al Qaeda. Since the death of Osama bin Laden and the disappearance of Ayman al-Zawahiri, Mohammed has taken on an increasing role as a mouthpiece for Al Qaeda, though he claims no leadership in that or any organization."

70

"Where is he now?" Susan said.

"No one knows for sure. We believe he's in the tribal regions of Pakistan, or possibly under protection of the Taliban in eastern Afghanistan. He may cross back and forth across the border, depending on what kind of heat we're bringing. His people are careful to use generic and obscure backgrounds whenever he makes a video. In the video you're about to see, all meta-data has been erased, including time, date, and location. The video itself was uploaded to the internet from an empty warehouse in Belgium frequented by squatters and heroin addicts."

"So how do we know it's authentic?" said Richard Monk, Susan's chief-of-staff.

Kimball was undeterred. "We've used voice recognition software to pattern Mohammed's voice. We have numerous good samples from previous video and audio, and the voice on this tape is a match. We know it's him. In the beginning of the video, he refers to former Speaker of the House William Ryan and the attempted overthrow of the United States. No discernable splicing has been done, which means the video was filmed sometime in the past week."

The footage began. It was nothing exciting. It showed the man sitting in a chair near a wall made of what appeared to be red sandstone. He spoke in Arabic, into a microphone clipped to his robe. He seemed to read from prepared remarks. Susan couldn't understand a single word he said. The clip lasted slightly more than a minute.

"Okay," she said. "So what did we just watch?"

"The whole video is quite a bit longer than this," Kimball said. "There's a lot of typical stuff in it, and he hits notes everyone in this room is probably familiar with. He criticizes the apostate leaders of Iran, and calls for all pure Muslims to resist Iranian incursions in Syria. He criticizes Israel's treatment of the Palestinians, and likens it to the Holocaust. He describes the kings of both Jordan and Saudi Arabia as the minions of Satan. He implores God to bring about the destruction of Russia."

"Is there anybody this guy likes?" someone said.

A smattering of laughter went around the room.

"Well, he saves the best for last. He describes the United States as the lair of Satan, and suggests that President Hopkins is Satan's concubine."

"Terrific," Susan said. "It's been quite a while since somebody called me a whore. As far as I know, anyway."

"I was careful not to use that word," Kimball said. "But that is the implication. Now here comes the dangerous part. In that last section, he tells all of his followers to have hope, because the soldiers of Allah have acquired the greatest weapon in Heaven and on Earth. They've stolen the weapon from Satan's lair, and God willing they will use it to bring pestilence and plague down upon the heads of the Crusaders, such as Allah did in the time of the Prophet."

The room was quiet.

"The obvious reference here is to plague and pestilence, and to stealing a weapon from Satan's lair."

"The Ebola virus," Susan said.

Kimball nodded. "He knows about it, which is bad enough. The theft isn't public knowledge yet. And he's telling us it's in the hands of Islamic terrorists, which is even worse. In all likelihood, this means the virus was stolen by extremists affiliated with Al Qaeda. He wouldn't be nearly as excited if Hezbollah or Iran had taken it. Worst of all, he is clearly suggesting they know what they have, and they plan to release it, either on American soil, or on American military stationed overseas."

"Hence the reference to Crusaders," Susan said.

"Yes."

"What do you suppose he really wants?" Susan said.

Kimball shrugged. "He doesn't say, so I won't speculate. It could be he wants to do exactly what he describes, which is bring a plague of Biblical or Quranic proportions down upon the United States."

"Jesus," someone in the back of the room said.

"Do you think they can do it?"

Kimball shook his head. "I have no idea."

"So where do we go from here?" Susan said.

"Well, that's the thing," Kimball said. "We have an overture in front of us. It's a little bit unprecedented..."

"It's ridiculous," said Richard Monk.

"Try me," Susan said.

Kimball raised a hand. "Bear with me. Don't say no until you hear everything I have to say."

"Susan, if I were you, I'd say no now," Monk said.

"Okay, Richard. I'm clear on your position, but I haven't even heard what it is we're talking about."

"There's a man named Robert Hassan Cole," Kimball said. "He's of mixed African-American, Irish-American, and Syrian descent. He was born and raised in the Brownsville section of Brooklyn."

"I know who he is," Susan said.

An involuntary shiver ran through her at the thought of him. He was a young American, a failed rapper, who had become a radicalized Muslim, then disappeared into the vortex of war-torn Syria. Eventually, it became clear to US intelligence that the same man was also a black-masked executioner of orange-clad hostages. He often beheaded helpless prisoners with a machete while it was videotaped, to be released later on the internet. Hostages who had been ransomed said that the prisoners had a nickname with which they referred to their sadistic jailer.

"Robert Hassan Cole is Brooklyn Bob," Susan said.

Kimball nodded. "That's right."

"What about him?"

Now Kimball seemed somewhat sheepish. "He's waiting on the phone. He's using a satellite phone from inside the city of Raqqa, the ISIS stronghold in eastern Syria, and we have him on the line. He says he's been empowered to talk to us, and he insists that he will only speak directly to you. We think he wants to offer a trade. We can patch him in to the conference call speaker right here on the table."

Susan glanced around the room at all the faces. They stared back at her. She didn't know three-quarters of them. They stared at her, almost entirely men, waiting to see what she would say. Their eyes were hard. Masculine energy came off them in waves. They reminded her of sharks.

"What do we know about him?" Susan said.

"Well, he was raised in poverty. His father abandoned the family when he was young, then he, his mother, and his younger sister lived on welfare. His sister was run over and killed at the age of seven by a drunk driver. Cole tested well and was accepted into the elite Brooklyn Technical High School, which he attended for two years, before dropping out at the age of sixteen. After that, he was a petty drug dealer, had numerous run-ins with the law, and he attempted a music career. He seems to have become serious about

73

Islam around the age of eighteen, when he joined a Brooklyn mosque known for harboring radicals."

Susan pictured someone raised in that way. No father, no money, a dead sister, and surrounded by poverty. It was obvious to her, as a mother, that his feelings had been deeply hurt. He was a wounded child, and he had lashed out as a result. But he had taken it way too far.

Kimball went on. "He disappeared at the age of twenty, and turned up in Syria sometime after the civil war started, maybe 2013. He may have been in Afghanistan before that, and possibly Somalia before that. He's young, he's reckless, and he's a little bit of a clown, but he's also very smart and very dangerous. You've all seen the videos where he beheads prisoners."

"It's barbaric," someone behind Susan said.

"It is barbaric," Kimball said. "But it's more than that. It's a very effective recruiting tool. In that sense, Cole represents a new type of jihadi. He's a social media machine. His YouTube rants against what he calls the racist West, often set to driving hip-hop music, receive tens of millions of views. He's a talented recruiter and instigator on Twitter. He's thought to have raised several million dollars from wealthy Muslims in the English-speaking world. He's actually so effective at what he does that he's been accorded special respect by jihadi groups. He speaks Arabic, and he's a go-between from Al-Qaeda affiliates to ISIS. He's believed to have been instrumental in developing the recent truce between them."

Susan got that sense again. Everyone in the room was watching her. It was an uncomfortable feeling. What would these men think if they knew that not fifteen minutes ago she was upstairs crying in the bathroom while her husband hugged her?

They were asking a lot from her. None of them were in the position she was in. None of them had been the target of repeated assassination attempts in the past week. None of them wore body armor every time they went out in public. None of them had been thrust into a situation they neither asked for, nor were ready for.

"What do you think, Susan?" Kimball said.

"Don't talk to him, Susan," Richard Monk said. "Please don't. It's so far beneath you, and everything you've stood for in the time I've known you. He's a terrorist. He's a cold-blooded murderer. In fact, we have his coordinates from the satellite phone he's using. I say we just bomb him and do everyone on Earth a favor by getting rid of him once and for all."

Susan glanced at the black eight-sided conference call speaker at the center of the table where she sat. It was sunny out today, and light from outside streamed in through the windows. A square of yellow light almost reached the speaker.

Susan thought of all the events they had done when she was Vice President. They had seen so many people in so many places. She had done a whistle-stop train tour, riding from Chicago to Oakland, California, on Amtrak one time in the first year after Thomas Hayes had been elected President. It was a publicity stunt conceived by Thomas's people, and it worked astonishingly well.

Throngs of people came out to the train stations at every stop. She spoke to people of every political stripe. They loved the tour, and they loved her. They brought her roast turkeys and apple-rhubarb pies, home-cooked meals to eat while riding the train.

It was fun being Vice President. In contrast, this was...

This was something else again. It had the quality of a nightmare, one from which she could not awaken.

"Susan?" Kimball said.

She looked up at Kimball and nodded. "I'll talk to him," she said.

CHAPTER TWELVE

"If you want to see me," the voice said, "we're live streaming on the internet right now. I've got a guy here that will send you the link. The link is encrypted, so no funny eyes in the sky can see. It's just me to you."

Susan had a funny feeling in her gut. A man in a blue military suit and a crew cut brought an open laptop to the table and placed it in front of her.

"We're muted," the man said. "He's waiting. He can't hear a word we say."

"Can he see me?" Susan said.

"No. We're not going to show him anything. Our people are going to study his video feed to see if we can learn more about where he is. We have his location pinpointed, but we want to see if it's hardened, who's there with him, what weaponry they seem to have, what technology, and all the rest."

Susan nodded. She felt like a little girl, with all these big knowledgeable men running around. "Okay."

On the screen in front of her, a grainy image began to resolve. It was of a human hand, male, with the middle-finger pointed up.

"You guys see me okay over there? You see me, Lady President?"

There was a low chatter of voices in the room.

"Okay," Kurt Kimball said. "We need absolute quiet in here. Cell phone ringers off. If you need to be in contact with someone else right now, then ask yourself why you need to be here in the first place."

Susan glanced around the room. They had already cleared the place out from before. There were maybe fifteen people in the room now, whereas a few minutes ago there had probably been forty.

"Mute is coming off the phone in ten seconds," Kimball said. "I'm the only one who speaks. Susan, of course that doesn't include you. If you choose to speak, I will defer to you. I only caution you not to get into a prolonged conversation with this kid. He's clever, he's infuriating, and he'll try to bait you into saying something you'll regret, and which he can upload to the internet as an audio track."

"Girlfriend, you with me?" Brooklyn Bob said from half a world away.

A voice behind Susan: "We are audible in three, two, one…"

Brooklyn Bob appeared close to the camera. His face was narrow, with a scruffy black beard and long black curly hair. He had blue eyes, a stark contrast to his skin and beard. He was good-looking, of course—most YouTube and social media stars were.

He rapped on the surface of the camera with his knuckles. It sounded like he was knocking on a window. "Hey! Anybody there?"

"We're here," Kimball said. "Can you hear us?"

"I hear you, but I don't hear my girl Susan."

"She's here with us, and is listening to every word you say."

"Can she see me?"

"No. We have a couple of laptops streaming you, but she isn't near one."

Brooklyn Bob glanced away for a second. "Who you kidding, man? You got twenty-nine separate computers streaming me, by our count, clustered in just that one house."

"Most of them are in other parts of the building. Lots of intel people are monitoring you, Bob, but you probably already know that. You're a young man with a short future ahead of you. Anyway, suffice to say that the President can hear you, but she can't see you. She's not interested in seeing you."

Bob shook his head and smiled. "That's too bad. I was planning to show her my joint."

"Let's get to the point," Kimball said. "We've got a Predator drone locked on your position, and we're already running out of patience."

Brooklyn Bob shrugged. "Do it. Then you won't even be warned before Allah's punishment arrives."

He moved back from the camera lens. The camera panned to follow him as he paced a small room. The room was made of cinderblock and was sparsely furnished. He sat in a rickety four-legged chair by a table. He picked up a piece of paper.

"Nice place you got there, Bob," Kimball said.

Susan wasn't sure what to make of Kimball taunting and threatening this person. If this were any other situation, she would find herself appalled by his behavior.

Brooklyn Bob smiled. He shook his head. "Believe me, this place is better than anywhere I lived when I was growing up in the Land of Opportunity."

He looked down at the paper in his hand, then glanced back up at the camera. He gave a sly grin. "You feeling me, Susie Q? You really ain't gonna talk, are you? I wish you would. I'd love to talk to you. When I was a boy, I used to jerk off to your pictures in magazines."

Susan felt her face flush. He was ridiculous. He really would say anything.

"Enough with the foul mouth," Kimball said. "Let's hear it. One more word like that, and I'll call in the air strike. I am not kidding around."

Bob looked at the paper again. "You heard the message from Imam Saddiq Mohammed?"

"Yes."

"You idiots translated it correctly?"

"Of course."

"Okay, then here's the deal. In his speech, the blessed one talked about a plague or a pestilence. That's some old-school lingo, right? He was referring to a quantity of Ebola virus that our brothers took from one of your own laboratories. But you probably figured out that part already. Here's the bad news, from your point of view. There are brothers in the United States right now, in possession of the virus. They know it's weaponized, and they know how to deploy it. Also, the quantity taken has already been multiplied by a factor of at least one million."

A burst of murmuring erupted throughout the room.

Kimball raised his hand.

Brooklyn Bob broke out into a big smile. "That got your attention, huh? Well, here's more bad news." He looked away from the camera for a moment. He spoke in Arabic to someone else in the room with him. Then he turned back to the camera again.

"So I've got about one thirty-five p.m. in Washington, DC, does that sound right? Our brothers are going to deploy the Ebola in a small American city, beginning at five thirty this afternoon, your time. I'm not going to tell you the name of the city, but when the attack hits, I think you'll know very quickly. The fun part will be watching you try to stop it."

"What's the trade?" Kimball said.

For a second, Brooklyn Bob seemed confused. "Trade?"

"Yes. What do you want?"

Bob raised his eyebrows, then smiled wider than ever. "Ohh… I get it. Like what do we want that you can give us, and we won't launch the attack?"

"Right."

78

He shook his head. "We don't want anything. Not yet. See, you can't stop this attack. The whole idea is just to show you what we can do. Later on, after... you know, whatever happens this afternoon... then we'll all get back on the phone and talk about what we want from you."

Susan felt a lump forming in her throat. This boy, for he was little more than a boy, and he acted very much like one, was a monster. How had this country created him, or anyone like him?

"I can tell you," Bob went on, "that although it's a small city, and it's unimportant in a lot of ways, it's also much beloved. People are gonna hate to see it go. That's my little hint, though I doubt it will help you any."

"How can you do this?" Susan said. The words were out of her mouth before she realized she was going to speak, and she instantly regretted it. Even so, she pushed on. "You're going to kill innocent people, don't you know that? Women, children, families..."

Brooklyn Bob's grin lit up. His eyes suddenly came alive.

"There's my girl!" he said. "I love you, Susan. You know why? I love you because *you're* an innocent. Somehow you don't know that your own people kill women and children over here every day. And you know what else I love? I love that the CIA or whoever it was didn't manage to waste you last week. They got everybody else, but not you, right? Hot damn! I bet they're still trying, though."

He shook his head, seemingly at the wonder of it all. "The first woman President, and a fine-looking one at that. I wish I was there with you right now, because you know I just want to..."

"Hang it up!" Kimball shouted. "Hang up the goddamn telephone."

The conference call speaker went dead, but the video feed was still running on Susan's laptop. She stared at the screen as the young lunatic raised his hands in the air and did a deranged, pelvic-thrusting dirty dance while still sitting in his chair.

CHAPTER THIRTEEN

1:45 p.m.

Galveston National Laboratory, campus of the University of Texas Medical Branch – Galveston, Texas

"Who is he?" Luke said.

Swann had loaded a photograph of a young man of Mediterranean descent on the laptop screen. Luke and Ed were back in their little classroom command center. The photo in question was a grainy, faraway paparazzi-type photo of a man in a swimsuit on the deck of a boat.

The four of them huddled around the computer as if it were giving off heat.

"His name is Omar bin Khalid al Saud," Trudy said. "It sounds like a mouthful, but all it really means is Omar, son of Khalid, of the House of Saud. You're looking at an old picture of him. He's forty-two years old now, and he's a member of the Saudi royal family. He's one of the more than a thousand grandchildren of King Abdul Aziz, the founder of modern Saudi Arabia."

"Pretty snazzy," Luke said.

"Right, but we don't want to get carried away. It's not like being a British royal. There are over fifteen thousand people in the Saudi royal family. He's one of them."

"What's his deal?" Luke said, willing to play along for the moment. "But give me the Omar elevator pitch," he said, "not his memoirs."

"He's a billionaire," Trudy said. "Forbes 400. He controls an investment fund called World Holdings, which invests in Western companies, often in the United States. No one knows the portfolio size of World Holdings, but it's thought to be in the hundreds of billions. No one knows who the investors are, either, but it's assumed there are a lot of bad actors in there."

"So he's a go-between," Ed said. "Pouring dirty money for drug lords and weapons dealers into theme parks and soft drinks."

"Bingo," Trudy said. "Among many other investments, World Holdings owns major stakes in Disneyland Paris and Coca-Cola products."

Luke made a circular motion with his hand. "Let's keep this moving," he said. "I'm sure Omar is a wonderful businessman. Why do we care?"

Now Swann chimed in. "He was here in Galveston four nights ago. Or at least his boat was. We have satellite imagery of his mega-yacht, the *Cristina*, at a deep water mooring outside of a place on the peninsula called Pelican Bay Marina."

"Getting warmer," Luke said.

"It gets better," Trudy said. "We've obtained street camera footage of Aabha's BMW turning right into the Pelican Bay Marina parking lot at approximately nine forty-three p.m. on the night of June seventh. We also have street footage of the car leaving the parking lot at ten twenty-two p.m."

"What does the marina say?" Luke said.

"I called them," Trudy said. "They say they don't share information about guests, so they can't confirm the name of anyone using a mooring there on any specific date. I didn't ask for anything specific in case we wanted to subpoena and raid them at a later date. So they wouldn't destroy anything. You understand."

"I do," Luke said. "I understand." He turned to Swann. "Swann?"

Swann smiled. "Yeah. I took the liberty of glancing at their database. That's how we stumbled upon Omar. A two-hundred-fifty-foot yacht owned by a Chilean shell company called Mundo, Inc. leased a deep-water anchorage for three days beginning on June fifth. It also leased a dock berth for its ship-to-shore tender. It set sail at ten thirty-eight p.m. on June seventh, about sixteen minutes after Aabha's car left the marina. There was no destination given."

"And Mundo, Inc?"

"Right," Trudy said. "Mundo, Inc. is a subsidiary of a Bermuda-based company called Nexxxus Holdings, which itself is a wholly owned subsidiary of World Holdings. Which is Omar's company."

"So to sum it up for you," Swann said, "a Saudi billionaire was here in Galveston on the same night the Ebola virus was stolen. Or at the very least, his yacht was here. The woman who stole the virus stopped at the same marina where the yacht was moored soon after she left the lab. And minutes after she left the marina, the yacht also left. Sounds like we found our man."

"Where is the yacht now?" Luke said.

"We tracked its path via satellite data. It headed east from here and arrived in Port of Tampa, Florida, in the late afternoon of June eighth. It remained there several hours, where it refueled and took on food and other catering supplies. About one a.m. in the early morning of June ninth, it left Port of Tampa and motored south. About nine p.m. that night, it arrived outside the Cuban resort city of Varadero. It's still there, in a deep-water anchorage a mile out at sea."

"Is he there?"

"We can't tell," Swann said. "What we can tell is that the yacht tender is running back and forth to shore pretty continuously, bringing a steady supply of young women out to the boat."

Luke nodded. "Okay, we'll assume he's there. I imagine a man like that would frown on his yacht crew partying without him."

"Omar is legendary for his partying," Trudy said. "And his fondness for the ladies, especially ladies of the evening."

"What are the chances he still has the virus on the boat with him?" Luke said.

Trudy shrugged. "Hard to say. We'd have to know the chances he ever had the virus with him in the first place. The whole thing could be a coincidence."

"It doesn't look like a coincidence to me," Ed Newsam said.

"There are no such things as coincidences," Swann said.

"Okay," Trudy said. "If he did have the vial on board, my bet is he offloaded it in Tampa. Why would he keep it with him on a boat? He's basically on a slow cruise to nowhere. Meanwhile, Tampa is a major port city, and a commercial shipping hub. There are more than a dozen large trucking companies based in Tampa, and dozens of smaller ones. It's also a commercial travel hub, with flights to everywhere on Earth, and access to two major interstate highways. Drop the virus off in Tampa, and once again, it could go anywhere very quickly."

Luke's wheels were spinning. "But even if he did drop it off, in all likelihood, Omar will know where it was headed."

Trudy nodded. "Yes, that's probably true."

"I'll need a helicopter," Luke said. "And a place to fly it from. Key West is probably best. It's the closest thing we have to Cuba. Swann, what's the fight time between here and Key West?"

Swann typed a few words on the keyboard in front of him. "They say it's an hour and forty-three minutes, but with our plane, if we gun it I'd bet we can cut fifteen or twenty minutes from that."

"Okay," Luke said. "We'll call it ninety minutes. I'm also going to need two special ops drop teams, four men on each team. Seasoned guys, no nonsense. Delta if there's any immediately available, SEALs if not. There are probably some SEALs hanging around Key West. I also need a door gunner, and a couple of crack pilots. How soon can we pull all that together?"

"Your door gunner is standing right here," Ed said.

Luke gestured in the air with his hand. "Of course. Good. One less thing to track down. What about the rest of it?"

Trudy frowned. "I don't know. A few hours, I suppose. Maybe sooner."

"All right, make it three hours, and you've got a deal," Luke said. "We can get rolling right now, and we'll meet the rest of our people at the Naval Air Station in Key West."

"Luke, what are you planning?"

He smiled. "I'm going to pay Omar a little visit. I might even invite him back here to the United States for a little while, with a black bag over his head and zip ties on his wrists."

She shook her head. "Omar is a Saudi national, and he's currently in Cuban territorial waters."

"I'm aware of that."

"To extract him, you would have to violate Cuban airspace. You're not going to do that, are you?"

"No," Luke said. "I'm not going to violate Cuban airspace. I'm just going to borrow it. I'll give it right back to them as soon as I'm done."

Just then, Luke's cell phone began to ring. He glanced at the number. It was from the 202 area code, Washington, DC. He looked around at his team.

"Guess who," he said.

He pressed the green button. "Stone."

A deep male voice came on the line. "Please hold for the President of the United States."

He held. In a moment, she came on the line. He listened to her for a few minutes. He watched as Trudy began making calls. When the President was done speaking, he thanked her for her confidence in him. He hung up the phone.

He remembered how, when they first came to Galveston, Trudy was uncharacteristically quiet. She felt shaken because they were so far behind the ball. And Luke felt that if they could just focus their energies and begin to move in a direction, if they could just find out where Aabha went, they would be okay. He didn't feel that way anymore. The project was barely underway, and they were already too late.

Trudy was talking into her phone. She had her official voice on, and was obviously trying to move chess pieces around despite reluctance on the other end of the line.

"Trudy," he said. She was immersed in the conversation.

"Trudy!"

She stared at him.

"We don't have three hours. Everything's been moved up. We need those special ops teams, and the chopper, on the pad at Key West two hours from now."

"Bad news?" she said.

He nodded. "Very bad."

CHAPTER FOURTEEN

2:15 p.m.
The Skies over the Gulf of Mexico

The dark blue Secret Service Learjet zoomed over vast blue water.

Once again, Luke and his team used the front four passenger seats as their meeting area. They stowed their luggage, and their gear, in the seats at the back. The narrow tube of the plane was a Babel of voices, as four conversations went on at once.

"I need chatter," Swann said into his phone. "I don't care. It's never completely dead. Give me anything. The slightest clue."

"Six hours is too long," Trudy said into her phone. "We don't have that kind of time. Five thirty this afternoon is the drop dead date. Yes, five hundred full personal protection suits, and one hundred infrared thermometers per airplane. Yes, full means full. Suits, masks, boots, gloves, goggles, air-purifying respirators. Yes, all of it airborne, and the planes flying with overlapping radiuses. Yes, I know it's a tall order. Why do you think I called you?"

"Seventy-Fifth Rangers are cool man, but we need to hit hard," Ed Newsam said. "I don't know if they're up for what we're going to do. Hard, you hear me? That's how we roll. They have combat experience? No? I don't know, man."

Luke was on a conference call to the New White House in Washington, DC. He plugged his right ear with one finger to drown out the voices of his team, and pressed the satellite phone to his left ear. The plane was moving fast, and the phone kept dropping the call.

It sounded like chaos up at Susan Hopkins's house. Supposedly, he was giving them a report, but there was so much background noise on her end Luke wanted to scream at them. *Shut up! For the love of God, shut up already.*

"My intel officer is about as good as they come in this business," he said to the unseen gathering. "She's come up with a number of different scenarios as to how they could deliver the virus." He glanced at the notes Trudy had given him. "Assuming it's aerosolized, they could use old-fashioned crop-duster airplanes. They could employ helicopters and small trucks that municipalities use to spray for mosquito infestations, especially in southern states."

A burst of static came over the line. Luke held the phone away from his face. When he came back, he listened.

"What city do you suspect?" Susan said. "Brooklyn Bob said it was a beloved city, and it was too bad to see it go."

Luke didn't want to get into the wisdom of the President talking to Brooklyn Bob on the phone. If he had been there, he wouldn't have allowed it. He would have thrown his body on top of the telephone.

"I don't know," Luke said. "Pick your favorite small southern city. St. Augustine, Sarasota, Key West, Miami Beach, Savannah, or Charleston. Maybe Richmond, Virginia. Myrtle Beach. Wilmington, North Carolina. Norfolk? Who knows? The problem is mosquitoes could have nothing to do with it. They never said it was a southern city, only that it was small and beloved. How about Portland, Maine? Or Boise, Idaho, or Boulder, Colorado? Burlington, Vermont. There are so many beloved little cities in this great nation of ours…"

He shook his head and smiled at the thought of well-to-do middle-aged tourists wearing khaki pants and LL Bean boots and lime green pullovers made of recycled plastic soda bottles. White kids with dreadlocks riding mountain bikes to art school. Twenty-something metrosexuals sampling craft beers. It was not Luke Stone's life, but it was good. These were good things. People were safe, they had wide freedom to choose lifestyles… let's keep them that way.

"Another problem," he said, "is the terrorists could be lying and they could attack a major city instead. Yet another problem is they could deliver the virus through air conditioning and heating systems, through letter bombs, or through people carrying hand-held aerosol sprayers into crowded public places. They could drop non-incendiary bombs that scatter the aerosol on impact. They could do the same with missiles. Our old friend Saddam Hussein used to employ those techniques on his own people on a regular basis."

Luke stopped. The sheer litany of possibilities was demoralizing, even to him. "They could use a combination of any group of these techniques, all of the techniques, or none of them. Instead of aerosols, they could use a bodily fluid–based approach and infect prostitutes who pass the disease to their johns. Ten urban prostitutes could easily infect two hundred men in one night, not even through unprotected sex, just through physical proximity.

Before the symptoms became apparent, the johns could spread out across a city or region, infecting their families or anyone else they came in contact with. By the next morning, thousands of people could be exposed. Or they could infiltrate a hospital staff somewhere, and they could contaminate the blood supply. They infiltrated a high-security BSL-4 lab. Compared to that, a city hospital is easy."

He paused, then went on.

"They could bypass the hospitals altogether and just give Ebola-contaminated needles to heroin users. In a small city, overnight you could have two hundred Ebola bombs walking around downtown, infecting other people. They'd be coughing and sick, but at first they wouldn't be bleeding. Hardly anyone would notice because street people are always sick."

He sighed heavily. "Do you understand what I'm saying? There is no end to the potential attack methods. We can safely assume that our opponents are creative, which means we can assume they will try an attack that we won't think of."

A voice came on. He didn't recognize it. It wasn't Susan. It wasn't Monk. Were they even still in the room?

"What do you suggest then?"

"Mitigation," Luke said without hesitating. "If the attack is going to happen, then we can't stop it. Be ready with quarantines, road closures, bus station, railway, and airport closures. Curfews, checkpoints, temporary martial law. Pick thirty or fifty small cities, as many as possible, and contact mayors, city managers, police departments, fire departments, hospitals. Put them on alert for the slightest suspicious activity or illness presentations that are out of the ordinary. Create a command center at the Pentagon or at FEMA to coordinate all activity. They have resources, and we need things to happen fast. Put hazmat suits in the sky, along with infrared thermometers, ready to be delivered to first responders anywhere within an hour. We've taken the liberty of beginning this process, but it has to go bigger than we can do. Also, put National Guard units on two-hour alert across the country. Get friendly governors to start mobilizing them now."

Another voice, a different one this time. "Agent Stone, what about evacuating possible target cities?"

Luke rubbed his forehead. He almost couldn't believe the extent of the problem they faced. There was a ton of back chatter on

Susan's end. He doubted anyone was even listening to him. Who were these people asking him questions?

"We can't do that," he said. "The attack might have already taken place. How can we know? If we start evacuations, it'll cause panic, and people will run. Some of those people might be infected, but not showing symptoms yet. If people run, we could drive the disease out into a much wider dispersal area. No. We have to monitor for signs of the attack, catch it as soon as possible after it happens, then lockdown and quarantine."

"Do you know what you're suggesting?" a deep male voice said. "You'll be trapping people in…"

The call dropped again. Luke sat up and sighed. He slid his phone onto the table in front of him. They weren't going to do anything he suggested. It sounded like a very large cocktail party was going on over there. It sounded like intermission.

Swann was watching him. As soon as Luke put his phone down, Swann wiped the thin sandy hair out of his eyes. "Luke, how much space do you have left in your head?"

"Enough."

Swann looked at his notes. "Okay. Jihadi social media basically went dead about an hour ago. There are kids still screwing around, of course, but the real jihadists have stopped talking. Also, their satellite phones are dead. Their safe house phones are dead. The video streams have dried up. Email has dried up. Everything is off the air. Our people monitor their networks twenty-four/seven. They tell me they've never seen anything quite like this before. Nobody is saying anything."

"They don't want any slip-ups," Luke said. "They don't want to say anything that gives us a hint or a lead to go on."

Swann nodded. "That's right, not even enough to make a guess. They're showing remarkable discipline. They know we're listening, and they're not saying a word."

Luke shook his head. The terrorists got more and more sophisticated all the time. The technology became more advanced, cheaper, and readily available. Companies made innovations, released them all the time, and the jihadis adopted the innovations the next day. Meanwhile, US government procurement officers took six weeks to move a memo from one side of the desk to the other. All of that stuff was a given.

But their ability to go silent was what bothered him. Luke had heard tell of how during World War Two, entire cities in the United

States would go dark in seconds, as soon as the air raid sirens started. In major cities, like New York and Boston, everyone would shut out the lights at once. In those days, people were on the same page, everybody pulling in the same direction.

Now, people in the US were going eight hundred different directions at once. And it was the enemy that could turn their own lights off, so to speak, in seconds. Luke wasn't sure what that meant.

Trudy hung up her phone. "We've got six planes that will be airborne within an hour, five hundred personal protection suits and one hundred infrared thermometers on each one."

"Six planes? Trudy…"

"I'm going as fast as I can, Luke. That's three thousand hazmat suits and accessories, in the air, an hour from now. And I started making these calls fifteen minutes ago."

He shook his head. There was a shortage of hazmat suits in the country, and the ones that existed were at a premium. The idea was to get as many suits and infrared thermometers airborne as possible. When the attack came, if it came, the suits could fly directly to the city affected, and be put into the hands of first responders as fast as possible. It was a cockamamie idea, and it made Luke all the more worried because he had thought of it. So far, it was the best he could come up with.

But six planes? Jesus. Sixty planes wouldn't be enough. It was a big country.

He looked at Ed. "What about you?"

Ed shrugged. He was still on the phone, but apparently waiting for someone to come back. "Pretty good, not perfect. We've got a chopper, an MH-60 Black Hawk with some anti-radar stealth technology. Night Stalkers are going to loan it to us, as long as I promised not to lose it. We've got our own SRT pilots, Rachel and Jacob, en route to Key West right now. They're hitching a ride on two Navy F-18s, moving down the coast at about a thousand miles per hour."

"Good so far," Luke said. "What about the drop teams?"

"We've got a three-man SEAL sniper team, just got into Key West from a mission in parts unknown. Their CO left it up to them. They're tired, but they're willing to go airborne again. I figure you can round out that foursome."

"Good," Luke said. "What else?"

Ed shrugged. "Maybe not as good. We've got four Seventy-Fifth Rangers doing underwater crash survival training at the pool in Key West. They're all young, and none of them have seen combat."

"Okay," Luke said. "If I'm riding with the sniper team, we'll go in first. The young guys will support. We'll tell them not to shoot us in the back."

Ed nodded. "Fine."

Luke picked up his phone again. He dialed in to the Washington conference call. A robot voice asked for his security code. He punched it in and at the tone, he announced himself.

"Luke Stone," he said. "Back again."

"Luke, where are you right now?" Susan Hopkins said. Finally, Susan Hopkins, and she was speaking to him.

"I'm over the Gulf of Mexico, maybe an hour from Key West."

"Why?"

"I'm going to talk to a man who might know what city will be hit."

A male voice chimed in. "In Key West?"

"No."

"Where is he?"

"Uh, I can't really tell you that right now."

"Stone," Richard Monk said, "this isn't the wild west. If you have information, or you plan to go on an operation, you need to tell us what you're doing. You need to coordinate your activities with the Joint Special Operations…"

Luke pressed the red button on his phone. He placed the phone on the table in front of him again. It was becoming a long day. He looked at his team.

"Damn phone. Keeps dropping the call."

CHAPTER FIFTEEN

3:23 p.m.
Joint Interagency Task Force South, Naval Air Station Key West

"You sure you're up for this?" Luke said.

"Up for what?" Ed said, huffing and puffing the slightest amount. "Man, I was born for this."

The sun rose high and hot over the palm trees. The low-slung buildings of the naval air station and the larger flight control tower squatted in the shimmering, baking heat of afternoon. A slight breeze did nothing to cool off the day.

The Black Hawk helicopter looked like a drab green insect parked on the flight line. Luke and Ed walked out onto the tarmac, Luke carrying a green satchel loaded with weapons, Ed gimping along on his crutches.

As they moved along, a fighter jet took off a quarter mile away, its engine noise nearly deafening. A moment later, the jet reached the sound barrier. If the takeoff was loud, the roar of the sonic boom was more than loud—it seemed to rip a hole in the fabric of reality.

Luke smiled. "We got a bunch of hard-headed Navy SEALs and a gaggle of Seventy-Fifth Rangers right out of grade school waiting for us on that chopper. They're going to think you're some far out old man, waiting to collect his social security check."

"You're older than I am," Ed said.

"Yeah, but I'm not debilitated like you are."

"Fair enough," Ed said. "I guess I'll just have to prove my mettle by grabbing the biggest SEAL in there and kicking his butt up and down this chopper pad."

Luke laughed. "That'll spice things up some. Maybe you should wait until we're out over the water."

The chopper's engine whined into life as they approached. The four rotor blades began to turn, slowly at first, then with increasing speed. Luke and Ed reached the cabin and climbed on board.

Seven men in jumpsuits and helmets watched them as they entered.

"Gentlemen!" Luke shouted over the noise of the chopper blades. "I'm Luke Stone of the Special Response Team. I'm your commanding officer on this trip. Thanks for joining us today. I'm former Seventy-Fifth Rangers and former Delta Force, so I know what you guys are about. This is my partner, Ed Newsam. Don't let the crutches fool you. He's former Eighty-Seventh Airborne and former Delta. He's hell in a wheelchair. I'll brief you guys on the operation as soon as we get in the air."

"Sir!" a voice rang out. "When did you join the Rangers, sir?"

Luke looked at the face attached to the voice. The other guys looked young, but this kid was positively cherubic. Basic training, AIT, and Ranger School hadn't burned the baby fat off his cheeks. Luke glanced at the name tag sewn into his jumpsuit.

SOMMELIER.

"You go by the English or the French pronunciation?" Luke said.

"So-mee-yay, sir! Charles! Private First Class!"

The kid next to him smiled. "Sir, we call him Charlie Something."

Luke nearly laughed. "Oh yeah? Why's that?"

"Sir, no one can pronounce his name, sir."

Luke looked at the wiseass kid again. "Well, Sommelier, how old are you?"

"Nineteen, sir."

"Then I joined the Rangers around the time you were born."

"Yes, sir. No surprise there, sir."

Luke moved up front to the cockpit. A man and a woman in visor helmets and green camouflage flight suits sat surrounded by blue sky through the cockpit windows, and a bewildering array of controls and displays practically against their knees.

These were the SRT mission pilots, Luke's pilots, Rachel and Jacob.

They were old friends of his, and they'd flown together for years. Both of them were former U.S. Army 160th Special Operations Aviation Regiment. The 160th SOAR were the Delta Force of helicopter pilots.

Rachel was as tough as they came. You don't join an elite group of Army special operations pilots as a woman. You brawl your way in. Which was perfect for Rachel—her off-work hobby was cage fighting. Luke liked Rachel. She had dark auburn hair. She was brawny like the old Rosie the Riveter posters. Big arms, big legs, big all over, and barely an ounce of it fat.

Meanwhile, Jacob was as steady as a rock. His calm under fire was legendary, almost surreal. His hobby was mountaintop meditation retreats. Physically, he was nearly the opposite of Rachel. He was thin and reedy. He looked nothing like your typical elite soldier. The thing he had going for him, besides his profound sense of calm, was that he was probably one of the ten best helicopter pilots alive on Earth.

"How we doing, kids?" Luke said. "Ready for another crime fighting adventure?"

"We live for adventure," Rachel said. "Where we headed?"

"We're taking this thing to Cuba," Luke said.

Jacob smiled. "Nice. I bet they'd love to get their hands on this thing."

"We're not going to land in Cuba," Luke said. "Though it would be fun to dance the night away in Havana with Rachel here."

"You know how to sweep a girl off her feet," Rachel said, smiling while her hands flipped switches in front of her.

"There's a yacht about a mile out from Varadero. We're going to fly in below radar and I'm going to drop in with some of these guys in the transport hold. There's a Saudi billionaire on that boat and we're going to extract him."

"So we're gonna drop the basket for him?"

Luke nodded. "That's probably easiest. I'm not expecting a lot of cooperation from this guy. With that in mind, I don't want to tip people off that we're coming. What's the odds of getting across the water without picking up a funeral procession of Cuban choppers?"

Jacob shrugged. "Here? This is one of the busiest air stations we have. You've got Navy strike fighter squadrons, Marine Corps attack squadrons, and Air National Guard rescue squadrons doing training exercises. You've got Navy P-3s looking for drug smugglers. There are so many American planes and choppers in the air, we own the skies west to the Dry Tortugas and south to the edge of Cuban airspace. To the Cubans, we'll look like more of the same for the first sixty or seventy miles. Then we'll drop low and come in just above the water. If you guys do your thing fast enough, by the time they pick us up, we'll be back among the friendlies."

"All right," Luke said. "Let's hit it, then."

CHAPTER SIXTEEN

4:05 p.m.
The Skies Approaching Varadero, Cuba

"We don't tolerate resistance," Luke said. "Someone shoots, someone so much as shows a weapon, they're out of the game. Copy?"

He glanced through the wide open doorway. The chopper rode low over the water, moving fast. It was probably close to its max air speed, around 180 miles per hour. The dark blue water went by in a dizzying blur, almost close enough to touch. A hot wind blew in, buffeting his face and body.

"Copy," the men around him said. "Copy that."

Luke crouched on a low-slung bench in the chopper's personnel hold. He felt that old trickle of fear, of adrenaline, of excitement. He had swallowed a Dexedrine pill twenty minutes before, and it was starting to kick in. It had been a long day already, but suddenly he felt sharper and more alert than before.

He knew the drug's effects. His heart rate was up. His pupils were dilating, letting in more light and making his vision better. His hearing was more acute. He had more energy, more stamina, and he could remain awake for a long time. Dexies were old friends of his.

His two teams sat forward on their benches, eyes on him. The two groups made an eye-catching combination. To his right sat three grizzled, thick-bodied Navy SEALs, each with full beards, Oakley sunglasses, bullet scars, and bizarre intaglios of tattoos wrapped around bulging muscles. Their eyes were sharp, but relaxed. To his left sat four young guys, sporting the lean and mean bodies of athletes not that far out of high school, clean-shaven, eyes wide and excited and nervous.

Luke's helmet was patched in to the pilots in the chopper cockpit, as well as to Swann back at the Naval Air Station.

"Jacob," he said. "What kind of time are we looking at before this airspace becomes unfriendly?"

Jacob's voice was calm as always. "If we catch the Cubans napping, we might be able to hold a position in here for as long as seven or eight minutes. Ideally, I'd like to see you guys drop in, acquire the target, and load back up in three to five minutes. I have a feeling we'll be racing for the exits at that point."

"Swann, what are we looking at on the bridge of that ship?"

"I've got a real-time satellite feed direct from the deck right now. I'd say we're looking at one part dance party, one part Oktoberfest, and one part freak show. Omar has about twenty or thirty girls with him on there, and a handful of men. I'm tracking a man I think is Omar on the top deck. He has short black hair, and a tattoo of a black horse on his right pectoral muscle. He's wearing a pair of red shorts and no shirt. Careful, though. He's dancing with four women around him."

Luke stared at his men. They had heard every word from both Swann and Jacob. "All we want is Omar. We don't want a gunfight, but we stop anybody who does. We don't hurt the girls. When we get on deck, use simple Spanish to clear them out of the way. *Caer al suelo!* is good. It means 'Drop to the floor.' You can shorten it to *Al suelo!* Push a couple of them down. The rest will get the idea."

A Navy SEAL had the stub of an unlit cigar in his mouth. He smiled. His voice had a little bit of Texas in it. "I don't say a word. When people see me coming, they start crawling on the ground all by themselves. Just like worms. Don't ask me why that happens."

Luke ignored his comment, but directed his words to the SEALs. "A-team, we go straight to Omar, bag him, and bring him out."

"Easy as pie," one of them said.

"B-team, you support and cover us. You secure the drop site, and you hold it while we bring Omar up. You're the last men out. Eyes sharp, heads on a swivel. Nobody moves against us. If A-team goes inside the boat, you two hold the drop site, you two move up and hold the entryways."

He pointed with his index and middle finger at each duo when he gave them their assignments. Their faces were so young! Was that what he looked like when he was a Ranger? He felt like he was diagramming a play for players on the junior high school basketball team.

"Are we clear?"

"Clear."

"Ed, you with me?"

Ed had wedged himself standing up in the doorway on the other side. He was propped behind a big door-mounted M240 machine gun.

"Always," he said.

"Crowd control, but we're not shooting girls today."

"Only with my love gun," Ed said.

"We are shooting bad guys, though. You've got all the latitude you need to interpret that. I want to drop eight men, and bring nine back up. Everybody healthy and happy. The men on the boat? I'm not going to lose sleep, all right?"

Ed nodded. "Naturally."

"All right, boys," Luke said. "Hard and fast today. No slacking. No bullshit. And drinks are on me tonight."

*

Omar stood on the upper deck of his giant yacht.

He was a king. He was a modern sultan. He was... a prophet?

Dance music boomed from the speaker system, and his body moved gently from the waist up. Most of the movement was in his shoulders. He held a half-full glass of rum in his hand, from which he took a sip now and again. He didn't have a high tolerance for alcohol, so he always drank a few sips at a time.

He had a nice buzz on. It made his thinking very pleasant. It was a bright day, with sunlight dappling on the vast blue waters all around them. The sun heated his skin, deepening the brown color. He could feel it happening.

Near the horizon, the white high-rise hotels of Varadero, the center of Cuban beach tourism, shimmered like a city in the sky.

Everything, to put a word on it, was beautiful.

The girls were especially beautiful today. Young girls, mostly dark-skinned lovelies, with fantastic, nubile bodies they loved to show off. Some wore bright yellow or white bikinis against their black skin—the effect drove Omar wild. They wore high-heeled stiletto shoes, they wore high-heeled sneakers, they walked around in bare feet with sheer wraps around their bodies and nothing else on at all. They chatted, they danced, and they laughed. A few drank rum and got very wild. Most drank Pepsi and stayed sober.

Whatever they chose to do, Omar loved these girls.

They were *jiniteras,* a Spanish word that Omar also enjoyed. It meant "horse-riders," and Omar of course had a deep affinity for horses. *Jiniteras* were the Cuban version of party girls. Were they prostitutes? Maybe. Were they young mothers with boyfriends and husbands at home? Maybe. They were more like girlfriends for rent than anything. The Cuban people seemed to have few of the judgments around sex that other societies were burdened by.

Omar smiled, and the smile reached his very soul. This life of his, it was the only life worth leading. Yes, he was a flawed example of a Sunni, and he was a long way from a dedicated Wahhabist. Some might even say he was a hypocrite.

On his trips abroad, he drank alcohol, he smoked pot, and he snorted cocaine. He was surrounded by half-naked young women, none of whom he had married, and he would have sex with as many of them as possible. He encouraged vice, both with his money and by his example. The mujahideen he funded, if they learned of his lifestyle, might seek to kill him.

He threw his head back and laughed. He was flawed, yes. But he was a prophet himself, wasn't he? He nodded at the truth of it. He had been sent here by Allah to bring the Crusaders to their knees, and restore the ancient Caliphate. He was sure of it. Recent days had proven it to him. He had prayed, for untold years he had prayed, and now he had received a sign so clear, it was unmistakable. An unstoppable weapon had been placed in the palm of his hand, and no one else's.

He had a Quran verse he often thought of. Chapter 9, verse 88. *But the Messenger, and those who believe with him, strive and fight with their wealth and their persons: for them are all good things: and it is they who will prosper.*

He fought with his wealth and his person. And that meant all good things were for him. He pulled two sexy girls close to him now. The three of them danced, their bodies just inches apart. He was becoming very drunk.

So many girls, so little time.

"Omar," a man's voice said.

Omar turned, and one of his bodyguards stood there. He was a man in a white suit. Omar could not think of his name. The man had pulled a gun, a squat, ugly automatic weapon. More men were moving to Omar's side.

The first man pointed at the sky.

A dark speck approached from the northwest. It moved fast, growing ever larger as Omar watched. In two seconds, it had resolved itself into a helicopter. A second later, it was much closer than before. In fact, it was almost here.

"We could have trouble," the bodyguard said. "You should come inside."

CHAPTER SEVENTEEN

"Go!" Luke shouted. "Go! Go! Go!"

Two ropes descended from the doorway of the chopper. Luke was last of his four-man team to go. He hit the green START button on his stopwatch. Right before he left, he looked at Ed in the opposite doorway.

"Keep us alive down there, brother."

Ed raised a hand from the top edge of the machine gun. "I'll keep the rest of them alive. I ain't seen a thing on Earth that can kill you."

Luke glanced below him. All was clear, and he went over the side. A second later, maybe two, he touched down on the deck of the boat. He looked around, getting his bearings. His team was ahead of him, moving fast.

He unslung his M-16 and started running.

"Down!" he shouted. "*Caer el suelo!*"

All around him, scantily clad women dove to the floor. The women screamed as he ran among them. Up ahead, the Navy SEALs sprinted up a small flight of stairs. They pushed people to the ground as they ran. Luke sprinted up the stairs behind them.

On the top deck, three men shoved a fourth through a doorway. Luke caught a glimpse of Omar's red shorts and bare skin. The metal door clanged shut.

Dammit! Omar was inside. The men faced out from the doorway, automatic weapons ready.

POP! POP!

Two of them fell. The SEALs dropped them without slowing down.

The third man managed to reach his trigger. He released a blat of automatic gunfire. Women shrieked. The man fired wildly. Luke kneeled, drew a bead on the man. He was a big man in a white suit.

BANG! A dark red circle appeared on his chest. Almost instantaneously, three more appeared.

The man slid bonelessly to the floor. A SEAL reached there a second later. He shoved the body out of the way with his foot, then tried the door. It was locked. It was a big heavy iron door. Luke reached there, almost within the circle of men.

He checked his stopwatch. They'd already been on the boat nearly a minute.

"Blow it," he said. "This is taking too long."

A SEAL kneeled by the door. He ripped open two plastic pouches and popped out two incendiaries. He stuck them to the door near the hinges, punched in a quick four-digit code on each, and leapt back.

"Hot stuff coming!" he shouted.

All four men darted back, hit the ground, and covered up.

BA-BOOOM. Two explosions went off almost as one.

Luke climbed to his feet. The door was so heavy, its iron hinges so thick, that it had merely fallen down sideways. It rested on the floor, still upright. It mostly blocked the doorway, the lock still engaged at the clasp. A SEAL tried to wrench the door off, but to no avail. It would take three strong men five minutes to move that door out of there.

"Blow the lock," Luke said. "Let's go, let's go."

The mega yacht was built for pleasure, but retrofitted for security. Of course it was. The new vogue was billionaires worrying about piracy on the high seas. If Omar had a panic room, and he made it there, they would have a hard time getting him out.

Luke had too many things on his mind, and he hadn't thought of everything. He had slipped.

"Come on!" he said. "Move it."

The SEAL knelt again. He stuck three incendiaries on the door, then four, then five, all clustered around the lock mechanism.

"I'm gonna kill this thing," he said.

Just then, a new burst of automatic fire erupted. It came from behind them. Luke spun. On the deck below, three men had emerged from a side door, guns blazing. They fired toward the helicopter, toward the Rangers holding the drop site.

In the first instant, a Ranger was hit. Luke saw it. He watched the red mist blow out from the exit wounds, and the skinny Ranger do a death dance before dropping. Then the other Rangers were on the deck, taking cover.

"Oh, no."

A burst from a heavy weapon came. The three men who had come from the side door blew apart, legs and arms and heads flying in a spray of blood and bone and gore. Luke caught the line of fire. He followed it up to the chopper, to where Ed had just ripped them up.

The Rangers were screaming. Luke couldn't make out what the words. A second later, a voice became clear. "Man down! Man down! Shit! It's Charlie Something. Oh my God."

The man down was the only one not screaming. Charlie Something. He was already dead.

"Dammit!" Ed's voice shouted in Luke's ear. "Dammit!"

"It's gonna blow!" a SEAL shouted from behind him.

Instinctively, Luke hit the deck. The explosions sounded like a string of M-80s on the Fourth of July. BAH-BA-BA-BA-BOOOOOM.

His face was pressed to the rubbery footing on the deck. He closed his eyes and took a deep breath. In his mind, he saw the young Ranger take the hits again. He saw the blood spray, the mist rising.

He shook his head. Jesus. But there was no time to think about that now.

He jumped up, turned, and ran through the blown open and shredded doorway, half a step behind the third Navy SEAL. The doorway led to an iron stairwell, which circled down into the bowels of the ship.

The men clambered down, heavy boots on metal stairs. The skeletal stairwell shook with the weight of their bodies and their footfalls. This was what Luke didn't like. Big men in a line, vulnerable in a tight spot. A shotgun fired from the bottom of the stairwell would do damage right now.

The stairs went down two stories and came to a door. The lead SEALs kicked this one down. Luke was half a second behind them.

All four men burst into a chamber. Across from them, two more shooters stood. Between them was Omar, crouched over a digital lock, feverishly punching in numbers. He stood in front of another heavy door, probably the door to the panic room. Once he got through that door, he would be sealed inside.

It didn't matter now. He wasn't going to make it.

The tall men on either side of him reached inside their jackets.

POP! POP! POP!

They were dead before they could pull their hands out again. Their bodies danced as the bullets pierced them. One man dropped instantly. The other put a hand on the wall behind him, tried to steady himself, then slid sideways and down. He left a red smear on the wall.

Omar gave up on the lock. He stood to his full height. The gesture seemed a bit out of place, considering his red satin shorts, and his bare chest and feet.

100

"You men are trespassing on my property," he said in perfect cultured English. "You must leave now or face arrest under maritime law."

Luke walked toward him. "Omar bin Khalid al Saud?" he said.

Omar nodded. "Who is asking?"

Luke punched him in the face, a hard right cross that swept across the man's jaw. Omar's head swung around to Luke's left, his body corkscrewing beneath it. He fell to the floor, landing on top of one of his dead bodyguards. He sprawled there, breathing heavily.

"Bag him," Luke said. "And let's get the hell out of here."

A shriek of static came through Luke's headset. Then there was Rachel's voice from the helicopter cockpit. Unlike Jacob, big strong Rachel wore her emotions right out on her sleeve. "Luke?" Her voice had an edge to it, an edge of fear.

"Yeah, Rachel. What's going on?"

"Any chance you can hurry up in there? We've got incoming all around us."

"What is it?"

"Two fighter jets just went by about a mile north of our position. We've got big choppers on radar, closing in east and west. We've got Cuban Navy patrol boats coming from shore. You name it, we've got it."

Luke grunted.

"Try to make contact on the radio," he said. "Tell them we have a prisoner and a man down, and we're bringing both of them out. Ask them for an escort to American airspace."

"We'll try it," Jacob said. "But I don't know how that's going to go over."

"Let me know what they say," Luke said.

"What would *you* say, if you were them?"

Two Navy SEALs had pulled Omar to his feet. A trickle of blood flowed from the corner of his mouth. His eyes were hard and angry. Evidently, he wasn't accustomed to this type of treatment.

"You men are murderers. This is an act of piracy, and an aggression against a sovereign nation. The Cubans won't let you take me. They'll probably put you in jail."

Omar was a little too verbal for Luke's taste. Luke pulled his sidearm, a black Glock nine. He put the muzzle to Omar's head.

"Where will the attack take place?"

Omar's eyes went FEAR wide, but still he smirked. "What attack?"

Luke jabbed him in the forehead with the gun. Hard. But he still hadn't gotten Omar's attention. He could see it. Bad things just didn't happen to Omar.

"You know what attack. The Ebola attack."

Omar smiled now. "Oh. That attack. The one with the vial stolen from your laboratory in Texas. Is that what all this is about? What makes you think I know anything about that?"

Luke took a deep breath. On a good day, he didn't like being taunted. This wasn't a good day. A mouthy, funny nineteen-year-old kid had died for this. A bunch of Omar's bodyguards had died as well. And Omar was treating it as a joke. It wouldn't take much for Luke to send this smug jet-setting bastard to see Allah.

"You were in Galveston the night the vial was stolen."

Omar nodded. "Maybe."

"The person who stole the vial came directly to this boat after she stole it."

"Was her name Aabha?" Omar said. "An exotic name, no?"

"Listen to me," Luke said.

"No, you listen to me," Omar said. "You're an American, so you think you can rain death on Arab people, and on Muslim people, anytime and anywhere you like. I'm a messenger. That's all I am. And the message is no. You can't do it. And the way you'll learn is when death begins to rain on your own people, like it will do this very afternoon. Death from the skies, just like the Americans do it. And even better, it's going to be an American. A sick, twisted American, because your society is sick, and it makes its own people insane. I tell you all these things because you can never stop it now."

"Where will the attack be?" Luke said again.

"I guess we'll just have to wait and see, won't we?"

The urge was there, to shoot the man in the head. He was frustrated enough to do it. But Omar was their only link to the stolen virus. If he died, the link died with him.

Luke grabbed him by the right wrist and pulled his hand up and away from his body. He pressed the muzzle of the Glock against the back of Omar's hand. Omar tried to yank it away, but he was too slow, too weak. Luke pulled the trigger.

The bullet shredded a hole through the fragile flesh and bone of the man's hand. The noise of the gun was loud in the close confines of the chamber.

Even louder were Omar's shrieks of agony.

A couple of the SEALs laughed.

"Wait and see about that," Luke said.

CHAPTER EIGHTEEN

They brought Omar up on deck.

Omar's head was covered in a black nylon bag. His wrists were zip-tied behind his back. He sniveled and moaned in pain.

"Okay, drop him a minute. We've got trouble."

The SEALs leading Omar let him fall to the deck. He lay curled in a ball.

Luke's eyes were dazzled by the bright sunlight. He was even more dazzled by the swarm of about a dozen Cuban helicopter gun ships hovering in the air around them. They were dark blue. Luke recognized them as old, Russian-made Mi-24s. The Cubans called the Mi-24 *el cocodrilo*, Spanish for "the crocodile."

Three American Apache helicopters would take out the whole lot of them, but Luke didn't have three Apaches today, and he wasn't going to have them. He had breached Cuban airspace, and he hadn't let anyone know beforehand.

The Cuban women, in their flashy multi-colored outfits, still lay everywhere on the decks. Now, Cuban naval cutters approached from all sides.

"What are we supposed to do here, Luke?" Rachel said inside his helmet.

"Uh… stay steady, everybody," he said. "I'm thinking."

"I say we hole up," the cigar-chomping SEAL said. "We've acquired the target. There's food and water. We bring him down inside to the citadel, and we wait them out. Unless they sink us, the four of us could hold this ship for a month. Hell, we make the captain pull out of here, we head north, and dare the Cubans to sink us."

The plan, audacious as it was, had some merit. Luke wanted to interrogate Omar. He could just as well do it here as anywhere else. "What about the chopper?" he said.

The SEAL shrugged. "They can either ditch in the water or run for daylight. It's up to them."

That had less merit. A run for daylight with a dozen crocodiles on your tail? They had already lost one man on this raid. Luke wasn't going to lose Ed, Rachel, and Jacob as well. Not for Omar.

A Cuban Navy boat had pulled even with the yacht. At the rear, Cuban commandos began to board the bottom deck. With in a minute, two dozen of them were racing up the stairs between decks, weapons drawn.

"Now would be a good time to decide, boss," the SEAL said.

The commandos swarmed and disarmed the three remaining Rangers. The SEALs drew their weapons and backed up into covered firing positions.

"Luke, what are you doing, man?" Ed said inside Luke's helmet.

Luke had decided. No more loss of life. "We're going to talk our way out of this."

Half a dozen Cubans came up the final set of stairs. Their weapons were trained on Luke, and on the SEALs. Luke glanced back at the SEALs. Their weapons were trained on the Cubans. A shootout now would become a bloodbath.

The commandos were led by a tall, muscular man in a blue jumpsuit. He carried only a handgun, and he kept it holstered. He removed his helmet. His face was a warm brown color, his hair graying, crow's feet around his eyes. He had been at this game a long time.

He extended a hand to Luke.

What else was Luke going to do? He shook it.

"I am Captain Soares," the man said in heavily accented English.

"I'm Agent Stone."

"Well, Agent Stone, you are in violation of treaties accepted by the United Nations concerning Cuban airspace and territorial waters. As I understand, the United States is a member state of the United Nations, is it not? We are free to consider this an unprovoked act of war."

Luke gestured at Omar. "This man is my prisoner. His name is Omar bin Khalid al Saud. He is wanted in the United States for suspicion of terrorism."

The man's eyes glinted. He almost smiled. "Suspicion?"

"Yes."

Captain Soares shook his head. "There is no extradition treaty. Our government knows this man. He is a friend of the Cuban people. And we are concerned about the thousands of so-called suspects imprisoned in America without the due process of law."

Luke nearly laughed. *The Cubans* were concerned about human rights? When did that happen, this morning? Luke had missed the news report about it.

"You may take your fallen comrade with you," Soares said. "And we will escort your helicopter back to United States airspace.

But you must disarm, and you must leave this man with me. Please understand that you are outgunned and surrounded."

Luke stared at the Cuban commando. What he had just described was total surrender.

"I'll give you three minutes to decide."

CHAPTER NINETEEN

"He said death from the skies," Luke said into the satellite phone. "He said a sick, twisted American would do it, someone who had gone insane."

Trudy's voice came back to him. "It's not much to go on, Luke."

"It's a start, Trudy. If it's true, it means they're going to spray from the air, maybe a helicopter or a crop-dusting plane. We need to do a search for chopper and small plane pilots with a history of mental illness, maybe people who've been in psychiatric hospitals, or even just in jail. Maybe former military with posttraumatic stress disorder, or nursing some kind of grudge."

"Luke, we're almost out of time."

"Trudy, what's the matter with you? I'm your boss. Don't argue with me. Just do what I say. Pull together twenty people and start searching databases. In the meantime, ground every pest control helicopter and crop duster in the country. Every single one."

"Luke, we don't have the authority to that. You've been relieved of your command."

Luke stopped talking. He looked out the right side door of the Black Hawk. It was the door where Ed had stood with the machine gun earlier. Ed and one of the SEALs had broken the gun down and dropped it into the ocean. They had no choice. The Cubans had the drop on them.

In the sky outside the door was a dark blue Mi-24 helicopter gunship escorting the Black Hawk back to American airspace. Luke turned and looked out the left side door. Another Mi-24 moved abreast of the Black Hawk on that side. At least three more followed behind. No Cubans had been killed. That was the reason they weren't all sitting in a Cuban jail right now, or at the bottom of the ocean.

Otherwise, the raid was a disaster.

On the floor of the transport hold, two SEALs were zipping Sommelier into a canvas body bag. The three remaining Rangers sat along the left side bench. Their body language was dejected, limp, drained—the exact opposite of how they had been before the mission started. One of them was crying. More than crying—he was weeping, tears rolling down his face, his shoulders jerking.

"You need to man up, son," one of the SEALs with the body bag said. "You wanted to see war? Well, you've seen it. This is what it looks like. You don't like the orders you got? You think your friend died in vain? Then now's the time for you to embrace the suck."

Trudy was still speaking into Luke's ear.

"The Saudi ambassador has called a press conference for six p.m. He's already made some remarks to the media, demanding to meet with the President. He's called for you to be extradited to Saudi Arabia, to be put on trial for the murder of nine Saudi nationals, and assault with a deadly weapon against a member of the royal family. Can you imagine what will happen if you're actually extradited? They'll cut your head off."

Luke almost smiled. If Charlie Something wasn't dead on the floor, he would have.

"Thanks, Trudy. That makes me feel better."

She went on. She sounded like a school teacher admonishing him. "The Saudi ambassador to the United Nations has filed a complaint to the Security Council. The Cuban ambassador has been recalled to Havana. This is an international incident, Luke. It turns out one of Omar's companies is a major investor in oil exploration off of Cuba's southern coast. You've way overstepped. You're on the shit list, and I don't mean that as a joke. I'm afraid you're in real trouble this time."

Luke sighed. "Can we take me out of this for a minute? It's four thirty-five by my watch. As far as we know, we've got a terror attack scheduled for five thirty. A man with knowledge of the attack has suggested it will come from the sky, and that an American, possibly one with mental illness, will carry out the…"

"I can't accept orders from you, Luke. I can't do anything. No one will listen to me. We're all on suspension until further notice."

Outside, the Cuban helicopters suddenly stopped and hovered, dropping back from the Black Hawk. They had reached the edge of American airspace. As if to emphasize this fact, three F-18 fighter jets roared by overhead, the shriek of their engines splitting open the sky.

"We're home," the cigar-chomping SEAL said.

"Trudy, do one thing for me, if you can."

"What is it?"

"We'll be back at base in twenty minutes. Make a formal request. Beg. Grovel. Remind her that I saved her life, but whatever you do, get me a phone call with the President."

CHAPTER TWENTY

5:11 p.m.
Charleston, South Carolina

A young man, well dressed in a blue button-down shirt and slacks, stood close to the helicopter. Too close, as far as James Walter Shouberty was concerned. The young man had brown skin, not James Shouberty's favorite skin color.

The kid held a fat book in his hand, and he read out loud from it. He had little sections of it picked out with those tassels that Christian preachers often used. The Holy Quran, the kid called it. James shook his head, but listened anyway. The kid was giving him a blessing, after all.

"Listen not to the unbelievers, but strive against them with the utmost strenuousness," the young man said. "Fight against them so that Allah will punish them by your hands and disgrace them and give you victory over them and heal the breasts of a believing people."

James stood about ten feet from the young man, his mind starting to drift. He was sixty-three years old, listening to a fool less than half his age read from a book the kid didn't understand, and spout nonsense about things he couldn't even begin to comprehend. James knew light years more than this kid.

They were in an open field, where James had landed the chopper he had spent the better part of the past twenty years flying. It was a Bell Jet Ranger 206, a peppy little twin-bladed utility chopper in use the world over. Police and fire departments flew it, TV news shows flew it, third-world militaries flew it, and even James Walter Shouberty flew it. The one he flew belonged to Charleston County.

On either side of the chopper, there was the county seal, along with the words *Charleston County Mosquito Control.*

The Muslim kid droned on.

"Let those fight in the way of Allah who sell the life of this world for the other. Whoso fighteth in the way of Allah, be he slain or be he victorious, on him we shall bestow a vast reward."

He looked up from the book now and over at James. "May Allah accept the sacrifice of brother James as jihad, and open the gates of paradise to him this very day."

Behind the kid was a white sixteen-foot aerial support trailer. Someone had left it here yesterday, with two full pallets of product inside. Normally, the product would be 220 gallons of larvicidal chemicals, which James would load into the twin broadcast sprayers mounted on either side of the chopper.

This time the product wasn't for mosquito control, however. This time it was for people control. James had waited for this day a long, long time. God had brought him to this moment. Not Allah, but God, the one true God, the real God.

James was God's avenging angel. James had known this for many years. Now God had brought James these Muslims... They were earnest, they were young, and they were clowns and buffoons. Their lives were meaningless. They were following an imaginary god, and they were trying to do something that made no sense. They wanted to rebuild a medieval kingdom? Good luck with that. The truth, God's Pure Truth, was annihilation.

He looked at the kid.

"You done?"

The kid nodded. "Yes."

James slid a hand into the pocket of his flight coveralls. He pulled out his gun, a tiny .25 caliber. They called it a pocket pistol, and that's why he carried it in his pocket. It was for person protection. It wouldn't stop a tank, it might not even take out a car windshield. But there was one thing it did very well.

Kill people.

James didn't hesitate. He didn't even think. He shot the kid four times. The shots rang out, loud, but not disturbingly so. If you were nearby, you might mistake them for firecrackers. Anyway, no one was round. They were just in a vast, empty field, surrounded by marshland, and all by themselves.

James walked over to the kid. The kid lay on the wet ground, gasping for air. The kid's precious Holy Quran had fallen near his head. James kicked the book away across the dirt. The kid's blue button-down was quickly changing color. Dark red circles had appeared and were expanding. As James watched, the circles reached for each other, flirted, kissed, and then became one. The shirt was soaked in blood.

James leaned over and looked into the kid's face. The kid's eyes were wide and afraid. Tears streamed down his cheeks and mingled into the dirt.

"Are you in pain?" James said.

The kid nodded crazily. He was like a toy bobble head doll.

"I want to tell you something," James said. He smiled. He'd been thinking about this a lot, but he had no one to tell it to. James was a loner, and the people he worked with seemed to think he was strange. He spent a lot of time thinking, and a lot of those thoughts went nowhere. But not today.

"Please help me," the kid said. His whole body trembled and shook. Blood ran from the corner of his mouth. Funny that the kid would ask James for help. Hadn't James just shot him a moment ago?

"Imagine you're trapped in an attic," James said. "And there's a lady in a wedding dress by the window. She's looking away from you. You walk up to her, she turns around, and she's a skeleton. You try to scream but you can't. You know why? Because you're a skeleton, too."

"Please…" the kid said.

"You think you're watching television," James said. "But really, it's watching you."

The kid looked away and winced in pain. It wasn't the response James was hoping for. He wasn't quite sure what he was hoping for. He pointed the gun in the kid's face and fired one last time. The shot echoed across the field.

"Unlocked doors are invitations," he told the kid's splintered and bloody skull. "And your door was wide open."

James turned and walked toward the chopper. Moments later, the bird was gaining altitude. He rose above the treetops, then flew south and east, toward the beaches, the harbor, and downtown. God, he loved this bird. He loved being up in the air like this, soaring like an eagle. And he loved raining down the apocalypse, whether on parasites like mosquitoes, or on vermin like the human race.

*

"Your Mercedes wasn't enough?" James Shouberty said.

The sun rode low to the west, and it was almost as if he were speaking to the big yellow orb. He sat inside the bubble of the chopper's cockpit, the sky wide open all around him. He was alone up here. He could be talking to the sun. He could be talking to God.

He often talked like this when he was in the cockpit. He often talked like this in the car, and at home as well. When no one was around, which was most of the time, he often slipped into quiet, seething rants. He wasn't even quite sure who he was talking to. The yuppies, he supposed. The yuppies, and their charmed lives.

"Your golden necklaces weren't enough?" he asked them. "Your trust fund wasn't enough? Your vodka and cognac weren't enough? All of your debaucheries weren't enough?"

He was about a thousand feet up, and he flew the chopper southwest along the beaches of Isle of Palms and Sullivan's Island, places he had sprayed many times. He usually dropped to about a hundred feet above the tree line here, and bombed those thick marshes just behind the dunes. Mosquitoes loved to breed back there.

A few people were walking on the beach after work. Not enough, though. Not nearly enough people. The camel jockeys, the ones worshipping a false god, had told him to drop the product in a densely packed area. That was how it would do the most damage. That was how the effects would spread.

James was a fan of genocide, and he wrote an anonymous blog about it. His employers never found out about it. His family never found out—he didn't talk to them, anyway. The police and FBI had never bothered him—heck, it was free speech to talk about mass murder and destruction. It was free speech to describe your fantasies of global destruction in detail for a few hundred people a month. And we had free speech in this country, didn't we? You bet we did.

Few people ever contacted him about the blog. But the camel jocks did. They were curious about him. He was American, obviously, but where in America? What were these references he made to flying, and these references to raining death and to wiping out breeding populations from the sky?

Was he a real pilot?

Oh yes, he was as real as they come.

Did he really know how to rain death?

On mosquitoes, yes.

Was he as interested as he seemed in wiping out humans?

More than you could possibly know.

He had finally met with a camel jockey at a diner just two weeks ago. He'd been talking to them on the internet for the past five months. Even so, he took precautions. He sat in a booth and watched the guy for an hour. The guy didn't speak to anyone. He didn't look around. He didn't whisper into a radio or make secret hand signals. Eventually, James felt fine about everything, walked over, and slid into the man's booth. They talked for about twenty minutes, mostly working out details and logistics.

Finally, near the end, James asked the question that to him was most important.

"Could it kill everybody?"

The expression on the young man's face didn't change in the slightest. "Do you mean everybody on Earth?"

James nodded. "Yes."

The man nodded. "It's possible, if enough people were infected, that the virus could spread out of control. It's a dangerous virus, very deadly, and very easy to catch. Once it gets loose, it will be hard to stop. But I think you would have to spray a lot of people for it to go around the world."

"Well, I guess I'll spray a lot of people then," James said.

Now, below him, the low five-sided walls of Fort Sumter were just ahead, guarding the mouth of the harbor, just as it had done during the Civil War. He kept the fort on his left and peered down into the open area within the old stone walls. A handful of tourists milled around inside the fort like ants. A handful was not enough.

"They're mocking you, Jimmy. They're making fun of you because of how you look, and how weak you are. But that's okay. Ultimate revenge coming, and right on time. You people could have shown me more respect, treated me better, asked for more guidance from me, and maybe this wouldn't have happened. All you rich snots who think you're higher than me and everyone else with all your money, just because you were born with it?"

He moved up through the harbor, dropping altitude. The bottom of the peninsula was dead ahead—the Charleston Battery, with its twenty-million-dollar pre–Civil War waterfront mansions, and its throngs of afternoon walkers and joggers and bench sitters and various other lingering wastes of skin. He would hit there first, then move right up the line. He came in low, lower, dropping down to three hundred feet.

The Battery was straight ahead; it was early evening, and people were out. There must be a hundred people. He could see them straight ahead, practically close enough to touch. The line of mansions grew closer, the pastel-colored Rainbow Row of fancy houses clearly visible now. He was coming fast. He pulled up just a touch. Here came the waterfront walkway. People were looking his way. They could hear the chopper, closer than they expected.

He was over the water, a hundred yards out and closing fast.

"You didn't see this coming, did you?"

He hit the sprayers. A dense cloud of purple-brown fog opened up on either side of him. He laid down a thick mist, banking left, and following the line of the Battery walkway, dropping product the entire time.

He rained death. People didn't run. They didn't know what to do. They didn't know what was happening. Maybe it was Malathion? Maybe it was Pepsi-Cola? No, you dummies. It's death. Death is on you. It's all over you.

He closed the sprayers and checked his levels. He had two more drops' worth, and that one was a direct hit. Good, very good.

"They never saw it coming," he said. He shook his head for emphasis. "They never imagined what I would do. They were just dreaming along in dreamland. Wake up, dreamers! Welcome to nightmare land."

He laughed and banked right. He knew this town like he knew his own face. He flew straight over the houses and buildings, moving north into the heart of the city. He put Meeting Street to his right and King Street to his left. Both streets were lousy with hotels and restaurants and rich tourists. Both streets were crowded, way more crowded than the Battery walk.

He hit the sprayers again. The mists went out two hundred feet on either side of him, enough to cover both streets. Look at all the people! Hundreds of them. Swarms of pests. He opened those foggers up and let it rip, block after block, a thousand feet before he closed it up again. Beautiful.

A little bit of the fog blew back into the cockpit with him, but he didn't care. He knew it would happen. It always did. He breathed it deeply. He wanted it inside him. This was his final statement. The act itself was his manifesto.

No one ran. No one did anything. They just stood there. A few pointed at the sky, at James Walter Shouberty and his chariot of fire. He checked his product level. Low. Enough for one more drop, a small one.

Better make it good. He banked right at Market Street and flew toward the Charleston City Market. It was crowded. He could see the crowds from here. The summer evenings brought out the maggots just like rotting summer garbage did. He opened the sprayers and dumped the last of his load on the Market and all the nice rich people buying sandwiches and overpriced pizza, and trinkets for the folks back home.

A moment later, the chopper was over the Cooper River. James banked right and headed down to the mouth of the harbor again. In front of him was nothing but wide ocean, dark green and stretching to the horizon.

He glanced at his fuel gauge. He had about forty minutes of flying time left. He hadn't really given much thought to what would happen… afterwards. He figured he would probably just set the bird down somewhere and eat his own gun.

On a whim, he headed straight toward open ocean instead. There was something romantic about it.

"Bury me at sea, darling," he croaked to no one. "Bury me at sea."

CHAPTER TWENTY ONE

5:35 p.m.
Joint Interagency Task Force South, Naval Air Station Key West

Luke sat on the phone, listening to elevator Muzak and trying not to feel sorry for himself. Piano notes tinkled in his ear, playing a watered-down version of some song that had been popular twenty years before. This was the hold music at Susan Hopkins's New White House?

A few moments before, Ed Newsam had stormed out of the room on his crutches. Ed was upset the kid had died. Ed was quiet for several minutes, and then he exploded, shouting at Luke.

"You design a mission, you got to do it up, man. You don't send us in on some half-assed mission. We gonna do a raid? We go in guns blazing."

"I didn't send you on a mission, Ed. I was there with you. Remember?"

Ed shook his head. "It was half-assed, man. Don't pretend it wasn't. We got kids with no experience. We got some Saudi Arabian on a boat we know nothing about. We got five minutes or less to get him out. Is he gonna run? Of course he's gonna run. So we got some dumb ass boy killed, and we didn't even get the target. And you had him, and what did you do? Shot him in the hand."

"What was I supposed to do, Ed? Have a gunfight with half the Cuban navy and air force? That would have gotten us all killed."

"Shoot him in the head, Luke. That's what you do. You shoot him in the head. But you... now you got him laughing at us."

That's when Ed walked out.

Luke felt bad about the argument. He understood what Ed was going through. He was feeling it himself. Charlie Something had died, and it turned out for nothing. Was it a half-assed mission? He didn't want to think that way. But maybe it was.

On the phone, one saccharine-sweet song ended, and another began. He glanced at his watch. They had kept him waiting until after the attack was scheduled to happen. That little fact told him all he needed to know.

He paced the room in the makeshift command center. It was a small room down the hall from the Dutch Air Force command offices, which operated a small subgroup out of here in concert with the Americans, and patrolled the Caribbean basin all the way down to Aruba, Bonaire and Curacao. Trudy and Swann were at a table, monitoring computer data for any evidence of an unfolding attack.

The Muzak stopped abruptly. Susan Hopkins's voice came out of Luke's handset. "Luke, I don't have a lot of time to talk. You've put me in an awkward position. You're probably the best agent we have, but there's no way we can use you for anything now."

"Can we please put me aside for the time being?" Luke said. "If there's been an attack, we need to respond to it. If there hasn't been an attack, we can still stop it."

Monk came on the line. "Stone, do you know that successive administrations have spent the past ten years repairing our diplomatic relationship with Cuba? In one afternoon, you've set that relationship back to the depths of the Cold War."

"Okay, Richard," Luke said. "You seem to have an ax to grind."

"I don't have an ax to grind, Stone. Your behavior is out of control. You accused the director of the Galveston National Laboratory of having an affair with the terrorist who stole the Ebola virus."

Luke rubbed his eyes. "He admitted that he did it."

"Well, he's denying it now. He says you extracted a false confession from him under duress."

Luke shook his head. "If that's what he thinks, then he's never experienced duress. All I did was ask him some questions. I can deliver a lot more duress than that."

"We know that much," Richard said. "Like shooting a hole through the hand of a member of the Saudi royal family. Don't even get me started on that. Our entire embassy staff is being ejected from Saudi Arabia as we speak. You've set that relationship back to a place it's never been before. What you've done there, we have nothing to compare it to. But now that we've studied your personnel record, we see that you have a long history of exactly this type of thing. Violent incidents. Allegations of torture. Overstepped authority. By the way, did someone tell you it was okay to invade Cuba? Or did you just think it up on your own, and decide to do it?"

"Is Susan still on this call?" Luke said.

Her voice came back on. "Yes," was all she said.

"Susan, Omar knew about the attack. He knew the vial had been stolen. He was probably the one who paid for the theft to happen. We need to have the Cuban government hand him over to us."

"That won't be possible," Monk said.

"It has to be possible. He's the only link we have."

"The Cuban medics treated his hand, and then he boarded a private jet that was already waiting for him at the Jose Marti airport in Havana."

"Where did he go?"

"He didn't file his flight plan with us," Monk said. "But we assume he was headed home to Saudi Arabia. You're very lucky you're not headed there yourself."

"Are you Susan?" Luke said. He had just about had it with this guy. "You don't sound like Susan. I called to talk to Susan."

"Luke," Susan said, "I'm not sure we have anything to talk about right now."

"Susan…"

Monk didn't back down. "Face it, Stone. You're excommunicated. What other choice do we have? Effective as of the moment you breached Cuban airspace, you're stripped of command of the Special Response Team. The SRT itself, in its entirety, is suspended until we have time to decide what to do with it. You can borrow the Secret Service plane to get home. I suggest you do that immediately."

The line went dead. It took a moment to sink in with Luke what had just happened. He had spent most of his career outside the normal boundaries. Don Morris had brought him on in the early days of the SRT, precisely because Luke didn't paint inside the lines.

In ten years, Luke had been in administrative trouble more times than he cared to count. He had been suspended, he had been arrested, he had been threatened with contempt of court. He had also been beaten, he had been shot, and he had been stabbed. He had survived car crashes and helicopter crashes and countless explosions.

Now, Richard Monk had just hung up on him.

Luke stared at the phone, wondering if he should try to dial in again. He called over to the other side of the office.

"Swann, did we get any satellite imagery of where Omar went?"

Swann shrugged. "Yeah. It looked like his yacht's own small chopper took him to the big airport in Havana. Then three Lear jets went out of there in rapid succession, moving fast. One went east and headed across the Atlantic Ocean. We can assume it was headed to Europe or the Middle East. Another went south. It's headed toward South America, my guess being Venezuela. We have no extradition treaty with them. The third one went west and landed at a private airfield in Ciudad Juarez, Mexico. A line of SUVs went out of there a few minutes later and split up. I lost them in the city traffic. Omar's a tricky bastard, I'll give him that."

Luke thought about it. Omar was dirty, that much was clear. Now he was trying to run and hide. That meant the attack was real, and it was coming.

"There are two planes still in the air," Swann said. "You want me to pull some strings, see if we can interdict?"

"No. He's a high-profile guy. A billionaire Saudi royal can't exactly hide forever. The guy's got a carbon footprint the size of Ohio. We'll find him again. We should save whatever strings we have left for when we absolutely need them."

For a long moment, Luke wondered if that was the right move. He could no longer be sure what the right moves were. If letting him go was the right move, then why had Luke wanted to so badly to capture him earlier in the day? Because it seemed easy? Because he had been overconfident? Because he had been desperate? If he was desperate then, what was he now?

The answer came to him, and he didn't like it. He had been desperate earlier. Now he was just resigned. If the attack was going to happen, at this point chasing down Omar wasn't going to stop it.

Suddenly, Trudy stood up from her chair. The chair fell over backwards, crashing to the floor. The sound echoed in the mostly empty room.

"Oh my God," she said. She turned to look at Luke.

Luke stared at her. "What is it?"

Her mouth hung open for a long moment.

"The attack is underway."

"Show me," he said.

He stood and went to her computer. It showed a live TV newscast out of Charleston, South Carolina. A pretty blond-haired news reporter stood on a crowded street, in front of a line of beautifully restored Victorian-era buildings. People milled around behind her, some looking uncertain, some laughing and clowning around.

"Mitch, I'm on Meeting Street in the heart of Museum Mile, near the Charleston City Market. People down here are in shock. Just moments ago, a helicopter from Charleston County Mosquito Control veered over this neighborhood and sprayed what appears to be a very large amount of pesticide on hundreds of people dining in outdoor restaurants, people leaving work, tourists, and others just out enjoying the mild spring weather. Charleston County officials we contacted seem baffled, saying there is no policy of aerial mosquito spraying in the city center. They are looking into who the pilot involved is, and what substance he might have been spraying. I'm standing with City Councilor Abe Thornton, who was strolling with his wife when the spraying happened."

The camera panned back to include a tall, older black man, with glasses and graying hair. He wore a bright green Polo shirt, and was much taller than the news reporter. She held her microphone up to him. Despite the circumstances, neither of them could repress a slight smile.

"Councilor Thornton? What are your thoughts?"

The man shook his head. "Cindy, it's shockingly irresponsible. This is the type of thing I've been talking about for years. The city is the economic engine of this entire region, it's the arts capital, and it's a national historic treasure. Meanwhile, we're roped to a county that is unaccountable, is run by people who don't live in the city, and who seem hell-bent on doing whatever they want. Today's incident is an extreme example, but don't think for a minute this is an isolated incident."

"Did you and your wife breathe in any of the spray?"

He nodded. "Oh, we got a lungful, all right. And we're not happy about it."

"Are you worried about potential toxicity?"

Councilor Thornton raised a hand as if to say STOP. "I think it's too early to go there, Cindy. Let's stay calm for the moment. We don't know what the pilot was spraying. We don't know what the health implications are. My hope is that a healthy person could ingest some amount of this material without long-term consequences. Personally, I feel fine. I'm concerned about citizens who may have asthma, or emphysema, or some other lung impairment, but as I said, we don't know anything yet. My staff are in contact with the county, and we're going to get to the bottom of this as soon as we can."

There were a few more seconds of banter between the reporter and the politician, but Trudy had already turned the sound down.

"They don't know what just hit them," she said.

"Hey, look at this," Swann said. He pulled up another screen. "This was posted to a social media stream three minutes ago."

The three of them watched the screen. It was narrow cell phone footage of a small helicopter flying low over some buildings. The footage zoomed in, became unstable, lost the chopper for a second, then panned sideways and found it again. Background chatter came through the phone's speaker.

"Jesus, he's too low."

"Who is this idiot?"

"Hey! What the…"

Suddenly purple and brown fog burst from thin, antenna-like sprayers on both sides of the chopper. It wasn't a small burst. The chopper laid it down heavy and long. The person holding the phone followed the chopper as it passed, fog pouring out the entire time. The background chatter went on, voices shaking, almost frantic.

"Oh my God, it's coming down!"

"Should we get inside?"

"Inside where?"

"It's wet, it feels like rain."

"Okay, okay, it's just a mist. Relax."

"Honey, hold your breath."

"Disgusting!"

The video ended. The screen showed a static image of a helicopter with a triangular arrow in the middle indicating PLAY. Luke, Trudy, and Swann stood around the small bank of computers.

Luke's mind revved up, started cranking along, and then took off like a missile. He was in a bad position. It had been a horrible day, and his credibility was shot. His command post was gone, and his entire team was suspended. Would anyone listen to him now? He had no idea. But he had to try. The faster the response, the more people could be saved.

"Swann, pull me up an aerial map of the Charleston peninsula. I need to see main arteries and possible choke points. I need hospitals, especially with helipads. We need to close all the marinas and marine terminals, and blockade them with Navy and Coast Guard if need be. This is it, the time to pull strings. Pull every string you have at FBI, NSA, CIA, Centers for Disease Control, Naval intelligence, anywhere and everywhere. We want real-time satellite data, and we want all video surveillance in the city coordinated and fed to our command."

"Where is our command?" Swann said.

Luke shrugged. "Here. Naval Air Station Key West, right? They've got to have a real command center here somewhere. Tell them we need it, we work for the Office of the President. Except for a skeleton crew to keep their normal operations intact, we need all of their intelligence, data, and logistics personnel. Anyone asks questions, refer them to me."

Luke paused, his mind racing ahead of his ability to speak. He took a deep breath. He gave himself five seconds to settle down, then he started on Swann again.

"Alert the control tower at Charleston airport. Tell them to put more people on—we're going to have military flights coming in and out every thirty seconds. We need to close the city, so we need portable roadblocks moving into place now. Whatever the local cops have will do for the time being. No one gets out, and controlled entries only. Tell the CDC we need to drop about a thousand medical personnel in there in the next few hours, all of them trained in infectious blood-borne and airborne diseases, and we need them protected from attack by panicked people and from the virus itself. Find out what nearby military units were in West Africa during the Ebola crisis there, and pull them in. We've got to get people in place fast. And, not for nothing, it has to happen in something like an orderly fashion."

Swann stared at him, eyes wide.

"Do it, man! We're already out of time."

Swann raised his hands. "Okay, Luke."

Swann slid into a chair at a laptop, started pulling up data, and picked up his telephone. Within a few seconds, he was already talking to someone.

Luke turned to Trudy.

"Trudy, get me back in touch with the President. We need the governor of South Carolina to declare a state of emergency right now, and we need National Guard mobilized in both South Carolina and Georgia. If he won't do it, Susan has to do it. There are a lot of military assets based in Charleston. She has to close the city, and the resources to do it are right there. We need every artery out shut down, including walkways and nature paths. When the roads close, people are going to try to get out by sea. We need boats covering the harbor and the rivers—use the Coast Guard first, they'll have cutters standing by and they'll get there fastest. No one gets off that peninsula. Also, you have to keep Ebola victims hydrated, right? So bring in about a hundred thousand gallons of water. That's for starters. More if you can get your hands on it. Also food. We're going to put an army on the ground, and we have to feed them."

Trudy didn't move. She seemed stricken.

"Who's going to listen to us, Luke?"

"What?"

"We don't have a mandate from anyone. We don't even have jobs. Who's going to listen to us?"

"This is the attack, Trudy. Do you understand me? Don't ask rhetorical questions. Move your ass. We've still got planes in the sky that we control, with hazmat suits and laser thermometers, right? Start there. Find the closest ones and divert them to Charleston. Get Ron Begley at Homeland Security on the phone and tell him what's happening. Then make a priority call list, and work down it. You're a smart cookie. You know what to do."

Trudy's face trembled. She seemed almost ready to cry. "We're suspended, Luke. We have no resources. We're probably going to be disbanded."

"Yes," he said. "I understand all that."

"What if no one takes my call?" Trudy said. "Why would they? Then what?"

In an instant, Luke had lost all patience. It was too much. They had been behind from the beginning, and they had never caught up. Not even close. The raid on Omar had failed. A disaster was unfolding. But this wasn't the time for Trudy to melt down and become weak. This was the time for her, and for everyone else, to blast headfirst through brick walls.

"Trudy, you see this building we're standing in?"

"Yes."

"It's on a fucking military base! If you can't get anyone to take your call, then run down the hallways screaming and tackle the first admiral you see. Lie. Impersonate someone. Overstep your authority. I don't care how you do it, but tell decision makers that an attack has begun, and start moving people and material to Charleston. Do it now!"

CHAPTER TWENTY TWO

6:29 p.m.
United States Naval Observatory – Washington DC

Susan Hopkins fiddled while Rome burned.

When she couldn't stand it anymore, she had excused herself from the Situation Room, and had retreated upstairs here to her study. She stood at the big bay window, staring out at the beautiful rolling lawns of the Naval Observatory campus. The afternoon sun was moving west, casting perfect spring light.

For years, Pierre had slowly been collecting originals by the late 1800s Scottish painter Patrick William Adam. Adam's paintings played with light streaming through windows in such a delightful way. The light coming through this window always reminded her of those paintings.

For the past five years, she had lived in this house as Vice President. She loved it here. In the old days, at this time of the afternoon, she might have gone out with a couple of Secret Service men and jogged a few loops around the grounds. Those years were a time of optimism, of stirring speeches, of meeting and greeting thousands of hopeful Americans. It seemed like a lifetime ago now.

Richard Monk stood behind her. She felt him there, more than saw him. It was interesting how you could know a person just by the feeling they brought with them into a room. Richard probably wanted to update her as a bad situation only grew worse. Richard had been a good chief-of-staff during her fun-loving, easygoing days as Veep. She was beginning to suspect that he was the wrong man for this job.

"Susan?"

She didn't turn around. "Yes."

"About ten minutes ago, Wesley Drinan shot himself in the head in his office at Galveston National Lab. Staff members down the hall heard the shot. When they reached his office, they found him with live coverage of Charleston on his computer."

"Is he dead?"

"Yes. He left a note on his desk."

"What did it say?"

"It said: *I'm so very sorry.*"

She sighed. "I guess he really did have that affair."

"I guess he did. His assistant told me Drinan worked in the private sector in Japan for twelve years. He had an affinity for Japanese traditional culture. It used to be important for a Japanese leader to commit suicide after a public failure or disgrace."

Susan shrugged. To her, it sounded more like Drinan took the easy way out, and found a way to avoid the punishment he deserved. She felt no compassion for him, no forgiveness, no... feeling at all.

"Drinan was a punk," she said. "He wasn't a leader."

There was a pause between them. Susan felt a hesitancy on Richard's part, but she still didn't turn around.

"Next order of business, please."

"City of Charleston," he said.

"Yes."

"The latest estimate is that more than a hundred thousand people have been quarantined in the southern half of the Charleston peninsula. There are widespread reports of looting. Crowds of teenagers are running through the streets, committing random assaults. No Ebola symptoms have been observed yet by drone-mounted cameras, or on footage uploaded to the internet by people trapped inside the quarantine zone."

"How many people were sprayed?" Susan said.

"Best guess? Between three hundred and five hundred."

"And the transmission rate again?"

"No one is sure among humans, but in the one test they did on monkeys, very nearly one hundred percent."

"Mortality rate?"

He hesitated.

"Mortality rate, Richard?"

"Again, all we have is that one experiment, and it wasn't on humans, but possibly as high as ninety-four percent."

She knew it was something like that, but to hear him say it was like a punch in the gut. Her hands tightened into fists. Her teeth clenched. She squeezed her eyes shut as silent tears streamed down her face.

"You're telling me," she said, "that ninety-four thousand people are likely to die?"

"I don't know, Susan. No one knows."

Those people were a lost cause, she realized. That alone was almost too horrible to think about, but if the disease made it out of the city and into the mainstream population... No. It was impossible. She wouldn't let it be true.

"We can't let the disease get out of the city," she said.

"On that score, we seem to be doing okay," he said. "The local police and fire departments closed the streets and roads a mile north of the spray zone within ten minutes of the attack. Permanent barriers and checkpoints are being erected as we speak by installation support personnel from the 628th Air Base Wing from Joint Base Charleston, which is located at the Charleston International Airport. National Guard troops are pouring into the area from throughout South Carolina and Georgia, and are amassing at the airport."

"That sounds all right," she said. It even sounded positive, but it was hard to feel positive given the circumstances.

Richard went on. "Coast Guard patrol boats were moved into strategic placements along the Cooper and Ashley Rivers, and at the mouth of the harbor, all within fifteen minutes, and have since been augmented by Navy gun ships. All water traffic is shut down until further notice. There is a general maritime shoot-to-kill order, which has been communicated on all radio channels used by commercial, private, and fishing interests. The unmistakable message is if you try to leave the city by sea, we will kill you."

Susan finally turned around. It was startling to see Richard there. She had forgotten what he looked like. He looked almost like a men's magazine model, maybe just a little too old and not quite handsome enough. But the body was right. Richard spent a lot of time in the gym.

"Shoot-to-kill?" she said. "Who ordered that?"

He shook his head. "Luke Stone ordered it. On your authority. He's a megalomaniac, Susan. He's in Key West, operating a command center out of the Naval Air Station, and has convinced everyone he still works directly for the White House. He has seized control of elements of FEMA, the Coast Guard, the Navy, the Air Force, and the Centers for Disease Control."

Richard looked at the tablet computer in his hand. "He mobilized more than three hundred doctors and nurses, volunteers with Doctors Without Borders, and is flying them to Charleston International Airport and Savannah Airport on any available aircraft. Then he apparently plans to airlift them by helicopter to the roof of Roper Hospital in downtown Charleston. He commandeered three thousand CDC hazmat suits and diverted them to the quarantine zone. He purchased a quarter million gallons of spring water from a massive Food Lion distribution center about forty miles north of Charleston, and has them trucking it down to the city. The first twenty thousand gallons arrived in a convoy of trailer trucks about fifteen minutes ago. I guess no one cancelled his SRT credit card, so he's running it up and letting it rip."

Susan tried to think about what Richard was saying.

"Stone has eviscerated the Posse Comitatus Act," Richard said. "He is putting military units everywhere, and mingling them with civilian resources. He is doing this on no one's authority but his own. He has misrepresented himself and his team to the highest ranking officers in the United States military. You're worried about a coup? Stone has more or less launched one this afternoon. And he did it in the middle of a terror attack, about an hour after violating Cuban airspace and torturing a member of the Saudi royal family. He's had a busy day."

"What are we doing?"

Richard put his hands in the air. "What choice do we have? He got out ahead of us. We're coordinating resources with him."

"Okay," Susan said.

"Okay?"

"Yes, it's okay."

"What do we do about him?"

She shrugged. "It sounds like he did the best job he could, and he did it in a pinch. Once the situation stabilizes, have someone go in and formally relieve him of command. Don't tell anyone that he was already relieved of duty earlier today."

"Should we arrest him?"

She shook her head. "No. Only if he refuses the order to stand down."

"So if he hands over command…"

"Yes, Richard. Just put him on a plane and send him home."

*

An hour had passed. She had barely moved.

She remained at the window. She watched the light change, then change again, as the sun moved lower in the western sky. It was now nearly 7:30 p.m. She stood and stood, half wishing that a sniper was out there, centering her in his gun sights.

Pierre came in.

127

She turned to him. He was just himself, always Pierre, in a pair of brown corduroy pants, a ratty favorite sweater of his with holes chewed through it by his dogs, and penny loafers with no socks on his feet. His hair was tousled and standing up in tufts.

"Hi," he said.

"Hi yourself."

He ran a hand through his hair. "I took a nap."

She nodded. "Good. How are the girls?"

"They're okay. Doing girl things. Fashion magazines. Facebook. YouTube. They're getting a little antsy, truth be told."

"I figured."

He seemed about to speak. Then he stopped.

She shook her head and managed a smile. She realized it was a faint ghost of the nine-thousand-watt smile for which she was known.

"Okay, Petey. Out with it. I've got the worst terror attack in human history on my hands, so I can't be begging you for the latest news."

He sighed. "We're leaving. I'm taking the girls home. We're going to the Malibu house, on the beach, away from all the craziness. I don't feel like the girls are safe here, and there's no way you can guarantee their safety."

"We're surrounded by the Secret Service," Susan said. "And we're inside a facility that has multiple checkpoints to gain entry. I think we're about as safe as anywhere in the country right now."

Pierre didn't miss a beat. "The Secret Service didn't save Thomas Hayes."

Susan had no answer for that.

"The country has gone insane, Susan. Did you know that in the past half hour, every store in America has run out of plastic sheeting and duct tape? It's true. People are wrapping their homes in plastic, and then barricading themselves inside. Supermarket shelves are emptying of everything. Water, canned food, flashlights, batteries. Forget about produce. Both Walmart and Kmart have run out of guns and ammunition. I don't mean a Walmart and a Kmart. I mean hundreds of stores, everywhere across the country. The country is awash in guns, and people are buying up whatever guns are left."

Susan nodded. "It's okay, Pierre. I understand. You want the girls to be safe, and I appreciate that. I want them to be safe, too. Washington, DC, could be the next target. I doubt Malibu Beach will be. I'll miss you all, but you should go. When do you plan on leaving?"

He shrugged. "Now. In an hour. Anytime. The plane is here. It's at Reagan National, gassed up and ready. I'm going to take a shower, get the girls packed up, and then we're going. I've said it before, and I'll say it one more time. I want you to come with us. There's no shame in leaving all this behind. You didn't ask for it. It was thrust upon you."

"I can't do it, Pierre. You know that. I took an oath. I promised to faithfully carry out my duties, and to the best of my ability. If I just leave now…" She shook her head. "I have more ability than that."

He nodded. "I know. I just wanted to make the offer. And it still stands. If you wake up tomorrow morning and you want to quit, just let me know. I'll send a plane."

They came together and hugged. There was less emotion to it now. Susan didn't need his support. She was tired. In fact, she was more than tired. She was ragged. She had been in shock, but she was going to rally. The country needed her, and she needed to stand up for them.

A knock came at the door.

"Yes."

"Madame President?" came a voice from the other side. "They sent me to ask if you're planning to return to the Situation Room."

She and Pierre pulled apart just slightly. She looked into his eyes and she couldn't help but smile. He was a good man. He was a great dad. He was very smart. He was trying to change the world.

She loved him. She loved their daughters. She loved the life they had lived together, as strange as outsiders might find it. There was no gap. There was no hurt. There was no misunderstanding. Everything was right there, and it was good.

"I'll be right down," she said.

CHAPTER TWENTY THREE

8:15 p.m.
Joint Interagency Task Force South, Naval Air Station Key West

Luke stepped out into a concrete yard between buildings and stared out at the sky. To the west, the sun was very low in the sky, a giant orange orb, heading to the water. The sky was pink, framed by the palm trees at the edge of the base. A hot breeze blew in from the Gulf of Mexico.

Five minutes ago, an admiral from the Joint Interagency Task Force, a logistics commander, had come into the command center with a phalanx of officers and four military policemen. He handed Luke his phone.

"Stone."

"Stone, this is Richard Monk, Susan's chief-of-staff."

"Hi, Richard, I'm a little busy right now."

"No, you're not. You're surrendering command to Admiral Van Horn. Right now. There are two ways to do it, the easy way and the hard way. The easy way is to shake hands with the admiral and announce the transition to everyone in the command center. The hard way is to be dragged out by MPs, and then charged with a list of felonies as long as my arm. I want to make something clear to you. Are you listening? You don't work for the Special Response Team. There is no Special Response Team. So that's the deal. Voluntarily surrender command, or go to prison. It's your choice."

The line went dead. Luke stared at the phone in disbelief. Monk had hung up on him again. The guy had zero phone etiquette. How had he slithered his way up to chief-of-staff?

Luke extended his hand to the admiral. "Admiral Van Horn? It's a pleasure to meet you, sir."

The admiral smiled. "You've done a hell of a job, son. Ever think of joining the Navy? We could use a man like you."

Okay. That was okay. There was no use fighting it. He was tired, and he had commandeered a lot of resources without actually asking anyone for permission. It was as good a time as any to hand them back. In fact, he was a little surprised it had all lasted this long. He had sent Trudy and Swann back to DC half an hour ago.

After her initial reluctance, Trudy had stepped up like Luke knew she would. It turned out no one knew the SRT was dead but the White House and the SRT itself. When Trudy Wellington called from the Special Response Team, Office of the President and demanded movement, people hopped to it. Her voice had grown more confident as the minutes passed.

Ed Newsam had disappeared and not returned. This was Key West, so... Well, he was a big boy and would find his way home on his own.

He sighed, staring out at the sky, raised his phone and called Becca.

The phone rang. It just went on and on. Luke felt a nervous tickle in his stomach. Was she ever going to answer? Shouldn't it have gone to voicemail by now? Was she...

She picked up. There was a long pause.

Her voice was guarded. "Hello?"

"Becca?"

"Luke." It was not a friendly greeting.

He let out a long breath. "Hi, babe," he said. "Are you guys okay?"

"We're fine."

"You're still at the country house?"

"Yes. Things have been very frightening. Fighter planes have been flying overhead for hours. I bought some plastic sheeting and duct tape at the general store up the road. We've got water and canned food in case we have to hole up here for a while. We're not going back to the city. This thing with Charleston..."

"I know," he said.

"Where are you?" she said, her voice sharpened by an edge of suspicion.

"I'm in Key West."

"I thought you went to Galveston."

"I did. It's a long story."

"To be honest, with everything that's going on, I just figured you were dead."

He paused for a second. Okay, this wasn't the kind of loving conversation he was hoping for. Absence didn't always make the heart grow fonder.

"Becca, I've had a very busy day. If you were worried, why didn't you call me?"

"Luke, I've called you about a dozen times today. You never called back. You never told me you were leaving Galveston. You never said a word, you never sent a text, and you never sent an email. You know what? It's the same old song from you, and I'm really kind of sick of it."

Luke looked at the phone he was holding. It was the satellite phone he had obtained earlier in the day. Where was his personal cell phone? He glanced down at the clothes he was wearing. He still wore the jump suit from when they boarded Omar's boat. He never had time to change out of it.

His cell phone was probably in his civilian clothes, which were in a locker... he looked at the building he had just walked out of. It was a low-slung office tower, with the base command center inside. The locker room where he had changed was in a flight crew dorm, near the helipads, in another part of the base. He wasn't even sure where that was anymore.

Becca went on. "There was some kind of attack in Cuba earlier today. An American soldier got killed. I thought you might have been involved in that. Now this biological attack. There's a news blackout on the ground."

Luke nodded. He knew about the news blackout. He had initiated it.

"There are no images, no footage, and very little information. Only that thousands of people are trapped inside the infection zone. They're saying thousands of people may have already died."

"I lost my phone," he said. As soon as he said it, he realized it was an excuse as lame as it sounded. Even so, he pressed on with the same flawed line of reasoning. "I didn't know you were trying to call."

"And you didn't think to call me, right?"

"Becca..."

"Don't, Luke. Don't even try it."

He stopped, and a long silence drew out between them.

"What are you doing now?" she said.

"Uh, I was just relieved of my command here. So I'm going to fly up to Charleston and look at the—"

"Luke, tell me that isn't true. Tell me you're not going there. I'm a biological researcher. It's a disaster area. People are dying in droves. Do you have any idea how infectious this virus is?"

He shook his head. That was just like her. Did he know how infectious the virus was? Was she kidding? Did she think she knew more about it because she had handled a few viruses and saw an hour-long Ebola documentary on TV?

"Becca, there's going to be another attack. This is the warm-up. The next one is a major city. I have to go to Charleston. I have to see it for myself. I can't stop the next attack if I don't know everything about this one."

"I'm done with this!" she said. "I'm done. Don't we count for anything? You're going to save this city, and rescue that country. You're going to fly here, you're going to fly there. You race around, popping pills to stay awake, playing Cowboys and Indians, shooting people, getting shot yourself. Do you ever think about your own wife and son? We were here, and we didn't know if you were alive or dead. And you know what? You didn't know if we were, either."

"Becca—"

"Gunner and I were kidnapped less than a week ago, Luke. Your son is traumatized. You may think he isn't, but that's wishful thinking. No, it's worse. It's selfish. You think that because it's more convenient for you."

Luke didn't say a word. Of course she was right. Gunner was traumatized. Becca was, too. But what was he supposed to do? Pretend this attack hadn't happened? Walk away from the whole thing?

"Luke, if you go to Charleston, I'm filing for a divorce. It's that simple. I can't live like this anymore. It's not good for me, or my son."

He tried again. "Becca…"

"Are you going to Charleston?"

"Yes."

The line went dead.

He didn't try to call her back. There was no sense in bothering. She was headstrong, and when she got angry... it was no use.

Instead of calling her again, he just stared at the phone in his hand. It was an older satellite phone, in an orange plastic casing, with a small readout screen at the top and the buttons below. It was a friendly looking phone. At the moment, it seemed like his only friend in the world.

"I'm sorry," he told it. "I'm really, really sorry."

CHAPTER TWENTY FOUR

7:45 p.m. – Mountain Time
Aspen, Colorado

"Doctor, do you know who I am?"

Omar and the doctor sat on the back deck of Omar's house near the summit of Red Mountain. The locals called it "Billionaire Mountain," and for good reason. Omar was far from the only billionaire who kept a home up here.

He and the good doctor were enjoying some red wine and gazing out at the green ski runs on Aspen Mountain, perhaps a mile across the valley. The sun lowered in the sky. It was a crisp early evening, but the winter snow was all gone.

Three of Omar's bodyguards stood behind them, as well as two servants waiting for instructions.

The doctor nodded. "Of course I do. You are Omar bin Khalid, of the House of Saud. It has been an honor to treat you."

"And what exactly did you treat me for?"

The doctor seemed confused. "For what ailment?"

Omar nodded gently. "Yes."

The young doctor was from Mexico, and from all the evidence presented was highly skilled. He was fluent in English and had in fact attended medical school in New York City. He had been waiting at the airport in Ciudad Juarez when Omar's plane came in.

The plane taxied into a hangar to confuse anyone who might be watching by satellite. Omar and his party, under cover of the hangar, transferred to a different airplane, waited twenty minutes, and then flew here to Aspen. They brought the doctor with them.

"Well, I treated you for what is clearly a gunshot wound to the right hand. I cleaned and disinfected the wound, and stabilized the injury. It appears to me that you will need, and I definitely recommend, further treatment at a hospital."

Omar was feeling buzzed already. It had been a long day, he was tired, and he had been quite drunk when the Americans so rudely interrupted his party.

"Can you describe the extent of my injury?" he said.

The doctor shrugged. "I explained this to your assistant, but I'm happy to explain again. In addition to the traumatic entry and exit wounds, you've sustained fractures of the bones of the hand and small bones of the fingers, some bone loss, soft tissue injuries to the muscles and related structures, as well as significant damage to the nerves and blood vessels. As you know, I've provided you with an opiate for pain management, and an oral antibiotic to reduce the chance of infection. Since I brought these with me from Mexico, you're going to need a prescription for similar medications here in the United States when these run out, which they will do."

"Do you know where I sustained this injury?"

The doctor held up his glass. A servant stepped up from behind them and refilled it with wine. The wine was dark. Like blood.

"You told me yourself. You were aboard your yacht on the Cuban coast."

"Very good," Omar said. "Now I want to ask you a few personal questions, if you don't mind."

It seemed the doctor must also be drunk, because he smiled. "I don't mind at all."

"Are you married? Do you have children?"

The doctor looked at Omar with a sly glint in his eyes. "So far I am married to my work. And I haven't, as you may understand, felt the urge to commit to any one woman."

"But did you tell anyone where you were going today?" Omar said.

"I was instructed to act in utmost secrecy."

The answer annoyed Omar, but perhaps only a touch. He smiled at the futility of it. It was a little bit cagey, and that was all. A non-answer masquerading as an answer.

"Did you?" he said.

The smile on the doctor's face began to fade. "Did I what?"

"Act in utmost secrecy."

"Yes. Of course."

"Good," Omar said. He rose from his chair. "I want to thank you for your fine work. I would shake your hand, but..." He raised his bandaged hand. "I'm unable at the moment."

He turned to go inside. "It's been a pleasure knowing you."

From the corner of his eye, Omar saw two of his bodyguards move in, seize the doctor, and drag him out of his chair. They quickly gagged him and handcuffed him. The doctor was either so surprised or so frightened, he didn't make a sound, and he offered only the most token resistance.

They pulled him ten feet away and pushed him to the polished marble of the deck. One of the bodyguards pulled a silenced pistol, raised the doctor by the hair, and shot him through the head. He did it at an angle, so as not to harm the stonework. The gunshot itself made a simple *clack*, like an office stapler. The bullet whined off into the wilderness.

Omar went inside the house. He passed down a long hallway, his servants following behind. He noticed the throbbing in his hand. It had eased somewhat, whether from the wine or the doctor's opiate, he wasn't sure. The wine and the opiate made a nice combination, though. In his head, he was definitely starting to feel that little concoction.

He entered his study. It was a solarium, with a glass bubble ceiling, and floor to ceiling windows on three sides, taking in astounding views of the surrounding mountains. There was a large telescope in the corner by one window. Omar was a stargazer when the mood struck. His assistant, Ismail, was here, sitting in a chair and studying a half-played chess game on the table in front of him.

He smiled when Omar walked in. "Omar, I have very good news for you."

"Yes, please. I need some good news."

"My eyes are everywhere," Ismail said. "Even in the den of the viper itself."

"Do tell."

"A private plane left Washington, DC, moments ago, en route to Los Angeles. It has some very special passengers on board. The husband of the President of the United States, himself one of the richest men on Earth, and their two lovely daughters. The plane has a six-seat capacity, which means there are three Secret Service agents on board, at most four, if there's a cockpit jump seat."

"Four Secret Service agents?" Omar said.

"At most. Three is more likely."

"Can we defeat that many?"

"In an unsecured location? We can defeat five times that many."

"And our presence in Los Angeles?"

Ismail nodded. His smile was contagious. "I would think that should be obvious. There is a robust presence. We have people moving into position even as you and I enjoy ourselves in this glorious mountain retreat."

"That sounds very good."

"It is very good," Ismail said. "Very, very good."

CHAPTER TWENTY FIVE

10:21 p.m. – Eastern Time
Charleston, South Carolina

The pilots called the plane FRED.

It was a military acronym, short for "Fucking Ridiculous Environmental/Economic Disaster." It was the C5 Galaxy, a fuel hog, and one of the largest airplanes in the world. Luke rode in the cockpit for most of the flight, but he went back to the cargo hold for a little while just to marvel at the amount the plane could carry.

The plane was a resource mover. Its enormous hold was 120 feet long, a foot longer than the Wright Brothers' first powered flight. The hold was full. Four Humvees were parked in there. Thousands of meals-ready-to-eat, packed on pallets. Cots, tents, more hazmat suits. Tens of thousands of pounds of medical consumables—disposable thermometers, syringes, rubber gloves, disinfectant wipes, plastic tubs, and more. It was hard to believe the thing could even get off the ground.

A light rain was falling when they arrived.

A young Army lieutenant met him on the tarmac. "Agent Stone? We've got a vehicle waiting, sir."

The road from the airport was empty except for military vehicles. The Jeep's windshield wipers slapped out a slow tempo. In the dark, they passed a convoy of troop carriers going the other way. Luke drifted into a dreamlike state.

In ten minutes, they passed through a checkpoint. Then a moment later, another. They passed him hand to hand until he reached the barricades. He had seen video of the area, but not of the barricades themselves. They were a makeshift tangle of sandbags, hurricane fencing, and looping razor wire, extending in either direction as far as the eye could see. Two- and three-story watchtowers had been quickly erected all down the line.

Bulldozers were working under cover of darkness, knocking down buildings across the street to create an open zone where no one could hide.

He found himself in a tower, about twenty feet above a long line of people moving slowly between barbed-wire-topped fencing. The fencing ran along a long wall of wire-mesh sand-filled Hesco bastion portable barriers, stacked two high. The Hescos were like giant sandbags, each one four feet high, and the wall of them

137

probably went three hundred yards. There were hundreds of people here, the line itself snaking back into the gloom. Three riflemen stood in the bird's nest with him. They watched the line move, hands on their guns.

The head of the line was just below them. Half a dozen men in full white hazmat suits stood at a long desk. They held yellow infrared thermometers, which they pointed at each person who came up in line. Then they directed the person either right or left.

"What's the setup here?" Luke said to one of the gunmen.

The kid gestured with his head. "The line below us is people who want out. They were vetted at an armed checkpoint further back. They're mostly docile. Regular citizens, we hope. No crazy people. No weapons. Also, no sneezing, no coughing, no bleeding. No obvious symptoms. They're behind that Hesco berm because we've been taking fire from across the way. You see those guys in the space suits? They're taking everybody's temperature. If it's too high, you go to the left. If it's normal, you go to the right. Left is a field hospital. It's hell on Earth over there. Right is a containment zone. Right is for the lucky duckies. You get a cot and a blanket and a bite to eat. You're under a big tent. You stay the hell away from everybody else, and in the morning, if you're still normal, you get to leave. That's the plan anyway. Personally, I think it's better if they hold them a few days, but they tell me the containment zone is already filling up. Anyway, all those people standing around in the rain down there? Who wouldn't have a fever by now?"

"What's your assignment?" Luke said.

"We're here to keep the guys in the space suits alive. They lost a few earlier this afternoon. It was pretty much chaos setting up these checkpoints. Things are a lot more orderly now."

Just then, a commotion started at the desk. A young black woman hugging a small boy was surrounded by men in white suits. She started screaming.

"No! He doesn't have it! I know he doesn't have it!"

Two men in white suits were pulling the child away from her. Two men tried to subdue her. She fell to her knees as they pulled the boy away.

"No! Don't take him! Eddie! No! Wait a minute. It's me! I have the virus. Please! I have it! He doesn't have it!"

Next to Luke, the kid raised his rifle and sighted the woman.

"Easy," Luke said. "Easy."

In the next second, the woman bounced to her feet. She was fast, and strong. She broke from the men behind her. She ran at the two men who had her child. She crashed into them, ripping and clawing at their suits. The suits were made of light vinyl. She tore a huge hole down the front of one. The men tried to back away. She ripped and tore. The man fell backwards, onto the ground. She climbed on top of him.

The man on his feet swept the boy up in his arms and ran with him down the walkway between fences.

The woman ripped and clawed at the man on the ground. "You leave my boy alone, you hear me? Eddie! You come away from that man!"

Next to Luke, the kid fired.

Boom... Boom... Boom.

His upper body jerked from the recoil.

People screamed. The entire line of people dove for the ground. Near the table, the woman had fallen into the mud. She lay there, barely moving.

A voice came over a loudspeaker. "Everyone stay on the ground. Remain calm. Do not move. Repeat, do not move. Remain calm."

The man in the white suit crawled away from the woman, then climbed to his feet. Luke could hear him. His voice was panicked. "Shit! I'm bleeding. Oh, man. She scratched me. Jesus!"

The kid kept his gun trained on the woman. "She's fine," he said. He spoke fast, seemingly to himself. "I'm firing rubber bullets. I didn't kill her just now. She's still moving. She's going to be fine."

A burst of automatic gunfire erupted off to the left, and the kid flinched. The crowd screamed again. The kid kept his gun trained on the woman. She writhed in agony on the ground, arms and legs slowly pushing mud.

A tracer went up from the barricade, lighting up the streets just across the way. As the tracer came down, it cast eerie shadows on the walls. It was really raining now.

"Can somebody please kill that guy already?"

Luke caught the light signature from the gun barrel. It was coming from a shattered second-story window of an old five-story apartment building. The building was set back in a courtyard. The bulldozers hadn't made it over there yet. Small arms fire from the barricade pelted the brickwork of the building.

139

A burst came from the window again. Automatic gunfire strafed the checkpoint a hundred yards down from Luke's tower.

"Everyone stay down!" the loudspeaker repeated. "Remain calm."

"The guy's a maniac," the kid said. "He's got an Uzi or a chopped Tec-9, and he keeps popping up in different places. He must have a million rounds. He's already killed about half a dozen people. I don't know what the hell his problem is."

Luke marked the window. "Do you guys have any heavy weaponry here? I can take him out."

"If we did, don't you think we would have done it by now? All we have is dum-dums for the rifles, and a few guys have sidearms. Not much good from here. We've called for a sniper, a mortar, an air strike, anything at all, but we don't get one. I don't know who set this thing up, but it's a hundred percent FUBAR. We're sitting ducks in these towers. The people on the ground are better off than we are."

As Luke watched, bullets strafed the defensive barrier the people in line were hiding behind. The giant sandbags stopped the bullets cold, but the people screamed, they crawled, they groveled in the dirt and the mud. The guy in the building fired a tear gas canister. The street began to fill up with smoke.

"Remain calm! Stay on the ground! Cover your nose, mouth, and eyes. It's only tear gas. It cannot hurt you."

Just below Luke, a woman squatted, her back to the sandbag wall, her eyes closed, her mouth moving frantically, her hands clasped together in prayer.

*

The chopper landed in the blowing rain on the roof of Roper Hospital.

The hospital was inside the quarantine zone, less than a mile north and west of where the attacks took place. A line of about fifty medical and support personnel snaked toward a doorway, just out of reach of the helicopter blades. A big Marine Corps staff sergeant paced back and forth along the line, talking into a megaphone.

"Attention!" he said. "You are now in the hot zone. You ARE NOT entering the hot zone. You're already there. Below this roof is the eighth floor of the hospital. The eighth floor is the staging area. No one... I repeat... no one goes below the staging area without fully donning a personal protection suit. The hospital is contaminated with live Ebola virus. If you go below the eighth floor without a personal protection suit, you WILL become infected, and you WILL die. Before you die, you will put other people at risk. We WILL NOT allow you to put other people at risk. So you WILL NOT go below the eighth floor without donning a personal protection suit. You can thank me later."

Luke was barely out of the chopper before it took off again. He approached the line, but was intercepted by a young Army captain. The guy looked like he had hardly shaved in his life. "Agent Stone? Come this way, please."

They bypassed the line and entered a dim stairwell. Stone followed the man down, their footfalls echoing on the metal grates. The captain pushed through a heavy door into a bright room. Stone walked in behind him.

It was a locker room. Twenty people were in the room sitting on wooden benches, slowly pulling on vinyl personal protection suits. Another ten people were helping them get dressed. Cases of bottled water were piled in strategic spots around the room, the plastic coverings ripped open. Piles of hazmat suits and equipment dominated the far corner. Every few minutes, a hydraulic door would wheeze open and a few more fully dressed people would pass out of the room.

A young woman in blue hospital scrubs approached. She was no nonsense. She didn't smile. She didn't greet Luke in any way. She seemed in a hurry to get started. Move 'em in, get 'em out.

"This is Nurse Rader," the Army captain said. "She's going to help you get dressed. Once you're dressed, another nurse will inspect your suit before you go in. They will read from a checklist, and confirm each item on the list, so it may take a little while. We ask for your patience. Have you worn something like this before?"

Luke nodded. "Yeah. This morning, as a matter of fact."

The captain looked at him.

"It's been a long day," Luke said.

"Good. It's about to get longer. And you already know it gets hot in the suits. There's bottled water, as you see, and I suggest you drink some before you go downstairs. Alert me before you leave. Dr. Connors will be waiting for you at the stairwell door on the seventh floor. He knows you're coming. He'll give you the grand tour."

"Is he the hospital director?" Luke said. He couldn't be sure, but this afternoon, it had seemed like the hospital director was...

"No," the captain said. "Dr. Gupta was the hospital director. He died about an hour ago. Dr. Connors is from Doctors Without Borders. He built and ran a two-hundred-bed field hospital in Liberia during the crisis there. He's taken over Dr. Gupta's responsibilities."

Behind Luke, the hydraulic door wheezed open again. It made an awful sound.

"Very important," the captain said. "Once you leave this room, you are considered exposed to the virus. That means you can't come back the same way you left. Every door you pass through is going to lock behind you, and you can only go forward. Am I being clear?"

"Crystal clear. But how do I get back out?"

"The staging area for removing the suits is on the other side of this floor, and we have no access to it. They have no access to us. Your equipment will be contaminated when you arrive there. You come up the stairwells on the northwest side of the building to reach them. There are hand-lettered signs indicating the way. If you find a door locked against you, do not panic. Don't try to find another route. Just wait. The door will open again. They're trying to prevent logjams in the disinfection process."

"Are people panicking?" Luke said.

The captain nodded. "I haven't been in there. But what I hear is no one has seen anything like this before. And people are panicking. I'm talking about experienced people."

"Okay."

It took half an hour to put on the suit. For once, Luke didn't try to rush anything. This was the real deal, live virus, and he was happy to take it slow and let his dressers get it right. He let himself drift as they worked through their checklist. When they were ready, he stood.

He wore a white vinyl coverall, with doubled-up rubber gloves, rubber boots, a hooded respirator with a full face shield, and a helmet. The respirator made it hard to speak. The helmet and mask made it hard to hear. The helmet had no intercom or speaker. This was going to be wonderful.

They sent him through the hydraulic doorway and he tottered down a flight of stairs. At the bottom, he pushed through a heavy door. He heard it latch shut behind him. A man stood in the hallway, waiting for him.

The first thing Luke noticed was the man was covered in blood. His suit was stained with it. His faceplate was streaked and smeared. There were other fluids and substances on him. Some of it was black like tar.

The man was older, perhaps sixty-five. He had white hair and was a touch overweight. His face had gone slack. When he saw Luke come in, his eyes brightened and he became alert.

"The red stuff is blood, as you know," the man shouted, evidently so Luke could hear him. "The black stuff is vomit. Mostly bile mixed with deep internal blood. You'll get some on you. I wouldn't worry about it."

"Dr. Connors?" Luke said.

"Agent Stone?"

"Yes."

"They tell me the President sent you."

Luke nodded. "Something like that."

"Will you report what you see to her?"

Luke shrugged. "If she's still speaking to me."

The man looked at him quizzically.

"Yes," Luke said. "I will report to her."

"Good. Then I'm going to show you everything."

"Fair enough," Luke said.

They went on a tour of hell.

CHAPTER TWENTY SIX

June 12th
3:15 a.m.
Georgetown, Washington, DC

The taxi dropped him off in front of a row of handsome brownstones. The tree-lined streets were quiet and empty. They seemed to shimmer in the light from the ornate overhead lamps. Luke paid the driver and got out. As the cab pulled away, he stood for a moment, deciding what to do.

Oh, well. He was nothing if not decisive.

The shades were drawn, but lights were clearly on in the street-level apartment of the building nearest to him. He climbed the wide stone steps on unsteady legs.

Luke had flown back to DC in a twenty-seat Lear normally used by Virgin Atlantic executives. It had been donated to the cause, and it came complete with a wet bar and a flight attendant. Luke was all alone on the plane. The flight attendant wore a painter's mask and rubber gloves, and she stayed in the back, as far from him as she could.

"Are you afraid I'm infected?" he asked her.

She pulled a bright yellow infrared thermometer from a drawer. She pointed it at him like a gun, and looked at the readout.

"Ninety-eight point six," she said. "You're in the clear for now. From what they tell me, if you're infected, by the time we get to DC, you'll know."

He nodded. "Do you mind if I make myself a drink?"

"Help yourself."

He opened the bar and set about pouring himself a strong one. Maker's Mark. One ice cube. He drank that one fast, and then poured another. Then another. He tried to drink away the things he had seen. It was impossible.

The hospital had 530 beds. They weren't enough. People were laid out in rows on the floors of open wards, and in gurneys along the hallways.

"CDC protocols are out the window," Connors shouted at him. "You're supposed to isolate Ebola patients, one person to a room. We ran out of rooms in the first two hours."

It wasn't a hospital. It was a slaughterhouse. The floors were awash in blood, in urine, in black and red vomit. All the sheets were stained with it. All the bedclothes were stained with it. There were white buckets in corners, filled with black vomit and feces. People bled from the eyes, from the mouths. It was hard to tell who was alive and who was dead. Once, a weak patient raised an arm to Luke, trying to touch him, trying to get his attention.

"Help me," the muscular young man mouthed. "Please help." The words didn't make a sound.

"We don't have enough personnel," Connors said. "We don't have any aides, we don't have enough nurses, or orderlies, or anyone at all. People come in here, people who were in West Africa, and they leave twenty minutes later. I had a dentist come in here and have a heart attack. I don't know what he was thinking, and I don't know if he's alive or dead. I've had experienced staff passing out at the sight of all this fluid. There's a river of it everywhere you look. Blood, piss, puke... Jesus."

The tired old doctor looked at him, eyes full of meaning.

"We were lucky," he said. "The alarm was sounded right away, and this city is a peninsula, so it was easy to quarantine. But if the virus had gotten off the peninsula..."

"It might have," Luke said. "We still don't know."

Connors shook his head. "If it had gotten off, you would know."

A thought came to Luke unbidden. *They're testing us. They gave us an easy one to see what the response would be. What about a big, sprawling, wide open city, one that wasn't surrounded on three sides by water?* It was a horrible thought.

Now, hours later, on the front steps of a brownstone, on the silent city streets of Georgetown, Luke was drunk. And he was numb. He should have gone home. He knew that. Becca didn't want him right now, but she was at the country house. He could have gone to their place in the Fairfax suburbs, but the thought of sitting in that big empty house alone...

He didn't like that thought. He didn't want to be alone, now or ever again. His hand reached out, practically of its own accord, and pressed the bell.

Ding...Dong.

It had that loud, formal doorbell sound.

In a moment, there was movement behind the door. The peephole slid open, then slid shut again. A big heavy bolt slid back. The door opened.

Trudy Wellington stood there. Her curly black hair was down. She had red-framed eyeglasses on her pretty face. She was braless, and wore a long baby blue T-shirt. It hugged her shapely body and barely came down to her thighs.

The shirt had a cartoon of various animals all standing together. A black bear. A moose. A white-tailed deer. A few ducks, and some furry rodents. An elephant. A rhinoceros. Even a small brown boy and a little blonde-haired girl.

Underneath the crowd was a caption: *Too Cute to Shoot.*

All the same, Trudy herself held a gun in her hand. It looked very large in her small hand. Luke nodded at the gun.

"You gonna let me have it with that?"

"Luke?" she said. "What are you doing?"

"Listen, I'm sorry I rode you so hard earlier today. It's just that this day has been a nightmare, we were in a crisis, and I needed you to do your thing. I could have been nicer about it."

Their eyes met and locked on.

"Is that why you came here?" she said. "To apologize?"

He shook his head. "No."

She pushed the door all the way open. "I think you'd better come inside."

"I think so, too."

He stepped into her apartment.

CHAPTER TWENTY SEVEN

1:15 a.m. – Pacific Time
Los Angeles International Airport

The airport was quiet.

A handful of people moved here and there under the soaring four-story ceilings. Airport service personnel, people who had come in on late flights, people who were stuck on layovers, waiting for early morning flights. The distant whine of a vacuum cleaner came from somewhere.

Pierre and his daughters had landed just moments ago. The girls were sleepy, and with good reason. It was a long flight. He held each of their hands as they stumbled along, eyes half open. They were flanked by Secret Service men and women. Red caps pushing their baggage in carts followed along behind.

An advance Secret Service man in a blue suit approached.

"Mr. Michaud? I'm Agent Ferguson. Sir, the cars are several minutes behind schedule. They'll be here shortly. It's the normal configuration. Three SUVs. You and the girls will ride in the second one. Your car is fully armored. We'll have a Los Angeles Police car at the front, and two motorcycles at the rear. We'll be spotted from above by a Secret Service helicopter. We'll have you home in about forty minutes."

The arrangements sounded fine. Even so, Pierre could barely hide his irritation. He was as tired as the girls. "Why are they late? They knew our arrival time."

"Sir, there was an accident. The lead SUV was in a head-on collision. The other driver crossed the median strip. Our driver is okay, but the man in the other car..." The Secret Service agent shrugged. "He didn't make it. We'll have a toxicology report and an ID in the morning. In the meantime, we had to bring up a replacement SUV. The first one is totaled."

Pierre let out a long sigh. "Okay. That's too bad."

"In the meantime, sir, if you and the girls want to relax in this waiting area, we swept it and it's secure. There are restrooms and a water fountain. Unfortunately, there's not much open in the airport this time of night."

"Okay," Pierre said. "Thank you."

He sat with the girls across a row of chairs. Across the way, an overhead TV was on, showing a twenty-four-hour news station. All the news was about Charleston. They kept showing the same smartphone clip of the helicopter flying overhead, spraying the people below. A GPS tracking chip mounted on the helicopter by Charleston County suggested that it had crashed into the Atlantic Ocean. Pierre looked away from the TV. Thankfully, the sound was off.

He closed his eyes. Normally, his brain gave him a steady stream of ideas. He came upon things out here in the world, and he saw how they could be improved. He saw gaps and opportunities everywhere. That wasn't the case today, and it hadn't been for at least a week. With his eyes closed, all he saw was nothing.

"Dad, can I go to the bathroom?"

It was Michaela. He opened his eyes and looked at her. Beautiful, beautiful girl. Just like her mother. Pierre never played favorites, and he didn't want to think it, but it was possible that Michaela was more beautiful than her sister, Lauren. He hoped that neither of them suspected he thought that.

"Go ahead, honey. Just don't dilly-dally. The car will be here soon." He turned to the female Secret Service agent assigned to Michaela. Pierre could never seem to remember her name. She had been with them a lot this past week. The woman stood about five feet behind them. She wore her hair pulled back in a ponytail.

"Of course," the woman said, without waiting for Pierre to say anything. "Let's go, Michaela."

The agent seemed very fit, with large arm and shoulder muscles for a woman. Pierre wondered idly if she took steroids or some other performance enhancer. People who used themselves as lab rats, testing the boundaries of human performance—this was a topic that interested him.

He looked at Lauren. Also a very beautiful girl. Lauren had her headphones on.

"Do you need to go, honey?"

She shook her head. "I'm fine."

"We'll be in the car a long time," Pierre said. "Better safe than sorry."

She rolled her blue eyes and flipped her long brown hair. "Dad."

Michaela and the Secret Service agent were already halfway to the bathroom. As Pierre watched, an older lady with gray hair and a big yellow suitcase on rollers reached the door just ahead of them.

The woman seemed to be having some trouble with the size and weight of the suitcase.

The Secret Service agent held open the door for the old woman.

*

The old woman was not old.

She did not have gray hair. She was having no trouble at all moving her oversized suitcase along. Her lined and aged face was an elaborate makeup job that included the use of putties and gels. She had waited, sitting still for over an hour while the artist transformed her from young and strong to old and infirm.

She stepped into the ladies' room, moving slowly. Just behind her, she heard the door slide to a close.

"Okay, Michaela," a female voice said. "Use any stall and do your thing. I'll wait here."

The old woman slid a silenced gun from her jacket, turned, and shot the Secret Service agent in the head at nearly point-blank range. The agent barely had time to flinch. The back of her head sprayed out in a fountain of blood and brains and bone.

She dropped instantly to the floor, as though a trap door had opened below her. The sound of the gun was the sound of two hands clapping once.

The little girl almost screamed, but didn't. The woman chopped the girl on the side of the neck with the blade of her hand. She didn't pass out, but she went limp, her eyes rolled back showing the whites, and she almost fell. The bones seemed to have gone out of her legs.

The woman caught her and eased her to the ground. The girl was very docile. The old woman wrapped duct tape around her mouth and the back of her head. She wound it around several times, catching the girl's long hair in it. She slipped a pair of eye shades over the girl's eyes. She gagged her mouth. She cuffed her hands behind her back. The girl offered no resistance at all. If not for a slight muffled whimpering, it would be hard to tell she was even awake.

"You stop that whining," the woman whispered fiercely. She gave the girl's body a violent shake. "If I hear another peep from you, I will kill your father and sister. Do you understand me?"

The girl nodded.

The woman zipped open the giant suitcase all the way. The sides were hard plastic. On the inside, the case was molded to accept a body just about the girl's size.

She stuffed the girl into the suitcase. It took several moments. This was the critical time, and the time that made the woman nervous. It was taking too long. These Secret Service agents were all wired together. A moment of silence half a beat too long, and they would all come running.

Finally, she had the girl inside. The woman zipped the bag shut again.

Alone now, the old woman, who was not old, wheeled the suitcase around the body on the floor, giving it a wide berth. A pool of blood was spreading out and becoming a lake, and she didn't want to track her wheels in it.

She pushed open the door leading to the terminal.

*

Pierre opened his eyes and yawned.

Across from him, the old woman he'd seen before slowly made her way under the giant TV set and toward the bank of elevators. She dragged along that big heavy bag of hers. It seemed like something was wrong with one of the wheels.

Pierre almost had the urge to help her, but he figured she pulled the bag with her on a regular basis. It was probably better if she handled it herself. The practice would help her keep up her strength.

As he watched, she entered an elevator and a moment later, the door slid shut.

He glanced around.

A Secret Service agent approached. The same one as before? He wasn't sure. Sorry. They all zoomed in and out of his life so often, it was impossible to keep track. He didn't know who anyone was.

"Sir, the cars will be here in two minutes. I suggest you and the girls get ready."

Pierre nodded. He glanced toward the bathroom.

Michaela spent a lot of time in front of mirrors, carefully inspecting changes to her body, brushing her hair, making faces, and in general admiring herself. It was an occupational hazard of the beautiful people. And for now, it had gone on long enough.

He looked up at the other female agent. He noticed she didn't have an earpiece in. "Do you mind popping in there and finding out what's holding her up?"

"Of course."

The woman headed toward the bathroom. She walked quickly, and a moment later, she disappeared inside. The door slowly slid to a close.

A few quiet seconds passed.

Suddenly, five large men ran toward the bathroom door.

Pierre was surrounded by Secret Service. In an instant, they had him and Lauren up from their seats and running toward the sliding glass exit door. Pierre was out of control, moved along by the strength and speed of the burly men around him.

"Wait!" he shouted. "Michaela is in the bathroom!"

Lauren made a yelping sound of terror.

A black SUV roared up to the curb, its passenger doors already open. The agents shoved Pierre and his daughter into the back seat. Two agents piled in on top of them, pressing them to the floor of the car.

"Go!" one of the agents screamed at the driver. "Go! Go! Go!"

The car lurched forward, speeding toward the airport exit. A strong man held Pierre down across the seat.

"Very important," the man said. "Did you see anyone?"

Pierre shook his head. "I don't know."

"Anyone. Anyone at all."

"I don't know. I saw an old woman."

"What old woman?"

"An old woman came out of the bathroom. She had a big suitcase."

A Secret Service man in the front seat shouted into a handheld walkie-talkie. "An old woman. The suspect is an old woman with a large suitcase."

"What did she look like?"

"I don't know," Pierre said. His mind was a blank. His head was spinning. "Where is Michaela?"

Beside him, somewhere in the dark speeding car, he heard Lauren's low moan.

"What color was the suitcase?" the man said.

"I don't know! Dark. It had wheels."

"What was the woman wearing?"

"Michaela!" Pierre screamed, as if that might conjure her in the car with them. For an instant, he imagined how that could work. Magic. He would just turn his head, and she would be there next to him, squashed down on the car seat by a Secret Service man. So he did turn. He turned his head as much as he could, but she was nowhere in sight.

"Is she dead?" he said.

"She's missing," the man on top of him said. "She might have been abducted. That's what all signs point to. But I promise you we're going to find her. This happened only a few minutes ago, so she's still somewhere on the airport grounds. And we're closing all the exits. They will never get her out of the airport. We just need you to answer some questions about the woman you saw."

Pierre had no faith in what this man was saying, none at all. Magic had a better chance of working.

This was impossible. This was a nightmare.

The Secret Service man was still speaking, but Pierre no longer heard him.

"Michaela!" he screamed again.

CHAPTER TWENTY EIGHT

5:45 a.m. – Eastern Time
United States Naval Observatory – Washington, DC

"Is she here?" Brooklyn Bob said.

Kurt Kimball shook his head. "No."

Susan sat in the Situation Room. Even at this late hour, the room was nearly full of people. Empty coffee cups littered the tables. The office-sized garbage cans overflowed with empty takeout food containers. A smell was beginning to permeate The Room, a smell of people who had gone a long time without showers.

Susan looked at Kurt Kimball. He was running this show. Kurt was Susan's National Security Advisor. She didn't even know what that meant anymore. There was no security. There was no advice worth taking. Everything was out of control.

She couldn't bring herself to look at the computer screen with the live feed from Brooklyn Bob's hideout in Syria. She sat staring at the table, blessedly encased in a feeling of numbness she had never experienced before. It was self-protective, and that was good, but it was also weak.

There was too much to be done. Something had to be done. If she couldn't rouse herself... *Oh God, Michaela.*

She glanced at the clock on the wall. Ninety minutes had passed since she had first heard the news they had taken Michaela. Ninety minutes since they had tried to make contact with this monster Brooklyn Bob. Ninety minutes he had made her wait.

"Why don't I believe you?" Bob said. Susan was beginning to think of him as just Bob, like an old friend, like your friendly neighbor Bob. "Why do I think she's sitting right there with you? Susan, if you can hear me, yes, it's true. The mujahideen have taken lovely Michaela. Now you know what it feels like to lose someone. Now you know what you people have been doing to us for all these years. Can you feel it, Susan? This is loss. This is pain. A piece of you has been taken away, and it may never come back. Not pretty, is it?"

"Bob," Kurt Kimball said. Kimball's voice was angry, seething. Susan looked at him. His round bald head was dark red. A thick vein stuck out on his forehead. "We are locked onto your location. You could die at any minute. I will call in the air strikes and gladly watch you get obliterated."

"Shut up, errand boy! I'm talking to the President. I'm talking to Susan."

In the first moments, the doctors had offered Susan a sedative. More than a sedative, really. A powerful tranquilizer. They had offered the same drug to Pierre and he had taken it. It was the right thing to do. He was sleeping now, he and Lauren both were, out at the Malibu house. Security was tight there. They were safe.

But Susan couldn't take the drug. She had to be alert. She had to... direct things.

"We're not stupid," Bob said. "We know you can find Michaela. We know you have all the latest gadgets. You might even already know where she is. That wouldn't surprise me at all. But know this. She is surrounded by mujahideen who have taken an oath. They will die before they let you have her back. At the first sign they've been discovered, they will kill her without hesitation. And by the first sign, I mean one security guard snooping around with a flashlight, a news helicopter flying too low, a homeless guy taking a piss in a rose bush and talking to himself. Anything that doesn't look right, and Michaela dies. If a SWAT team pulls up, or a bunch of paratroopers fall out of the sky... well, let's just say she'll be dead before they even touch the ground."

"What do you want?" Kurt said.

"Wait a minute," Bob said. "Don't get ahead of yourself. That's just for starters. The second Ebola attack is still on. That hasn't gone anywhere. You guys did okay with the first one. It looks like you might even have things under control a little bit. But Charleston is really kind of a small city, isn't it? The next one is going to be bigger. And it's going to be badder. It's going to be the baddest thing you've ever seen."

Susan looked up. On the computer screen, skinny, bearded Bob was standing with a dark blue New York Yankees baseball cap on. Would he really attack his own hometown? Was that what he was suggesting? Did he have any control over where they hit next?

Bob smiled. "But you can stop it from happening, at least for now. And you can have Michaela back. It's easy. All you have to do is a few things for us."

"We're listening," Kurt said.

Bob's smile died in an instant.

"I know you're listening, dummy. That's why I'm on here with you. Of course you're listening. So listen to this. There's an open air prison in the Iraqi desert near Qafa. You know the place. When the Crusaders took Mosul some time back, over five thousand of our brothers were captured and crowded into this place."

Kimball turned and snapped his fingers at two of his young staff members. "Qafa?" he mouthed at them. Instantly, they both started working on the laptops in front of them.

"We know our brothers are dying of starvation there," Bob said. "We know they are dying of thirst. We know they have no cover from the sun. We know you are torturing them to death."

"We don't torture people, Bob. We're not like you."

Bob ignored him. "We want that prison closed immediately, and we want all of our brothers released and given safe passage fifty miles west to our territory. Are you writing this down? That's the first thing."

Bob glanced down at a list he was holding. "Next thing, very easy. We want the Guantanamo Bay prison closed immediately, and all brothers remaining inside given safe passage to their home countries, or any destination of their choice."

"Bob..." Kurt said.

"Next and final thing, for now. We may decide we want more later on. We probably will. But for the moment, this is it. There is a CIA black site prison called the Salt Pit. It's in Afghanistan, at an abandoned brick-making factory outside Kabul. It's an evil place. Our count is that there are more than two hundred prisoners inside, trapped at the mercy of your most psychotic and demonic torturers. Most of these prisoners are not mujahideen. They are ordinary people arrested falsely. Whether they should have answered Allah's call is not for us to say. That is between them and the Great One. But we want them out of there. We want that prison closed, and we want the people inside transferred to the custody of the Red Cross so they can receive medical and psychological care. And we want the perpetrators of that site arrested and brought to justice. Not your justice. Ours."

"Bob," Kurt Kimball said. "You know these things are impossible."

Brooklyn Bob glanced away from the camera. "I have about six a.m. your time, correct? Good morning, East Coast. I'll give you six hours to make your decision. Let's get back on here at noon

155

your time. At noon, you should begin the process of releasing prisoners at Qafa, and transporting them to our borders. Safely and humanely, please. We will know if you are doing this, of course. By noon, you should be in touch with Red Cross personnel in Kabul to begin the transfer of prisoners from the Salt Pit. And you should be placing the torturers under arrest, ready for transfer to the custody of mujahideen. We understand that the logistics of closing Guantanamo may take a little longer."

"Impossible," Kurt said again.

"If these things aren't happening by noon, then Michaela dies immediately and we launch the next attack soon after. Okay? You have six hours. That seems fair. Thanks for chatting with me."

"Bob," Kurt Kimball said. There was an edge to his voice.

On the screen, Brooklyn Bob hung up the satellite telephone. He reached in front of him for something that was out of the picture. A second later, the video feed cut off.

*

"Madame President? The Saudi ambassador has arrived."

Susan sat at her desk in the upstairs study. The windows were west-facing, so the early morning light was a bleak shade, almost blue. Susan was more of a sunset person anyway. She stared down at the surface of the desk and ran her fingers along the smooth wood. It was a nice old desk. It had been in this office a long, long time. There was something reassuring about that.

"Okay," she said. "I'll summon him in a few minutes."

The aide went out and Susan looked up at Kurt Kimball and Richard Monk, both sitting across from her. The issue of Michaela, and the issue of another impending Ebola catastrophe, hung between them. Susan wasn't ready to talk about either thing.

"Give me the update on Charleston," she said.

Richard glanced at his tablet. He heaved a sigh. Of relief, of exhaustion, Susan had no idea. Richard had been here for at least forty-eight hours straight.

"We got very lucky," he said. "It's a disaster of gigantic proportions, but nothing on the scale of September eleventh. Latest estimates suggest that about a thousand people have been infected, nine hundred and fifty of whom have died, or are likely to die. About sixty people died in violence related to the outbreak, especially at the barricades. There have been over three hundred

156

arrests. But the city was closed so fast that nearly every single infected person was contained inside. A few small hotspots appeared in the suburbs overnight, but these were quickly locked down and quarantined. The disease has not reached a wider radius, and many people within the quarantine zone were never exposed to the infection. With most hosts dying quickly, the virus should burn itself out over the next week to ten days."

"Kurt?" Susan said. "What are the implications of this?"

Kurt didn't look at his tablet. "Dire," he said. "Charleston is a small city, and because of its geography, a city you *can* close. The attack was visible and unusual, and our forces responded to it immediately. We have computer models that suggest if an hour had passed between the attack and our response, a hundred or more infected people would have passed out of the quarantine zone before it was imposed. A hundred people doesn't sound like a lot, but they would have basically rendered the quarantine useless."

"In what way?" Susan said.

"They would have spread the infection at a rapidly increasing rate, generating hot spots throughout the region, in municipalities without the resources to deal with them. Highway rest areas, bathrooms, gyms, restaurants, public places of all kinds, would have led to explosive, and possibly exponential growth in the numbers of infected. The infection likely would have traveled north and south on Interstate 95, reaching nearby states very quickly. By trapping the virus in Charleston, and concentrating our response there, we've been able to smother it. But if it had broken out, the worst-case scenario is we would have had no way of stopping it, or even slowing it down."

He paused. He glanced at Richard, then back at Susan. "We came very close to a disaster with few precedents in modern history. The bird flu of 1918 killed perhaps fifty million people. This could have become that bad, or worse."

In the past few minutes, an idea had started to form in Susan's mind. It was an idea about Luke Stone. Stone had acted instantly, and with no authority, to close the city. He did that knowing many people trapped inside would die. But he had also done the more important calculation, which was that without quarantine millions of people might die. He made a difficult decision very, very quickly, and then acted on it.

"And they're going to attack us again," Susan said.

Kurt nodded. "It seems so. Only in a bigger city, and if they learned their lesson, a sprawling one with no obvious way to lock it down. Think the outer boroughs of New York City. Think Detroit, or Philadelphia, or Atlanta. Think Los Angeles or Houston. The obvious response is to impose twenty-four-hour nationwide curfews starting now, but you can't keep a curfew going forever. Economic activity would come to a halt. Anyway, people need to eat. The minute we lifted the curfew, we'd be vulnerable to attack again."

Susan turned to Richard. "Do we know where Luke Stone is right now?"

Richard shrugged. "We tracked him to Trudy Wellington's apartment in Georgetown late last night. I'm not even going to speculate about that. Don Morris, Trudy Wellington, Stone... you can connect those dots however you like. Before he arrived at Wellington's place, Stone was in Charleston, inside the quarantine zone, and still pretending he was acting on your orders. I don't think he'll stop until he's in jail."

"I want Stone here," Susan said.

"Susan, we haven't even talked about Michaela yet."

"I know. We'll talk about her as soon as Stone gets here."

Richard shook his head. "Okay, but..."

"No buts, Richard. I want him. So get him."

She turned back to Kimball. "What's next?"

"The Saudi ambassador. You summoned him. He's waiting downstairs. We can make him wait some more, or we can send him back. You don't need to speak with him if you don't want."

"No. I want to. Bring him up here. It won't take long."

A few minutes later, an aide showed the ambassador in. He was a portly man with dark hair. He wore a custom-made blue suit. Susan was a fashion person, so she noticed the suit. But she was also so tired, she couldn't remember the man's name. She didn't care about his name.

"Madame President," he said, and reached to shake her head. He smiled. He didn't seem anxious in the least. Ambassadors tended not to be nervous types. He spoke perfect English. "It's a pleasure to meet you."

Susan shook his meaty hand. She did not offer him a seat. They stood facing one another. Richard Monk and Kurt Kimball flanked them on either side.

"Ambassador," Susan said, "I'm going to be very clear with you. We know that Omar bin Khalid was involved in yesterday's terrorist attack. We want him surrendered to us immediately."

The ambassador shook his head. "Omar bin Khalid is a member of the royal family. As royals go, he's probably the blackest of black sheep. But our intelligence sources don't believe he was involved in this atrocity, and in any event, we have no idea where he is. He has no official role in our government, and therefore is a private citizen. We don't keep tabs on private citizens."

"I imagined you'd say that," Susan said. "So we'll move on for now. Please relay this message to the king."

The ambassador nodded. "Yes, of course."

"If my daughter is harmed in any way, or if another American city is attacked, I will personally consider either one of them an act of war by the Kingdom of Saudi Arabia against the United States. In the event of either occurrence, we will commence a bombing campaign of Saudi Arabia within hours. We will not stop until your capital city of Riyadh is in rubble, and your entire oil-producing infrastructure is destroyed."

The ambassador's face hardened. "We have no control over this situation," he said. "You cannot make these threats."

Susan was already done with him. She waved her hand as if to banish him away, and turned to go back to her desk.

"That wasn't a threat," she said. "It was a promise."

CHAPTER TWENTY NINE

6:25 a.m.
Union Station, Washington, DC

Luke sat at a table near the towering great hall of the train station, a cup of coffee in his hand. He studied the cup. It was blue with Greek columns on it. He must have held this exact cup in his hand one million times. The station was just coming to life, early commuters arriving on the first or second trains of the day.

There was an ongoing disaster in Charleston, but here in DC, people were getting ready to go about their daily business. Luke didn't want to think about it.

He had left Trudy's place before sunrise. She was deep asleep, her hair tousled, her beautiful body half-covered by a green fuzzy blanket.

Luke hadn't slept at all.

As he watched, an old man arrived at a high-backed shoeshine chair along the concourse and put down his heavy shine box. The man was thin with very white hair. He wore dark blue coveralls. He moved slowly, with what seemed like infinite care.

Luke stood and walked over to the chair.

"Hey, old timer," he said.

The man barely looked at him. "Good morning, sir."

"Can you give me a high-gloss spit-shine, like we used to do when I was in the United States Army?"

The man bent over his shine box and began removing the tools of his trade. Rags, polish, buffers. Now he looked at Luke. His face was lined and cracked. His eyes were deep set and piercing. "Like a bull polish?"

"That's what a civilian might call it, sure."

The man gestured at the chair. "It's pretty involved. Might take a while."

"I have time," Luke said.

He climbed onto the high throne of the shoe shine chair. The chair itself was worn smooth by thousands of men sitting there over the decades. Below him, the shine man went to work. He slapped on a layer of thick paste. Luke pawed through a stack of magazines and opened a copy of *Men's Health*. He skimmed the headlines.

6 Foods to Increase Your Sex Drive
7 Surprising Health Benefits of Green Tea

"What can I call you?" Luke said.

The man shrugged. "Raymond will do."

That was funny. Most recently, he had been named Paul. Today he was Raymond. When Luke was young, the name had been Henry, or Hank. He was the man without a name, the man without a country. What could you say about someone who was a Cold War spy, who sold his own country's secrets to the Soviets, then turned around and sold the Soviets' secrets to the British and the Israelis? What could you say about a man who had been marked for death again and again, and yet had never actually died?

One thing you might say is he was lucky to be alive. Another thing is that he was a man with a lot of information, even now, long after he had supposedly retired, long after most people had forgotten he was ever alive.

"Well, Raymond. This is quite a job for a man to be doing at your age. Did you forget to max out your 401k?"

The man named Raymond sighed. "I guess we're not all destined to return the rightful queen to her throne one week, then engage in piracy on the high seas and launch entire armies into quarantined hot zones the following week."

Luke shook his head. "No, I suppose not."

"Quite a display you put on yesterday. From zero to hero in just a few hours."

"It's not over," Luke said. "We've got another one coming. Yesterday was the practice. But I don't know where the big game is."

Raymond nodded. He worked on one knee. Luke's eyes wandered over a page of the magazine. He was too tired to read the words. Here was a photo of a bright yellow banana. Here was a restaurant plate of oysters on the half-shell.

"Do you know who Mohammad Atta was?" the shine man said.

"Naturally. The lead 9/11 bomber."

"Good. Besides being a suicide bomber, if that's what he was, Atta was also a Pakistani intelligence asset. Six months before the attacks, the ISI transferred a hundred-thousand-dollar payment into an account held by him. That's one thing to know. Another thing to know, maybe the most important thing, is that when he entered the United States for the last time, he flew into Los Angeles. He was picked up at LAX by a man calling himself Lawrence Munroe.

Munroe was a man with an interesting past. In the 1970s, under a different name, he was a low-level associate of Italian-American mobsters in California and Nevada, and a sometime informant for the Los Angeles field office of the FBI. In the 1980s, he was a freelance pilot running cocaine from the Nicaraguan Contras to African-American crack gangs in Los Angeles and Houston. But no matter who or what he claimed to be at any given time, he was always CIA."

Luke smiled. He glanced up and down the concourse. "I forgot to wear my tinfoil hat today," he said. "So are you trying to tell me the CIA and the Pakistani ISI were responsible for the September eleventh attacks? Weren't you CIA once upon a time? Now you'll probably tell me you killed John Kennedy."

Raymond the shoeshine man glanced up. His eyes were full of sharp intelligence. "I envy you, Luke Stone. You live in the darkest of possible worlds, and you still get to keep your childlike innocence right until the end."

He shook his head. "What I'm telling you is nothing is ever quite what it seems. These terror networks can't exist without the intelligence agencies. Terrorists are mostly misfits and morons. Left to their own devices, half of them wouldn't make it off the couch. They need an impetus, something to get them moving. And they need someone to protect them from local law enforcement."

"The intelligence agencies do this?"

The old man nodded as he worked. "Maybe. Sometimes. Now, do the CIA and the NSA and the FBI want their assets committing atrocities on American soil? No, I don't think so. What they do want is a reason. A reason to open ten million private emails. A reason to enter people's homes at night. A reason to increase their funding, expand their surveillance, and extend their reach."

The man's ancient hands held a soft blue chamois. The hands worked quickly and expertly now. "Terrorist networks give them that reason. But it's a slippery slope, because terrorists have a tendency to disappear, and situations have a tendency to get out of hand. You think things are going one way, then they turn and go somewhere else."

"Someone knows where the terrorists are?" Luke said.

Raymond nodded. "Possible. Not guaranteed."

"But they want something in return?"

"Indeed."

Not for the first time, Luke marveled at the cold-bloodedness of it all. Tens of thousands of lives, possibly millions, hung in the balance, and somebody wanted something. Somebody always wanted something.

"What do they want?"

The man shrugged. "What do people ever want? Money, of course. But in this case, amnesty is more important. They want to come back into the fold. As you know, in any game, there are winners and losers. Susan Hopkins won. Now, whether she knows it or not, there's a hunt going on behind the scenes. Her people, the winners, are using the resources of the state to track down the ones they think are responsible for the coup. The losers. It's understandable, of course, considering everything that happened. So there have been at least two dozen summary executions in the past week. Some were right, some were wrong. But it's starting to take on an open-season quality, and people are being driven deep underground. A few of those people have quite a lot of information at their fingertips."

Raymond reached into the breast pocket of his coveralls and came out with a business card. He handed it up to Luke.

"When the people in charge want to talk, they can call that number. The man to ask for is Rick. If they call, they should be ready to offer a truce, and mean it. Total amnesty for all involved. Otherwise this all goes nowhere."

Luke looked at the card in his hand. ACE Rug & Carpet Cleaning.

He shook his head. "I don't have the ability to grant anyone amnesty. I can't protect anyone, and I have no influence. I don't even work for the government anymore."

The man glanced up again. There was a wild light in his eyes. He grinned.

"Don't you? If not, then who are these gentlemen joining us right now?"

Four large men in blue suits with earpieces walked briskly up the concourse. They were nearly identical. They all had close-cropped hair and the kind of big, muscular bodies upon which suits just never hung right. They made a bee line for the shoeshine chair. The first man to reach the chair already had his badge out.

"Agent Stone, I'm Agent Troyer. Secret Service. Will you come with us, please?"

"Am I under arrest?"

"Your presence is requested at a meeting with the President of the United States."

"Requested?"

The man didn't smile. "Strenuously."

At the bottom of the chair, on one knee, the shoeshine man was already putting away his gear. His workday was over. The Secret Service men didn't even seem to notice him. Just an old man and his shine box.

Luke glanced at his own shoes. They positively glowed. It was the brightest shine he'd had in years, except for one small area at the tip of his left shoe. That spot was still dull and lifeless.

As Luke got up, he handed Raymond a fifty. "Looks like you missed a spot."

The old man shrugged. "You know? Even when something looks like it's over, it isn't. It's never over."

"I'll take that under advisement," Luke said.

The old man pocketed the fifty. "That's a good idea. You do that."

CHAPTER THIRTY

6:55 a.m.
United States Naval Observatory – Washington, DC

"It's the smallest functional battery ever built," the young man in the Coke-bottle glasses said.

He paused, looking sheepish for a second. "I don't want to overstate it, but it's true as far as we are aware. Of course, we can't know about everything being developed."

Luke sat in a high-backed leather chair in the upstairs study at the New White House. The guy with him was probably mid-twenties. He wore a blue short-sleeved dress shirt with a white T-shirt beneath it. He wore khaki pants with some sort of mustard stain on one leg. Stylish he wasn't.

He placed a laptop on the table in front of Luke. He stood next to the computer and pulled up an image. It was a photo of what appeared to be interlocking stacks of metal staples. It almost looked like an old-style steam radiator.

"This was taken by a microscope. The image is less than one-hundredth of an inch across. Given the way we use it, the battery theoretically has an infinite lifespan."

"Amazing," Luke said. A couple of aides had shown him in here five minutes ago. The kid was already here when Luke opened the door.

The kid nodded. "Amazing is right. And this stuff gets more amazing all the time."

"Why are you showing me this?" Luke said.

At that moment, the door opened again. Susan walked in, followed by Richard Monk, a large man with a bald head, and a couple of Secret Service agents. Susan had dark circles under her eyes. Her mouth hung slightly open. Her tan suit was wrinkled. Her hair was pulled back to her scalp. She looked like she hadn't slept in days.

"Hi, Susan," Luke said. "I heard you wanted to see me."

"Luke," she said without cracking a smile. "Thank you for coming. I see you've met Timothy Penn. He's a designer in research and development at my husband's Boston office." She gestured to the big man behind her. "This is Kurt Kimball, my new National Security Advisor. And you know Richard Monk."

Luke shook hands with Kimball, nodded to Richard.

"Stone," Monk said.

"Before we begin, I want to thank you," Susan said. "Our computer models suggest you may have saved millions of lives yesterday. Certainly you saved thousands."

"That's good to hear," Luke said. "I never doubt computer models, not even for a minute. Am I still excommunicated?"

"When you made calls yesterday and claimed to be working for this office, did anyone call you on it? Did anyone even blink?"

Luke shook his head. "No."

She shrugged. "Then you were never excommunicated."

"Okay," Luke said. "So what's going on? Why am I here?"

"My daughter was kidnapped by the terrorists late last night," Susan said. Her voice made no inflection and betrayed no emotion. It was flat and businesslike. "I need you to get her back."

The horror never seemed to end. Luke looked into Susan's exhausted eyes. The rest of her face was expressionless. All of the pain, all of the fear, all of the sorrow… it was in her eyes.

"Tell me," he said.

*

Timothy Penn had placed two laptops in front of Luke. He had pulled up a folding chair next to Luke's leather one. He sat next to Luke and manipulated both screens with a laser device he held in his hand.

Susan sat to Luke's left. Monk and Kimball stood behind them.

"Both the girls were chipped three years ago," Timothy said. "I won't say I was against it at the time, but I'll admit it did seem a little Big Brother to me. Pierre insisted, so we did it. It turned out to be a very good idea."

"What do you mean they were chipped?"

Timothy looked at Luke like he thought Luke might be putting him on. "Well, they're chipped. They have computer chips inside them. Like people put little chips inside their pets, so if the pet ever turns up in a shelter, it can be identified? Or you know, people with Alzheimer's disease wear little GPS units around their necks or on bracelets in case they ever become lost?"

"Yes. I'm familiar…"

"Both the girls have tiny GPS units inserted between their big toe and their second toe on their left foot. The units are half the size of a grain of rice. The batteries I showed you earlier? That's what powers the units. At the time, three years ago now, we believed this to be the most cutting edge GPS technology in the world. Things have moved on since then, but the units are still working, so we didn't bother to remove them."

Luke turned and looked sharply at Susan.

"When I became Vice President, Pierre became terrified for the girls. He was afraid that something like this would happen. We went back and forth about it for nearly two years. People like Timothy were developing this chip technology. And finally we chipped the girls. They were only eight years old. They thought they took a trip to the dentist. They don't even know the chips are there."

"I thought there were side effects to these things," Luke said.

Timothy shook his head. "Not anymore. At least, not that we've seen. The chips are tiny. They're encased in biodegradable plastic. We insert them in the foot so they're as far as possible from vital organs. Most of the time, they're in sleep mode, and send a split-second pulse every twenty-four hours, just letting the system know they're still out there and still working. That's why the batteries last so long. Only in the event of an emergency do we wake them up."

Timothy pulled up an X-ray image of a human foot. There was a tiny sliver in the webbing between the toes, and every few seconds, a red circle emanated from it.

"This is kind of an artist's rendering, but you get the point. The chip doesn't set off metal detectors. The only way you can find it is by X-raying the child's foot. And why would you do that?"

He shook his head and answered his own question. "You wouldn't. I think you can see how this technology is far superior to a chip that the kid wears as part of her clothes, or as a necklace. A product like that makes it too easy for a kidnapper to simply discard the chip."

"So you know where Michaela is right now?"

Susan didn't nod or move in any way. "Yes."

"Where is she?"

Timothy brought up a new image on the second laptop. It was a stylized photograph of a blue glass and steel skyscraper, backlit by the last light of day. The photo suggested that a glimmering night was coming on.

"This is another artist's rendering. It's of a forty-story luxury condominium building, Skyline Number Nine, which is located at 9 Lansing Street in downtown Los Angeles. The building doesn't actually look like this. It's only half-built. Some kind of dispute between the city and the developer has stalled the project, and it's been sitting there as a construction zone for the past several months. The GPS unit's location can be pinpointed anywhere on Earth, accurate to within two hundred feet. Currently the unit is awake and broadcasting from inside this construction site."

"Why don't we send someone in there and get her back?" Luke said.

"We can't," Kurt Kimball said from behind him. "The people holding her are a suicide squad. They will kill her at the slightest hint of unusual activity."

"Can the GPS unit show altitude?" Luke said.

Timothy. "No. That's hard. In another couple of generations, maybe. But now…"

"So if SWAT shows up at street level, or a sniper takes out one of the terrorists from a helicopter…"

"Yes," Kimball said. "The remaining terrorists will kill her."

"And we don't know where in the building she's located?"

"Right."

"Can you do it?" Susan said.

Luke shrugged. He didn't want to disappoint her. The terror she felt must be almost overwhelming. It looked like she was doing a good job of keeping it tamped down, but it was the kind of thing that could break through to the surface at any moment. Even so, this mission sounded like the tallest of tall orders.

"Go in there, take them by complete surprise, kill every single terrorist almost before they can move, and then bring Michaela out safely?"

She nodded, and now tears began to fall slowly down her face. "Yes."

A heavy sigh escaped from Luke. "I'll need my team," he said. "My pilots, my muscle, my tech guy." He glanced back at Richard Monk. "Even Trudy Wellington."

*

Luke didn't find Ed Newsam. He didn't have to find him.

The spooks were following his team everywhere they went. Luke walked into a McDonald's near Dupont Circle, and there was big Ed, sitting by the window, slowly and methodically demolishing a stack of pancakes, sausages, Egg McMuffins, and a large coffee. His face was lumpy and bruised. He had a new shiner under one eye. His crutches lay beside him.

Luke slid into the booth and faced him.

"Mind if I join you?"

Ed's expression barely changed. His eyes were bloodshot. He looked, in a word, like shit.

"You keeping tabs on me?"

Luke shook his head. "Not me. Them." He gestured at a black SUV parked outside the picture window. Ed grunted when he saw it.

"How was Key West?" Luke said.

"You're looking at it."

"Rough night?"

Ed shrugged. "I went out with a couple of the Navy SEALs from our little Cuban fiasco. Might have drank a little too much. They started badmouthing you, said you were weak. So I showed them what weak looks like."

Luke smiled. "Okay, I'll bite. What does weak look like?"

Ed stuffed a chunk of pancake into his mouth. "Them."

"I need you, buddy," Luke said. "It's that simple. We've got a bad one, and I need you. They took the President's daughter."

Ed's eyes opened very wide, but only for a second. He breathed deeply. He took a big slurp from his coffee cup. "We going to do it right this time? Hit hard, and no apologies?"

"I promise you this," Luke said. "We are going to hit them as hard as anyone has ever been hit. We have no choice."

Ed nodded. "All right. In that case, I'm in."

CHAPTER THIRTY ONE

7:50 a.m.
Somewhere in the Sky, United States

The F-18 Super Hornet screamed across the sky.

Luke slumped in the rear seat, usually reserved for the weapons system officer. He was fitted with a helmet, a flight suit, a g-suit, and on top of that a parachute harness and a survival vest. Inside the cone of the fighter jet, the sky was wide open all around him. He glanced at the instrumentation just in front of his knees. They were traveling just under 1,000 miles per hour.

The pilot was a lieutenant, a guy named Reginald Maxwell. People called him Max. As in Mad Max, and Max Airspeed. His voice came over the intercom.

"You feel all right back there? I usually get more from guests."

"More what?" Luke said.

"I don't know. Excitement... War whoops. Terror. Sometimes people puke, or pass out from the positive g load."

"I'm good," Luke said. "A little tired. Haven't slept in a couple of days. I might even take a nap. If I do, it doesn't mean I passed out. Sound okay?"

"Okay with me. These birds suck fuel like nothing you've seen, so we're scheduled for a refueling in South Dakota. If you wake up and we're on the ground, you'll know why. I'm told we're high priority, so we should drop down, gas up, and go."

Luke nodded. "Good."

"Care to tell me what we're doing today?" Max said.

Luke glanced behind them at the pyramid formation of fighter jets. He and Max were the lead. Behind them were five jets, each one carrying a member of the team in the rear seat: Ed Newsam, Swann, Trudy, and the chopper pilots Rachel and Jacob.

"What we're doing?"

"Sure. It's not often we carry a load of six civilians across the country at near top speed. With yesterday's attack in mind, it makes me a little curious."

"Yeah... well. Curiosity killed the cat, Max. This one is classified. Suffice to say you've got two former Delta Force operators, one former Naval Intelligence systems analyst, and two

170

former 160th Special Operations chopper pilots. There's only one true civilian in the bunch. And she's FBI."

"Ah."

Luke nodded. "Yeah."

"Well, enjoy the flight," Max said. "Estimated time of arrival at Point Mugu Naval Air Station is maybe ten minutes before eight a.m. local time, eleven a.m. East Coast time. From there, you have about a twenty-five-minute chopper ride into Los Angeles."

Luke closed his eyes and drifted.

They were flying in fighter jets because no other planes would get them to Los Angeles in time. As it was, they were going to cut it very close, with less than an hour to set up and execute the operation. And then there was the next Ebola attack.

Luke didn't want to think about it. He almost couldn't think about it. He was over-tired and his brain was badly taxed. They were going to hit a major city this time, a big city, one that couldn't be quarantined. Charleston was easy, relatively speaking. But how do you shut down a city like Chicago or Philadelphia?

Simple answer. You don't.

There were too many arteries in and out. There were too many people, and too many high-density living arrangements. There were too many transportation options. There were too many methods of attack available, and too many ways the disease could spread.

This time, they had to stop the attack before it happened.

Before leaving the New White House, Luke had taken Kurt Kimball, Susan's National Security Advisor, aside.

"You guys are killing people," he said. It wasn't a question.

"I don't know what you mean," Kimball said.

"The invisible war," Luke said. "Spy versus spy. The coup plotters. You're out there taking down the remnants of Bill Ryan's people."

Kimball looked away. "That's not my department. I know very little about it. The one thing I do know is it has to be done."

Luke shook his head. "It has to stop. We need those people. When one of them dies, our access to that person's networks dies with him. If we're going to find the terrorists before they hit again, those networks are how we're going to do it. So you need to make it your department, starting now."

He handed Kimball the business card. ACE Rug & Carpet Cleaning.

"Call this number. Talk to Rick and tell him who you are. Tell him you have access, and you want a truce. But the only way the truce will work is if you actually put a stop to the killings."

"And what should I expect Rick will tell me in exchange?"

"In exchange for his life?"

"Yes."

Luke shrugged. "Hopefully, he'll tell you where the next attack takes place, where the terrorists are hiding, and how we can beat them."

Now, aboard the fighter jet, Luke was nearly asleep. He had put his trust in Kurt Kimball fifteen minutes after meeting him. He had done so mostly because Kimball seemed better than Richard Monk. He had no idea what Kimball would do with the information Luke had given him.

Luke couldn't think about it anymore. He was exhausted. He couldn't be everywhere at once. He had to leave that part to other people. He had told Kimball the deal, and asked him to do the right thing.

All he could do now, as his head slowly fell forward, was hope for the best.

CHAPTER THIRTY TWO

6:15 p.m. (11:15 a.m. Eastern Time in the United States)
The Skies Above the Persian Gulf, near Dammam, Saudi Arabia

Two American F-18 Super Hornets flew combat air patrol along the Saudi coast.

Commander Henry "Hank" Anderson glanced at his radar. There was a lot of tension out here today. It was so thick you could slice a hunk off and chew on it. His patrol had diverted a couple of mock attacks from Royal Saudi Air Force F-15s in the early afternoon. Now, up ahead, three fighters had just taken off from King Abdulaziz Air Base. He radioed air control.

"Bare Ace, Bare Ace, this is 101, do you read?"

"Copy, 101."

"We've got three bogeys leaving Abdulaziz. Number one appears to be on intercept heading."

"Distance?" the air controller said.

"I'm at twenty thousand feet," Hank said. "Bogey at eight miles and closing. He's turning left, giving us a little bit of a left aspect. I'm in single target track."

"101, hold your heading."

"Roger that," Hank said.

They played these games all the time. It was usually American planes and Iranians, once in a while Americans and Russians. In the past twenty-four hours it had been the Saudis. Hank didn't watch the news much, but he knew about the bioweapon attack on American soil. Everybody knew. He also knew that an American intelligence agent had tortured and maybe shot a member of the Saudi royal family. And things were tense up here today. That much was true.

Hank didn't have much use for the Saudis. That was also true.

The Saudi fighter jet had turned and was heading directly toward him again.

"Bare Ace, this is 101. The bogey's got me on his nose now, six miles out." He waited a moment and watched that approaching plane. They were both going very fast, headed on a near collision course. "I'm at altitude, twenty thousand feet, three miles out now. Uh... two miles."

"Hold your heading, 101."

"One mile, Bare Ace. Here we go."

Hank had a visual on the Saudi plane. It was an F-15 Strike Eagle, coming at lightning speed. Suddenly, the plane fired.

"Bare Ace, I'm fired upon!"

Hank's heart skipped a beat in his chest. His hands moved automatically with no input from his conscious mind. His plane banked hard left and gained altitude. He over-steered and put himself nearly upside down. He rolled, still banking hard.

A missile flew by within a hundred meters. It zipped past and exploded in the air less than a mile away. The shockwave hit him and his plane shuddered.

"101... 101?"

"Copy," he said.

"Status?"

"Still here."

"101, you are cleared to engage. You are clear to defend yourself."

"Roger, Bare Ace."

Hank knew his rules of engagement meant he could fire back when fired upon. It wasn't on his to-do list when he woke up today, but it was always a possibility. He banked the plane around to his left and back. He fell in behind the F-15, which was running south. The other two F-15s were nowhere in sight.

Hank controlled his breathing and maintained his posture. That was close, but he was operational, and he was on the bogey's tail.

"I can take him anytime," he said.

"Take him," Bare Ace said.

"I can shoot him down?"

"Affirmative, 101. Shoot him. Shoot him down."

Hank locked on with a Sidewinder missile. "Fox Two," he said, using the brevity code for the Sidewinder. "Fox Two, Bare Ace."

"Roger."

Hank launched the missile. "Fox Two away."

The missile shrieked across the sky between Hank and the F-15, closing the distance in a few seconds. The F-15 didn't even seem to take evasive action. Hank pulled up hard as the missile hit home. He saw a flash of white light, and the F-15 spinning out of control.

"101, did you kill him?"

Hank glanced back and below. The Saudi plane spiraled down toward the waters of the Persian Gulf. As he watched, the pilot ejected.

"Affirmative. Fox Two kill."

Hank looked for the pilot's parachute to open. It didn't happen. The man's body in his dark flight suit dwindled and disappeared as it fell toward the water.

"His chute is not deploying. He is falling free."

"Roger, 101," Bare Ace said. "Confirmed F-15 kill. Nice shot."

As Hank turned back to rejoin his patrol, he could feel his heart rate and his breathing start to normalize. He wasn't much for politics. He felt it was best left to the politicians, who he wasn't much for, either. The whole thing seemed like it could turn on a dime, and frequently did. All the same, he didn't want to be the guy firing shots that started World War Three.

"You know? Could have sworn these guys were our buddies when I woke up yesterday."

"Roger that," Bare Ace said.

CHAPTER THIRTY THREE

8:25 a.m. (11:25 am Eastern Time)
Los Angeles, California

"Okay, Swann," Luke said. "We're running out of time. Give me what you've got."

They had set up a makeshift command center in an empty office suite on the thirtieth floor of an office building a mile from the construction site where Michaela was being held. Pierre Michaud owned the building. Pierre was under sedation, but Susan got them access to the offices.

The windows faced toward the construction site. In the distance, Luke could see a large construction crane towering above the half-finished building. In the background behind the city were the parched peaks of the San Gabriel Mountains.

Trudy stood at a telescope, watching the roof. She had counted about a dozen men up there, as well as a few on the stairwell to the crane's operator cabin, and at least one on the working arm itself.

Swann had five laptops set up across a long white table.

"Okay," he said. "I want to show you something. They can't know we're here, right? I've got command of a Solar Eagle surveillance drone. This is the latest thing. It's solar powered and super lightweight, so it can stay up there for years on end. It operates in the stratosphere, high above your typical air traffic. It's a toy belonging to the Defense Advanced Research Projects Agency. For obvious reasons, they're letting us have whatever we want today. The one I've got is at about eighty thousand feet and slowly circling that building. At that height, they can't see it, but it can sure see them."

"What does it show?" Luke said.

"This." Swann pulled up an image on one of his screens. It was of the narrow metal walkway on the working arm of the construction crane. There was what looked like a package lying across it.

"Okay, what is it?"

Swann used his fingers to zoom in on the image. "It's the girl."

He zoomed in, and in, and in.

The package resolved itself into a little girl, on her back, wrapped in some kind of straightjacket and belted to the deck with

176

leather straps. She wore an airplane nightshade over her eyes. It was about the only act of mercy the kidnappers had indulged in. Michaela was close to five hundred feet above the ground. At least she couldn't see it.

Ed and Trudy had gathered around.

"What is she wearing?"

"It looks like a suicide vest," Ed said.

"Sure," Swann said. "That's what is. If I zoom in some more, you can see the vest pockets are filled with metal cylinders. Six pockets that we can see, six cylinders. Trudy?"

"Yeah," Trudy said. "The vest itself is probably filled with nails, shards of scrap metal, and other forms of shrapnel. And cylinders like that are usually similar to pipe bombs, packed tight with either TNT, C4, or in the worst-care scenario, something very dangerous like acetone peroxide. We'll have to hope it isn't that."

"Trudy, we don't have a lot of room for hope," Stone said. "What's the problem with…"

"Acetone peroxide?" she said. "It's unstable. If you shake it too much, it goes off. Michaela is strapped to the jib of a construction crane hundreds of feet in the air. That crane is subject to high winds, and has a certain amount of give, so we know it's definitely shaking. If it shakes too violently…"

"Boom," Ed said.

"Exactly. Swann, can you pull that in any more? Maybe we see if there's a detonator."

Swann pulled the image even closer.

"There it is."

Clearly taped to the front of the vest was an old Nokia cell telephone. Two red wires extended from the phone and ran inside the vest.

"Those wires are likely soldered to the speaker output circuit inside that phone. The wires run from the phone, and are probably clipped with tiny alligator clips to fuses which will set off the explosives. If you call that phone, it'll send a current along the wire to the fuses. When the phone rings, that's it. Game over."

"They're dinosaurs now, but in the early 2000s, Nokia cell phones were the gold standard," Swann said. "They were super-reliable, simple to use, and could stand up to the elements. For a consumer product, they were also rugged as hell. I once ran one over with my car, just to see if it would still work. It did."

"So that's how they plan to do it," Luke said. "If they see us coming, if they see anything out of the ordinary at all, they call that phone and Michaela dies. Meanwhile, she's five hundred feet in the air, strapped to a walkway that's hard to reach."

"Yes."

"Trudy, can you give me the dimensions of that crane walkway?"

Trudy typed something into her computer. She pulled up a diagram. "The walkway itself is a meter and a half wide, so about five feet. It's steel grating and men walk back and forth on that thing all the time during a typical workday. There's a steel railing about four feet high. The longer side you see is called the jib or the working arm. That's the side they use to lift heavy equipment to the rooftop. It's fifty meters long. The shorter side of the arm is twenty meters long. Those boxes you see that look like shipping containers are machinery to drive the arm, as well as counterbalancing weights. They lift immensely heavy objects using that crane. The little windowed box beneath the arm is the operator's cab."

"So how do we get to the girl before they kill her?" Luke said.

There was a long pause during which nobody spoke.

"For starters, we could jam the telephone," Swann said.

"Tell me," Luke said.

"It's basically a denial of service attack," Swann said. "Very similar to when hackers take down websites. The major difference is there's a lot less security on cell networks. The whole system is based on trust. We can breach that trust."

"How do we do it?"

Swann sat down at one of the laptops. "Cell phones go through a five-step process before they answer a call. It goes like this. During step one, the base station sends out a broadcast page with an identification code for the phone. Step two is the phone recognizes the identification code. Step three is the phone wakes up and responds to the base station, more or less saying, 'Yeah, that's me. I'm here.' In step four, the base station assigns a private channel for the call, and the phone accepts it. Step five is the phone authenticates the incoming call. That's when the phone rings. It takes just a couple of seconds, but it's a little bit of a cumbersome process. The fact that it's cumbersome is what gives us our opportunity."

"So you can interrupt the process?" Trudy said.

"Better than interrupt it. I can hijack it. I need to do a quick search for modified baseband code which can run ahead of early generation Nokia phones. Normally, I'd modify the code myself, but there's no time. It shouldn't matter though, because you can find tons of this stuff ready-made across the hacker networks. Because the phone doesn't authenticate the incoming message until step five, we can broadcast a signal that will race the system and get there before the phone answers the call. We'll listen to the broadcast pages in step one, pick up any targeted for a broad array of old-school cell phones, race their phone to step five, and win. Their call won't come through."

"Where will it go?" Luke said.

Swann picked up his black iPhone off the table. "If I do it right, it should come right here to me."

"And if you do it wrong?"

Swann shook his head. "I'd prefer not to think about that."

"So if you can block that phone call..." Ed began.

Swann waved his hand. "Then you guys are free to do your rock and roll thing with guns and bombs and karate chops and whatever else you do."

Ed was already on his crutches and moving toward the elevators. Luke picked up his big gear bag, slung it over his shoulder, and followed Ed. On the top floor of this building was a helipad. Rachel and Jacob were parked on the pad up there. As the elevator doors slid open, Luke looked back at Swann and Trudy.

"Don't do it wrong, Swann. I'm counting on you. So is the President."

Swann raised an eyebrow. "When do I ever do something wrong?"

Luke entered the elevator just before the door slid shut. Instantly, the car started moving upward toward the roof. For a moment, he and Ed stared straight ahead at the door. Then Ed turned to him.

"There's a first time for everything," he said.

CHAPTER THIRTY FOUR

They called it the Little Bird. Sometimes they called it the Flying Egg.

It was the MH-6 helicopter—fast and light, highly maneuverable, the kind of chopper that didn't need room to land. It could come down on small rooftops, and on narrow roadways in crowded neighborhoods. The chopper was beloved by special operations forces, and Rachel and Jacob had borrowed one from the Air Force this morning.

Luke and Ed climbed into the small cargo hold. Downstairs, about twenty minutes before, they had both dropped a Dexie. The effects were starting to kick in.

This far up, you could begin to see the curvature of the Earth. He looked across at the target building, Number 9 Lansing Street. The construction crane rose close to ten stories above the building proper. Near the top of that crane, on the working arm that extended out over nothing, a little girl was tied up and terrified.

It had been a long and brutal couple of days. Luke had slept on the flight out here, but it wasn't enough. As the Dexie hit him, he began to feel a surge of guarded optimism. Even so, he also felt that familiar tickle of fear. Today it was even more than a tickle. He was about to do something he hadn't done in a long time.

Ed sat near the open cargo door, loading thirty-round box magazines for an M4 assault rifle. He already had a little stack of them going. That was Ed's way now. With his cracked hip holding him back, he had improvised a way to belt himself into a standing position and man the heavy weaponry.

"I'm not sure if you're brave or stupid," Ed said.

"I thought I was weak," Luke said. He opened his gear bag and pulled his black wingsuit and helmet from it. Then he pulled out his parachute pack.

"Yeah, let them SEALs try this. If they're out of the hospital yet, that is."

Luke began to shrug into the suit. As he did so, the chopper's engine kicked to life and the blades began to turn.

The helicopter was tiny. Luke could reach out and touch both the pilots. He poked his head between them. Jacob and Rachel sat inside the cockpit, going through their pre-flight checklist. They seemed serious today, more serious than ever.

"How you kids doing?" Luke said.

"Tired," Rachel said. She looked back at Luke. Inside her helmet, Luke could see it. Her eyes were little bigger than slits.

"We're tired. We've been zooming back and forth across the country in fighter jets for two days, then flying choppers on insane missions that you dream up. And this time we're also worried. We're worried that you're finally going to die, that you've dreamed up an impossible mission even you can't survive."

Luke didn't like the sound of that. What he didn't want was doubt from anyone. There was no room for that right now.

He looked at Jacob. "You worried, Jacob?"

Jacob shook his head. He looked tired, but not worried. "Nah."

"Good man."

"How do you want to do this?" Jacob said.

"Okay," Luke said. "We take off and loop around, away from that building. We want them to think we're just some typical city chopper traffic. So we don't go anywhere near them. We go up to about twelve thousand feet and take this thing out over the water. Trudy will give you the exact distance she wants you from the building. Math isn't my thing. All I ask is you get me an open straight line from the chopper to the roof. If there's anything in my way, I'm not going to make it. Once I leave, loop back the way you came and race me to the building. Try not to give anything away until it's too late for them to act. But do me a favor and beat me there."

"Luke," Rachel said, "you are the craziest man I ever met."

Luke smiled. "From an old 160th Night Stalkers Special Ops pilot, I'll take that as a compliment. I'm sure you've met a lot of crazies. Now let's hit it."

He backed away from the cockpit and the chopper lurched into the air. As the chopper banked to the right and gained lift, he slid his helmet on.

"Trudy, you on here?"

"I'm here," she said. "Can you hear me?"

"Loud and clear."

"Are you sure you want to go through with this? I mean, do you even know what you're doing? You never even mentioned you were a wingsuit flyer before."

"I used to do it for kicks back before Gunner was born. When Gunner came, Becca..." Luke hesitated. He thought back to the night before with Trudy. An awkward moment passed between them. "Anyway, you see my point. I was a dad now, so it was reckless and irresponsible to get myself killed for some weekend thrills."

She didn't say anything.

"Trudy?"

"Yes."

"I'm going to need you to walk me through this thing."

"I know," she said.

"Good. I'll get back with you in a few minutes."

Luke looked at Ed.

"You ready, partner?"

Ed nodded. He was wedged against the open cargo door and belted into an upright position. He held the big machine gun, one hand on the trigger hard, one hand resting along the top of the barrel. He gazed out at the vast city moving below them.

"Born ready."

"Today we're going hard," Luke said.

"Yes," Ed said.

"Hard as we can."

"Yes."

"Be conservative around the girl. But other than that, when I hit the roof, you kill anything up there that isn't me."

Ed smiled behind his sunglasses. "With pleasure."

Luke finished pulling on his suit. It was a tri-wing suit with three individual wings, one under each arm and one between his legs. It hung flat right now, but he knew it would fill when he jumped. He yanked his parachute pack on. It fit over his wingsuit like a backpack.

A few moments passed. The flight didn't take long. Soon, they hovered high above the city. The chopper turned, giving Luke a sweep of the Pacific Ocean. Giant container ships coming into port were like grains of rice on the sparkling water.

Jacob's voice spoke into Luke's headset. "Luke? How does this look to you? Is that a clear enough shot?"

Luke looked out the bay door. The sky was pale blue with streaks of white cloud. He could see the crane and the skeletal frame of the building below them, and what seemed like far away. The big San Gabriel Mountains were there again, a distraction now. He tried not to think about the distance, both to the building, and to the ground. There was an open channel between skyscrapers from here to there.

"Looks okay to me," he said. His voice sounded small. "Trudy, you on here?"

"I'm here."

"What's my story?"

Her voice was firm. "The story is you're jumping from a static hover. With no forward movement, you'll have no initial airflow, which means you'll go straight into free fall. The free fall will generate the velocity you need to gain lift."

"Got it," he said. "Like riding a bicycle."

"Once you get some lift, I'm estimating a one point five to one or maybe two to one glide ratio, meaning for every meter you fall, you'll glide forward a meter and a half or two meters. If this holds true, you should still be a couple thousand feet up when you reach the building. You'll want to pull both your main chute and your auxiliary at that point, and drop down slowly."

"Trudy, if I drop down slowly, I'll lose the element of surprise. We've got gunmen on that crane tower and all over that roof. I'll be a sitting duck up there, and they'll have time to get to Michaela."

"Hopefully, that's where Ed comes in," Trudy said.

"What if I go for a sharper angle of attack, like a ratio closer to one to one? And I come in almost level, or just above the roof?"

"Luke, the lower the glide ratio, the faster you'll be moving when you hit. You don't want to hit that roof, or that crane, at seventy or eighty miles per hour. Even if you get your chutes open, there won't be time to slow down. You want to come in above the building, at a low instantaneous velocity, pull your cord, and then drop in vertically. Do it any other way, and we'll be scraping you off the side of a steel girder."

"I'll take that under advisement. Will you be monitoring my air speed and altitude?"

"Yes."

"If I'm almost to the building and I'm going too fast, scream."

"Luke…"

He took a deep breath. He was almost ready to go. There was no sense doing a lot of thinking about this. It would either come back to him or it wouldn't. Ed would either be there ahead of him or he wouldn't. Michaela would still be alive or…

"Yes," he said.

Trudy's voice was quiet. "Please be careful."

"I'm always careful."

"I love you," she said.

Luke looked at Ed. Had he heard that? Of course he had. So had the pilots. Ed made no sign.

"Jacob? Rachel?"

"Yes," they said, almost in tandem.

"Beat me there."

He was still staring at Ed.

Ed gazed out the door. "Ever been to the Capital Grille?" he said. "Best steakhouse in DC. If you're still alive, we should go there some night. My treat."

"See you on the ground," Luke said.

He spread his legs, held his arms aloft, and leapt out the open cargo door.

CHAPTER THIRTY FIVE

The man's name was Pious. He stood alone on the metal walkway.

He was just above the cabin from where the operator would normally control this crane. A low railing flanked him on both sides.

He was very high in the air. Never mind that. He was high above the building's roof. The roof itself was forty stories above the street. The crosswinds made the whole confounded apparatus he stood upon tremble and shake. Sometimes it seemed like it would tumble into the abyss. But Pious was not afraid of heights today. Allah gave him the courage to stand here.

Perhaps thirty meters from him, the girl was strapped to the same walkway. From here, she looked like a bundle of rags. She was still alive, though. He knew this because once in a while, she tried to kick the straps from her ankles. She was a brave little girl. Perhaps she would not be as brave if she could see where she was.

It was Pious's job to make sure the girl died. If anyone tried to rescue her, the girl died. If noon came and went and there was no word about her fate, then the girl died. If anything out of the ordinary took place, the girl died.

It was almost noon now. In five minutes, he was to call the cell phone that served as the girl's detonator. Pious had a prepaid phone, and the detonator was the only number in its address book. He could call it with the touch of a button.

Perhaps he would wait one extra minute, or even two. He wasn't sure. The jihadis below him on the roof wouldn't like that. But it was his job, his responsibility. He would decide when. He didn't want to make a mistake, kill her, and find out it would have been better to keep her alive.

Someone began shouting. He couldn't make out the words. Down on the roof. They pointed to the sky.

Pious watched where they were pointing.

Something was coming from above. At first, it looked like a bird. Then it looked like a large bird, much too large. Was it a missile? Was it a man? It looked like a man, flying through the air.

Of course. It was an attack.

He threw himself to the metal grating. He pulled the phone from his jacket. Sorry, girl. This was no time to hesitate. You won't get your extra minute of life.

The number of the detonator came up. He pressed the button and covered his head, waiting for the explosion.

The phone was ringing.

Should it ring?

A man's voice answered. "Hello?"

"Hello," Pious said. "Who is this?"

"My name is Mark Swann," the man said. "And your name is mud."

CHAPTER THIRTY SIX

11:56 a.m.
United States Naval Observatory – Washington, DC

"Allahu Akbar! Allahu Akbar! Allahu Akbar!"

Susan was ready to vomit. She was having trouble breathing. She couldn't seem to get enough air. The chanting came out of speakers all around the room.

Kurt Kimball moved to her seat. He leaned down and spoke into her ear.

"We had an incident with the Saudi Air Force about forty minutes ago."

"An incident?"

He shrugged. "It seems they took your threat seriously. They fired on a patrol of our F-18 fighter jets over the Persian Gulf. We've stepped up patrols for obvious reasons, but they were the aggressors. One of our guys shot down one of theirs. Their pilot was killed. That was the end of it. But the Saudi air defense is on high alert, and their pilots are on a hair trigger. I think they're really expecting us to attack Riyadh."

"Are we in position to do that?" Susan said.

"Yes."

Susan nodded and swallowed. "Okay."

All around her in The Room, video screens on the walls and laptops on the tables showed footage of the walls surrounding Qafa prison in the shimmering Iraqi desert. It was early evening there, the light was just beginning to fade, but the air was still hot. Boom microphones picked up the shouted chant of the prisoners inside those walls. All the guards had left, pulling back to the several hundred yards from the walls.

"What does it mean?" someone said from behind Susan.

"It means God is great," Kurt Kimball said. "Or, depending on the translation you prefer, God is the greatest."

"What does it mean to us?"

Kimball shrugged. "It means the prisoners know something is up. These guys are ISIS. Some of the Iraqi guards are sympathizers. A rumor started going through the camp a couple hours ago that we were going to release them."

"Where are we with the terror cells?" Susan said.

Kimball glanced down at his tablet. "Using information from Luke Stone's contact, a man who calls himself Rick, we've pinpointed sixty-three possible terror cells throughout the United States, as well as the apartments, empty buildings, storefronts, mosques, and especially warehouses they may be operating from. Only nine of these are located in what we would call major cities, including Atlanta, Philadelphia, Houston, New Orleans, Los Angeles, Cleveland, Brooklyn, Miami, and Newark, New Jersey. All the same, we have SWAT teams from local law enforcement, as well as teams from FBI and ATF, prepared to raid all sixty-three facilities at the same time."

"Do we even know who this Rick person is?" Richard Monk said. "Have we figured that out?"

Susan almost cringed at the sound of Richard's voice. He had a problem with Stone. That much was clear. Whatever Stone did or said, Richard wanted it to be wrong.

Kimball shook his head. "No."

"Then how can we believe what he's telling us?"

Kimball stared at Richard. "I'm not at liberty to discuss that in this venue."

On a few of the video screens, the image suddenly changed. Now a slightly blurry feed appeared with the face of Brooklyn Bob on it. He was laughing and talking with someone off screen. As he talked, the image sharpened. He held a satellite phone in his hand. He punched in a few numbers.

"It's eleven fifty-eight," Kimball said. "Bob's call will come through any second."

"Have we heard anything from Stone?" Susan said.

"No, and we won't. As you know, in case anyone is intercepting our communications, we're keeping total radio silence until his mission is over."

"I know," she said. "I just thought maybe it was already..."

The speaker phone device on the conference table began sounding its musical tone.

"This is Bob," Kimball said to the room. "I want complete silence in here. Personal devices off. No one speaks except me, and possibly Susan. If I hear your voice, I will have your ass. I promise you that."

Kimball looked at someone in the back of the room. "Ready? Three, two, one..." He made a hand gesture as if welcoming a guest.

Brooklyn Bob's voice filled the room. "Hello, my fellow Americans. Are you there?"

"We're here, Bob."

"I figured I'd wait until noon. But then I figured why bother? What's two minutes between friends? By now you've either done what you're supposed to do, or you've prepared yourselves for the worst. I understand your guards have deserted Qafa prison. Are you prepared to open the gates?"

"We are," Kimball said.

"Good. It'll take some time for me to confirm that you've done it."

"Bob, we have a live video feed," Susan said. "We can send it to you, if you can receive it. That way you can see exactly what we're doing in real time."

Brooklyn Bob's eyes widened. He smiled. "Is that Susan?"

"Yes."

"Susan, I'd love to watch your video. Please do send it to me. Maybe after all this is over, we can get on a private line and chat about it. You can beg me for your daughter's life, and I can... oh, I don't know."

Susan suppressed an urge to cry out her daughter's name. She knew all along that even if she released the prisoners, they would never let her daughter go. They would make her beg. They would make her grovel. And still, it wouldn't matter. They would kill her anyway. Oh, God.

If she could only turn back the clocks somehow, to a time before this horrible series of disasters had begun. She would change it. She would never have taken the oath of office. She would never have agreed to become Thomas Hayes's running mate in the first place. She would never have been Vice President. She would never...

"Video is on its way, Bob," Kimball said.

On the screen, Bob looked away from the camera for a moment. His phone went silent and he spoke a few words to someone in the room with him. Then his sound came back on and he looked into the camera again.

"We have the video. I can hear the brothers chanting to Allah. It's a beautiful sound."

"Listen to this sound," Susan said.

Right on cue, the sound on the video feed changed. The chants were quickly drowned out, replaced by a growing roar. The camera man zoomed out, showing more of the area surrounding the prison. In a few seconds, a plane appeared. It was black, flying low, but still several thousand feet in the air. The plane had a bubble shape, almost like a flying saucer.

Something began tumbling from the bottom of it. Lots of little somethings. Dozens of them. The plane glided past, the little black somethings falling away behind it. The first ones hit the walls of the prison, the ones following landing dead in the center of it. Explosions rocked the compound. The camera shook from the concussions. Bright red flames flickered and dust clouds rose.

"That's a B-2 bomber," Kurt Kimball said. "It's dropping five-hundred-pound Mk-82 Snake-eye bombs. The B-2 carries a payload of eighty bombs. Looks like it just put most of its load smack in the middle of your friends."

As Susan watched, a second B-2 passed overhead. It released its bombs over the prison, as the first had done. They fell, seemingly backward and away from the plane. The bombs dropped in a fiery rain, most of them landing inside the prison. As the explosions subsided, another plane appeared. Then another.

Kimball ran a hand across his throat. Abruptly, the footage of the prison disappeared.

"Seen enough, Bob?" Susan said. She couldn't resist speaking to him now. The bombing had been her idea. They wanted to kill people? We could kill people, too.

During the long hours of waiting, the policy had become clearer and clearer to her. They would not bend to the demands of maniacs. It was out of the question. As long as she was alive, as long as she remained President, her government did not negotiate with terrorists.

Brooklyn Bob seemed shaken for the first time. "You people are animals," he said. "I guess this means one of your great American cities must be destroyed. And Susan, your little daughter is going to die."

"You know what, Bob?" Susan said. "So are you."

She glanced at Kurt Kimball. "Are we locked on?"

He nodded. "We are."

"Do it."

Over the conference call speaker, a sound grew louder and louder. On the video screen, Brooklyn Bob's eyes grew very wide. His line went dead as he looked at the ceiling above him. He raised his arms over his head. The video image began to shake. Then it froze.

Then it went dead.

Static showed on the video feed.

"Can we confirm anything?" Susan said. She felt numb. It seemed like there was no blood in her legs at all. She would remember the look on Brooklyn Bob's face for the rest of her life. She would never forget it. She never wanted to forget it.

Brooklyn Bob died in a panic.

An aide had given Kimball a pair of headphones. He listened. He looked at the room. "It's a direct hit on the house where Bob's satellite phone was located."

A small cheer went up throughout the room.

Susan raised her hands to tamp it down. "It's a little premature, people. We're not out of this yet. I want every single one of those sixty-three suspected terror cells raided. Starting now."

She took a deep breath. The Room became a storm of movement all around her. But in her mind's eye, all Susan saw was beautiful Michaela.

CHAPTER THIRTY SEVEN

9:01 a.m. (12:01 p.m. Eastern Time)
Los Angeles, California

He was coming very fast.

The wind whistled in his ears. His own reactions seemed slow. It had been too long. The building seemed to be quite a distance away, and then it was RIGHT THERE. He flew headfirst, but he was having trouble keeping his head up. He couldn't see clearly.

If he missed that roof, there was nothing but skyscrapers ahead of him.

Trudy's voice inside his helmet: "Luke! Pull the cord! Pull the cord!"

He did as she said. Instantly, he decelerated. His chute pulled his upper body backward, kicking his legs in front of him. Even so he was still coming fast. He pulled the auxiliary chute, slowing even more.

In front of him and below, a man moved along on the walkway of the crane. The man held a gun in his hand, and he was headed toward the forgotten bundle that Luke knew was Michaela. Luke steered his chute toward the man.

He was going to hit hard.

A burst of automatic gunfire sounded.

Duh-Duh-Duh-Duh-Duh-Duh-Duh

Luke looked, hoping to see the chopper. No. Far below, men on the roof had pulled their weapons, and were firing this way. He felt the breeze from their bullets. Nothing hit him. Lucky. Then his chute tore, automatic fire ripping it open. He heard it go rather than saw it.

Suddenly he dropped.

Between his shoes he saw the crane arm, and then nothing but open space. Everything seemed to swim and spin. The crane arm rushed up. It came at him on an angle. The man on the walkway was just below him. Luke fell too long and he was sure he had missed the whole thing. Then he hit like a meteor.

Luke crashed into the man, harder than hard. The force of it sent the man over the low metal railing.

The man fell away screaming, but then his scream suddenly cut short.

The railing caught Luke in the stomach and his air whooshed out. He slid, grabbing madly for anything. The rail jammed into his armpits, his hands found grips, and he held on for dear life. The iron walkway shook all the way up its length, and for a second he thought his extra weight would bring the whole thing down. It didn't. His weight was nothing to that crane.

Luke pulled himself over the railing and collapsed to the deck, tangled in his chutes. He gave himself a moment to let his wind come back. The cool metal slats pressed against his face. He was shaking a little, but not bad. He was alive and the chase was still on. He groped his way to his feet. He needed to move fast.

Another burst of gunfire came, an angry blat.

Luke ripped the chute off of his head. He looked down. The Little Bird was directly below him. If he had missed the walkway, he would have dropped straight through the chopper's spinning blades. That was where the guy who had fallen must have gone.

Aboard the chopper, Ed was at the door, ripping up the guys on the roof. He sprayed them with automatic fire. Luke watched them fall to pieces.

The walkway began to shake. Twenty yards away, two men were climbing past the operator's cabin and onto the long working arm. Luke was still wrapped up in the parachute. He reached inside his wingsuit, looking for his knife.

The men ran toward him, guns in hand. They barely noticed Luke, their eyes focused on Michaela. She was the task. *Kill the girl.* Luke was an afterthought.

The first one tried to leap over him. Luke timed it, then lunged upward with all his might. The man crashed into him and fell to the metal grating. They landed together in a tangled pile. Luke was behind the man. He pushed a hand out of his suit and grabbed the man by his hair, but the man flipped Luke over his shoulder.

Luke went head over heels and landed on his back with a thud. The man who had flipped him rose to his knees, just as the second man fired. The bullet blew through the man's chest. Luke saw the exit wound erupt, all blood and organ meat, heart and lungs. The man fell on top of Luke, his face all blank eyes and open mouth.

Luke had one free hand. He pushed the corpse aside and struggled to his feet.

The second man faced him with the gun. The man was ten feet away. Luke blocked the metal walkway, but he might as well have been wrapped in a tortilla. He was hopelessly tangled in his colorful parachute. And he was nearly helpless. He had no way to lunge at the man. He would never close the distance in time.

They stood, facing each other hundreds of feet in the air. Behind the man, Luke saw the blue ocean and the curvature of the Earth at the far horizon. The wind whistled around them.

The man pointed his gun at Luke's head.

"Drop the gun and I'll let you live," Luke croaked. He was conscious of being almost unable to speak. He was conscious of being the only thing standing between this man and Michaela.

The man grunted. It was nearly a laugh. "You're bluffing. You have nothing to kill me with. And you're delaying my work."

"It's over," Luke said with as much force as he could muster.

"It's over for you," the man said.

Suddenly, the man shredded apart in a blur of blood and bone and gore. His head practically separated from his body. What was left of him fell to the walkway in a bloody ruin. Pieces of it dripped through the grating.

Luke glanced to his right. The chopper hovered there, Ed in the open doorway with his smoking M4.

Luke shrugged. "Or you," he told the dead man.

"Luke?" a voice said inside his helmet.

"Ed?"

"Yeah, man."

"How are we looking, Ed?"

"Well, there are a lot of dead bad guys on that roof. I don't see anybody else, but there could still be a few inside the building. I wouldn't dilly-dally if I was you."

"You got me covered?" Luke said.

"If it moves, it dies. Anything that isn't you."

"Rachel, where can you land that thing?"

"There's plenty of room on the roof, but we'll hover until you get down there. No sense being a stationary target for anyone who might show up."

"How do I get down?"

"You see that tower the operator's cab sits on?"

Luke glanced down at it. Sure, it was like a tall steel cage. "Yeah."

"That's a staircase."

"That's a long way," he said.

He could hear the smile in her voice. "It's either that or jump ten stories. We'll wait for you either way."

Luke found his knife and cut away the remaining parachute. Then he shrugged out of the backpack and ripped away the wingsuit.

He turned and made his way back to the little girl.

She was alive, kicking her legs, making some sound behind her gag.

He kneeled beside her. He didn't want to touch the suicide vest. Trudy and Swann would have to walk him through taking it off of her. He just wanted to make sure she was okay first.

"Michaela," he said, "I'm going to take your gag off, but I don't want you to scream. I'm not going to take your blindfold off yet."

He might not take it off until they reached the roof. It was a long way down.

"Okay? I don't want you to scream. Nod if you won't scream."

The girl nodded.

Luke removed the gag. Michaela shrieked like nothing Luke had ever heard. The piercing sound of it went on and on.

When she was done, Luke cut her arms free. Michaela hugged him just like a little girl would do, and not at all like an eleven-year-old big girl. She squeezed herself tight to him, her arms wrapped around his neck. She kissed him on the cheek and whispered in his ear.

"Am I safe?"

Luke nodded. "You're as safe as can be. We have a little bit of a walk to get downstairs, but it's perfectly safe."

"I want my mommy."

Luke smiled. He looked out at the vast world around him.

"Your mommy sent me."

CHAPTER THIRTY EIGHT

The man's name was Adam.

They called him that because he was the first man hired for this job.

He stood on a catwalk two stories above the floor of the small warehouse, and watched the action below. It was a dusty old warehouse, and looked like it hadn't been used in years. It was full of hospital gurneys, organized in neat rows. There were ninety-six gurneys in total. All but a dozen had someone lying on them.

The people on the gurneys, the vast majority of them young Arab men, were volunteers for the cause. Each one was connected to an IV drip, with a clear fluid inside the plastic bag.

Bustling around the volunteers were six people, four men and two women. In sharp contrast to the volunteers, who wore normal street clothes, the six people in question wore white laboratory gowns, goggles, ventilator masks, rubber gloves, and booties on their feet. They were the workers.

The workers had been selected for their ability to give simple injections. Their job was to hang an IV bag, attach it to a needle, inject each of the volunteers, then to monitor the situation while the fluid in the bag slowly entered the volunteer's system.

It was a simple job. Any blood bank worker or hospital blood technician could do it.

Adam was feeling well-rested and ready to move on. He had inspected this warehouse upon his arrival in Los Angeles, and then spent the past couple of days in a hotel room, ordering room service and watching television. He had spent much of the day yesterday watching coverage of the Ebola crisis in Charleston.

Perhaps the attack hadn't gone as well as his employers wanted, but it was still quite an effective operation. Many had died. The city had plunged into chaos, and there was an icy sense of fear throughout the entire nation. And if it wasn't as dramatic or as devastating as some had hoped, was that Adam's fault? Hardly. He had done everything they asked of him, and had done it well.

He was doing it again today. He wore the same protective gear as the workers below him, though he had no intention of going down there. The volunteers were jihadis, and the IV drips attached to their arms were infecting them with the Ebola virus. Soon, they would leave here in groups of twelve, and fan out all across this great city in large passenger vans.

They would be dropped off on street corners much like religious proselytizers, who would then go out and convert the masses. Only in this case, they would convert the masses from healthy to very sick, and contagious.

These volunteers were human bombs.

Many were excited to do the work. Some were frightened and crying. A few needed to be browbeaten into it by the others. There had been a moment of pushing and shoving earlier, which briefly made Adam concerned that he hadn't brought in any armed guards. In any case, the violence had quickly abated.

Adam didn't know what could bring a person to want this task, but he felt it best to stay up here and well away from them. Soon the volunteers would leave, and he could turn his attention to acquiring his final payment, and getting out of this accursed country before the plague spread to every corner of it.

Soon they would be gone. He breathed a deep sigh of relief at the thought. Indeed, the first batch of a dozen had left the building's parking lot in a van perhaps twenty minutes ago.

God speed and good riddance...

BANG!

Without warning, the corrugated metal garage bay door in the far corner of the warehouse blew inward. It fell in on itself, writhing like a snake. The sound was loud. The door made a noise just like a thunderstorm.

Helmeted men in dark blue uniforms flooded in behind thick plastic riot shields. They moved fast, shotguns held ready in front of them. White lettering on the dark helmets said FBI.

"Down!" someone shouted. "Down! On the floor! Hands above your heads!"

The volunteers were slow to move. Maybe they were already feeling sick.

The FBI men seemed to hesitate for a moment. Adam watched them. He could see their hesitation for what it was: confusion. They had come in expecting a battleground, and instead they had found a sick ward.

They kept coming, more of them flowing in all the time. Soon, there would be as many FBI agents present as there were volunteers.

Already, five men were running up the stairs to Adam's catwalk.

Adam raised his hands and slowly eased himself to the floor.

He was a very confident man. In any contested situation, things almost always went his way. At times, he felt as if he could bend reality to his will. But even he could see that his plans for a trip abroad were going to be on hold for a while.

It was over. All his precious specimens would be for naught.

Except, of course, for the dozen who had already escaped. Perhaps, he thought with a smile, they would be enough to spread the death.

CHAPTER THIRTY NINE

12:17 p.m.
United States Naval Observatory – Washington, DC

"The target is Los Angeles," Kurt Kimball said.

They were upstairs in Susan's study. Stone had just sent word that Michaela was alive and well. Susan had sunk into a leather high-backed chair. She took a deep breath. The sensation of relief was overwhelming, even more so than the sensation of giving birth to Michaela in the first place. It was if Michaela had died, then by some miracle had returned from the grave.

Susan enjoyed that feeling. It was one of almost limitless possibility. She rested in that feeling, but only for a moment. There was more to do.

There was always more to do.

"We raided all sixty-three venues," Kurt said. "Most hadn't seen any activity in a long time. In south Los Angeles, the FBI hit an old warehouse. The terrorists stocked more Ebola virus there. Eighty-four people were in the facility, receiving injections of Ebola when our people came in. They were like suicide bombers."

"They were going to walk around, infecting people?" Susan said.

Kimball nodded. "Walk around, yes. Share dirty needles, perform sex acts for money, contaminate things. Some had jobs as food workers in cafeterias and restaurants."

"Would it work?" Susan said.

She felt blank and hard, like a cinderblock wall. She had given the order to kill five thousand men today. Death from the skies. If another attack had taken place on American soil, she would have ordered the attack on Riyadh. It was an eye for an eye. If the Arabs lived by that rule, she would do the same.

"Yes. It would work very easily."

"Are we done? Is it over now?"

Kimball shook his head. "No. Apparently a van with a dozen volunteers had already left by the time the FBI arrived. They're infected, and they're going to be dropped off somewhere in the city."

"Find them," Susan said.

"We're looking," he said. "We know the van says 8th Street Baptist Church on the side. The LAPD has an all-points bulletin on it. The NSA is feeding them real-time satellite data on large, fifteen-passenger vans driving on city streets."

Susan stared at Kimball. All she wanted was to get on a plane, fly to California, and see her family. She gave a brief thought to the infected volunteers. They were like suicide bombers, but the bomb was a disease.

"God will have mercy on them," she said. "But we won't. Understood?"

Kimball nodded. "Understood."

"Do we need to close that city down?" she said.

Kimball looked at her. "Los Angeles?"

"Yes."

"How do you close down the city of Los Angeles? Millions of people. A gigantic international airport. The two largest commercial shipping ports in the United States. Heck, the sixth game of the NBA Finals is tonight. Los Angeles versus Cleveland. The Lakers are up three games to two."

For an instant, Susan was alarmed by that thought.

"Shouldn't we tell them to cancel it?"

Kimball shook his head. "How can we? The NBA Commissioner was on all the news stations this morning. He said that security at the game would be the tightest in history, but the National Basketball Association would not bend to terrorism. He's been trending on social media ever since. He's the most popular man in America right now."

"Is this junior high school?" Susan said. "Does being popular trump keeping people safe?"

Now Kurt smiled. "Susan, when I was at Rand, I followed your career for years. Senator, Vice President, you were one of the few who always kept what you were doing front and center. And what were you doing all that time? You were winning popularity contests. In fact, you were the most popular person in America on more than a few occasions. It won't hurt you to remember that."

"Thanks, Kurt. One more thing to worry about."

"Well," he said. "Strike the basketball game off your list. They'll be doing searches, including strip-searches of selected attendees. If they don't like it, they don't have to come in. Metal detectors. X-rays. No bags or containers of any kind. Infrared thermometers at all entrances. I doubt anybody's going to get in there infected by Ebola. If I thought there was a chance of it, I'd be on the phone to the commissioner right now."

"Are you going to watch it?" she said.

"I wouldn't miss it," Kurt said. "I love basketball."

CHAPTER FORTY

9:41 a.m. (12:41 p.m. Eastern Time)
Skid Row, Los Angeles, California

The dark fifteen-passenger van pulled to the curb near the corner of San Julian Street and East 6th Street. As church vans went, it was different from most. The windows were blackened, making it impossible to see inside.

8th Street Baptist Church said the white stenciled lettering along the side panels.

Another church group, come to save the lost souls.

All along the street, homeless people lounged on discarded furniture, or on the sidewalk, or on bundles of blankets, clothes and rags. Some stood around. A few were already drinking from bottles in brown paper bags. A line of encampments hugged the fencing that ran the length of the sidewalk. Blue and green tents, bright yellow and red tarps, shopping carts piled high with belongings, makeshift clotheslines hanging here and there, a wide backseat cannibalized from an old car.

On this street and the surrounding streets, thousands of homeless people lived—the largest concentrated population of unsheltered homeless people in the country. Skid Row was teeming with them, a mass of throw-away people, many of them engaged in work at the bottom of the economy—prostitution, drug dealing, selling blood plasma, petty violence for hire.

As the denizens of the neighborhood watched, the back door of the van burst open. A man climbed out and down. Then another. Then a woman. Then another man. They didn't look like church people. They looked like homeless people themselves. For a moment, they seemed confused, or perhaps dazzled by the bright sunlight.

A person who looked closely might notice they looked unwell. Eyes rimmed with red on one man. A hacking cough on two others. Pale skin. A woman with a nose bleed. These people were sick.

"Down!" someone screamed. "Down! Get down!"

The roar of high-powered engines filled the street. The homeless people knew what that sound meant.

Police.

Everywhere, people hit the deck. Women dove on top of their young children. People crawled into tents, or ducked behind ancient home furnishings.

The people from the van began to scatter and run.

From nowhere, police dressed in full riot gear appeared. They came running up San Julian. They came running around the corner from East 6th. Police cars and vans blocked the street.

"Down! On the ground!"

Then the shooting started.

The church people outside the van did a funny death dance, before falling to the street. The ones who tried to scatter were gunned down as they ran. The van itself rocked with the force of hundreds of rounds. The windows shattered. The tires popped, and the van sank to its knees.

A man named Kendrick stood with a forty-ounce bottle of malt liquor twenty yards away from the slaughter. He was a long-term resident of Skid Row, and he hadn't even attempted to get down. Not a single bullet hit him. That result was consistent with a long-held theory of his. He had an invisible shield around him. He was protected from harm by God.

A cop in full riot gear moved passed, gun trained on the writhing bodies sprawled on the ground.

"Don't go near them," the cop said. "They're infected."

"Damn," Kendrick said. "You people have no mercy. No mercy at all."

*

"What do you think?" Ed said.

Luke shook his head. "I don't believe it. It's too easy."

The Little Bird banked over the Skid Row carnage. Ed still manned his machine gun. Luke stood next to him at the open cargo door.

They had dropped Michaela back at the office with Trudy and Swann, then quickly jumped back into the air. Rachel and Jacob followed police radio calls as the cops closed in on the van. Then they swooped in with the chopper to watch the show.

For Luke, it was important on a few fronts. He had been fighting this battle since the beginning, and he wanted to see it end. He wanted that closure. Also, if any of the terrorists got away, the Little Bird could help find them, or maybe even gun them down.

203

Of course, the air above the scene was lousy with LAPD choppers, so the Little Bird wasn't really needed for that. It was more like a traffic jam up here than the wild blue yonder.

But there was something else, a nagging feeling...

"Even when something looks like it's over, it isn't," Luke said. "It's never over."

Ed stared at him.

"A very smart man told me that once."

"Yeah?" Ed said. "When was that?"

"Early this morning."

Luke stared down at the vast grid of city streets. Police cars, ambulances, first responders of all kinds were converging on the spot where the cops had just massacred the human Ebola bombs. The wail of sirens cut through the air, and flashing lights were everywhere.

"Rachel," Luke said. "We need to get Trudy and Swann on the horn."

"We're patched straight through to them now."

"Trudy?" Luke said.

"Hi, Luke."

For an instant, Trudy's deep feminine voice gave him a start. Things had been so rushed today, he nearly forgot... they'd had a night last night. They had worked together for years, and a lot had built up between them. Trudy had given him a welcome he wouldn't soon forget. And Becca? It was too much to think about right now. He needed some time off to sort out his personal life. Two days ago he was telling everyone he planned to retire.

"How's the kid?" he said. "Michaela."

"Good. She's having a peanut butter and jelly sandwich from the restaurant on the ground floor. There's a chopper coming to bring her out to her dad's place in Malibu."

Luke nodded. "Okay, that's great. But our work isn't done."

"Is it ever?" she said.

"We're flying over Skid Row right now. It's a mess down there. Bodies everywhere. Cops everywhere. Looks like they got the suicide team, but there's people running through alleys, probably just people with warrants, but we don't know if anyone's infected. It's been handled pretty badly. From here, I can see cops running around down there in street clothes. This whole area below us has to be locked down and quarantined. Just like yesterday. Let's say forty blocks by forty blocks. No one gets out, controlled entry only. Personal protection for all medical personnel. First responders sit in a containment zone for six hours before they go home. Starting now. Okay? Let's get it set up."

"Okay, Luke."

"Anybody gives you trouble, we call the President. She owes us a big one. Need to move anything large and the locals can't do it, call that admiral in Key West... Van Horn. He likes us and he seemed like he was on the ball."

"Got it," she said.

Luke looked at Ed again.

He mouthed the words without making a sound.

She loves you.

CHAPTER FORTY ONE

11:45 a.m. – Mountain Time
Aspen, Colorado

"Omar, the plane is ready. We are leaving here soon."

Omar sat on the back deck of his house, trying to enjoy the view of the surrounding mountains. Today it was difficult. Despite the opiate the Mexican doctor had given him, his hand ached and throbbed. Every beat of his heart seemed to send an exaggerated pulse through the middle of his wounded palm.

He had pulled his bandage away last night, only for a moment. The wound was red and raw and very swollen. The simple act of pulling the bandage away had made his palm bleed.

Omar was no stranger to the study of religion. It was a painful irony that a soldier of Muhammad would be afflicted with the stigmata of Christ. He tried to make sense of it, he tried to decipher its hidden meaning, but he couldn't do it.

"Is it possible this is all a mistake?" he said.

Ismail stared down at him. "In what way?"

Omar shook his head. "I don't know. That this is not reality. That we're merely dreaming, and when we awake, there will be a different outcome." He shrugged. "Maybe we've slipped into a parallel universe where the outcomes are all wrong. Anything is possible."

Ismail sighed. "Omar, please don't let people hear you say these things. It's apostasy. Some might consider your ideas punishable by death. In any case, no. What appears to have happened is what has actually happened. The attack was a failure. The abduction of the President's child was also a failure. Now the Americans are looking for you again. If we stay here, they will find you. If not today, then tomorrow, or the next day. But soon."

"Shall we go home?" Omar said. Under the influence of the painkiller drug, he felt like a child. He needed someone to guide him. His assistant could be that guide.

"No," Ismail said. "They're also looking for you there. The Americans are putting pressure on your cousin the King to surrender you. He's weak. If he finds you, he's likely to hand you over. As a matter of fact, I spoke with your beloved cousin early this morning. He asked me where you are."

"Did you tell him?"

"I told him," Ismail said, "that he will never find you. Indeed, I told him that no one will ever find you."

Omar took a deep breath. "Are we complete failures?"

Ismail smiled. "Not complete, no. We have one more trick up our sleeve. We may yet succeed in the attack. Call it a parting gift to our enemies."

Omar smiled in turn. "You're a genius of an assistant."

Ismail nodded. "Thank you."

"Shall we go to South America, then?" Omar said. "I like South America. I especially like Brazil. The women are incredible."

Ismail frowned now. He shook his head, but only a little. "Omar, besides my work as your assistant, do you understand who else I work for?"

Omar was puzzled by this question. He tried to think through the fog of the opiate. As far as he knew, Ismail was only his assistant. Everyone who worked for Omar, worked only for Omar. It was not a rule, per se. Call it an assumption.

"Who?" Omar said.

"Your cousin," Ismail said. "And our country's intelligence apparatus. I was sure you must have known this."

Omar shook his head. "I didn't."

Ismail slid a gun from inside his jacket. It had a long silencer attached to the end. Two of Omar's bodyguards stood nearby, but made no move. They simply stood impassively, hands clasped in front of their bodies.

"The King told me that when you were young, you were one of his favorites. Very exuberant. Everyone was delighted by you. But now? You must understand... there is a special relationship between the Kingdom and the United States. The relationship cannot be placed in jeopardy."

Ismail raised the gun and pointed it directly at Omar's face. Omar's heart skipped in his chest. Looking at the barrel of the gun was like looking into a deep, dark hole in the Earth, one that went down forever.

"Ismail..."

"I will count on you to accept my apology," Ismail said. "We all have our orders."

"I was a soldier for Allah," Omar said. "I was a prophet."

He glanced again at the bodyguards. It was almost as if they were somewhere else, at a long speech or formal event of state— somewhere very, very boring.

"Now you are a liability," Ismail said. "And the King wants to cut his losses."

Omar stared down into the black, black hole. It seemed that now would be a good time to take action, to run, to fight, to try anything at all. But he couldn't bring himself to stand. He had no feeling in his legs.

"Goodbye, my friend," Ismail said. "I will always cherish our time together."

A burst of flame erupted from deep inside that hole. It was blue and orange, and it seemed to lick the outer edge of the tunnel, like the tongue of a great beast.

It was the last thing Omar saw.

CHAPTER FORTY TWO

3:45 p.m.
United States Naval Observatory – Washington, DC

"He wants to do what?" Richard Monk said.

Susan sat behind the desk in her office. She felt calm, and good. She was with Richard and Kurt Kimball, wrapping up what seemed like a few loose ends. For the first time in days, no one was downstairs in the Situation Room. Susan had sent everyone home. It was time. The place smelled like a barn.

Michaela was at the Malibu house with her father and her sister, surrounded by dozens of Secret Service. Rare for Malibu, the house had quite a bit of empty land on either side of it, but even so, all of the houses within a mile had been forcibly evacuated.

There was going to be some screaming at the next Malibu town council meeting. Susan smiled at the thought.

"He wants to interrogate the prisoner," Kurt Kimball said. "The one who was in charge in the Los Angeles warehouse. The one who calls himself Adam."

"Tell him no," Richard said. "That's my vote."

Kurt shook his head. "I don't think you get a vote, Richard. I brought it up to ask Susan about it."

"Luke Stone is out of his mind," Richard said. "He's a valuable agent, I see that. But he's also completely insane. You should see his service record. Have you looked at it? I have. In normal circumstances, he shouldn't even be allowed in the same building with the President. He's a danger to himself and others."

Susan took a deep breath. For an instant, she felt like Mother Nature, refereeing between her sons Winter and Summer.

"Why does he want to interrogate the prisoner?" she said.

Kimball shrugged. His bald head gleamed under the overhead light. "He thinks there's going to be another attack. The FBI has been questioning Adam for hours, but he insists he has nothing more to give them. He's been demanding to see a lawyer."

Kimball cleared his throat. "Stone thinks he can get more information from him."

Richard threw his hands in the air. "He wants to torture him. Is that what you're saying? Stone is asking the President of the United States to hand over an important prisoner to him, so he can torture that prisoner. Susan, you can't do this."

For the time being, Susan ignored Richard. "What do we know about Adam?" she said.

Kurt looked at his tablet. "Basically? Nada. His fingerprints and DNA don't match anything we have on file. We're checking with Interpol, with Scotland Yard, with the Saudis, and with the Russians. So far, nothing. He's about thirty-five years old, appears to be of Mediterranean descent, and he speaks English fluently, but with a slight accent. The CIA has language experts listening to tapes of him being interviewed, to see if they can take a guess at his first language. No one believes he's a Saudi, if that's what you're wondering. The only reason we know he was in charge at the warehouse is because the other prisoners told us. In general, he's a complete enigma."

"Susan, the answer is no," Richard said.

She turned to him. "Excuse me?"

He folded his arms. "This is the United States. The answer is no. The man has been arrested. He has rights."

Susan had grown more than a little tired of Richard over the past few days. He seemed hell bent on clinging to ordinary rules at a time when ordinary rules no longer applied. He also seemed to have lost track of who worked for whom.

"Richard, would you have a million people die because we didn't do everything we could?"

"There's no evidence that scenario is even on the table. All the intelligence we have points to the idea that attacks are over."

Susan tried again. "If Luke Stone is concerned..."

"Luke Stone! Come off it, Susan. Luke Stone is good at some things, but thinking isn't one of them. He's a maniac! If you intend to hand a prisoner over to him a day after he shot a member of the Saudi royal family..."

Richard didn't seem prepared to finish his thought.

Susan turned to Kurt.

"Give the prisoner to Stone. Tell him I don't want anyone physically harmed."

"Physically..."

Susan nodded. "Correct."

"Susan!" Richard said.

She looked at him. His face had turned red. He looked like a cartoon drawing of a small child with steam coming out of his ears.

"Richard, it's been a very stressful week. I think you could use some time off. Why don't you take a couple of weeks?"

She wanted to give him an out, a way he could go away, blow off steam, and maybe even come back. A couple of weeks might give both of them some perspective. It was a different country right now. Maybe Richard was better suited to another task. Or maybe he would return refreshed, energetic, and ready to play hardball with the big boys.

Instead, he said:

"Make it a month."

"Let's try this," she said. "You just go and I'll call you when I need you."

"Done," he said. He walked out of the office, closing the door hard behind him. It was almost a slam, but not quite. Richard had been a good chief-of-staff for five years. But he wasn't tough. In the current environment, he was a liability. He couldn't even slam a door a hundred percent.

Susan felt a momentary pang at his exit, but within seconds, it started to fade. They would work it out, or they wouldn't.

She looked at big, bald Kurt Kimball again. He looked back at her with a new respect. She demanded that respect, she thought. She felt it for herself. She was a new person now. A stronger, much tougher person than she ever thought she could be.

"The prisoner," she said. "I thought you wanted to give him to Stone?"

"Yes. I do."

"So what are you waiting for?"

CHAPTER FORTY THREE

2:15 p.m. (5:15 p.m. Eastern Time)
Over the Pacific Ocean, near Los Angeles, California

"Do you know who I am?" Luke said.

The man called Adam was slightly overweight. He sat cross-legged on the floor of the Little Bird's tiny cargo hold as the chopper gained altitude. He wore a yellow and white Nike T-shirt and blue jeans. He had sandals on his feet. His head was covered by a black bag. His wrists were zip-tied behind his back.

Luke crouched near him. The man ignored the question, so Luke gave him a punch in the side of the head. The man's head jerked to the side.

"You call that a punch?" Ed said.

Luke looked up at Ed. Ed was still strapped in a standing position at his gun. It was either that or lie on the floor for him.

"I'd have you do it, but for obvious reasons that isn't possible right now."

Luke turned back to his prisoner. "Adam, I'm speaking to you. Do you know who I am? It's an important question."

"You aren't allowed to hit me," Adam said. "It's against the Geneva Conventions."

"Last I checked, we weren't in Geneva," Luke said. He pulled the heavy bag off of Adam's head. Adam's hair was mussed, standing up in weird tufts. His eyes squinted against the sudden bright light.

"Can you see me, Adam?"

The man nodded. "Yes."

"Can you see where we are?"

Adam glanced around. "We're in a helicopter, a small one."

"Do you know why?"

"They told me. I'm being transferred to another custody. From the FBI to… some other agency. I told them it was useless. I have said everything I can say. There is nothing more to tell."

"Do you know whose custody you're being transferred to?"

Adam stared into Luke's eyes. "Yours, I suppose."

Luke nodded. "Very good. And who am I?"

Adam's eyes were flat and emotionless. "A torturer. One who never learned the art of interrogation, and so tortures instead. You can torture me, of course, but it will do you no good."

212

Luke shook his head. He gave it an element of sadness. "Wrong. I'm not a torturer."

"Then who are you?"

Luke smiled. "There's another Ebola attack coming, isn't there?"

Now Adam smiled, but his smile was less certain. "I told the others everything. I am useless to you."

Luke took Adam's head in his hands and turned it toward the open bay door where Ed stood. Ed's body was all muscle. His face was all sharp cliffs and drop-offs. Behind him was nothing but wide blue sky, and the shadows of whirring chopper blades. They were very high now.

"You see that big man there? What sort of man does he look like? An interrogator? A torturer?"

Ed stared at Adam. He didn't smile. His body language was relaxed, but his eyes were somehow huge, white, and hard. There was no mercy in them, no sympathy, no emotion at all. Ed looked like a man who would take a break from eating lunch, snap someone's pencil neck, then go right back to eating.

"He looks like a killer," Adam said. His voice made a subtle change. A small amount of his confidence, or his ambivalence, had suddenly seeped away. It had been replaced by a note of concern. "A psychotic killer."

"He's a janitor," Luke said. "So am I. When something, such as yourself, becomes useless to our superiors, what do you suppose they call that something?"

Adam turned back to Luke. Something new was creeping into Adam's dark eyes. It was fear. Luke could see that Adam was starting to realize something. Adam was vulnerable. He could die just like anybody else.

"I don't know," he said.

Luke jabbed him sharply in the side of the head with two fingers. He raised his voice. "When things are useless, what do you call them?"

"I don't know."

Luke jabbed him again.

Adam squinted and jerked his head away. "I don't know!"

"Ed?" Luke said. "When things are useless, what do you call them?"

"Garbage," Ed said.

Luke smiled again. "Thank you. Useless things are known as garbage. Okay, Adam, now what do janitors do?"

Adam's face began to turn red. He closed his eyes. He tried to take a deep breath.

Luke jabbed him again, harder now. Adam flinched.

"What do janitors do, Adam?"

Adam's face became a grimace. A sudden earthquake moved through his body, then stopped. He was starting to break. He wasn't quite there, but Luke was just getting warmed up.

"Open your eyes, and I promise I won't hit you."

Adam slowly opened his eyes. His eyes were rimmed with water. He breathed rapidly now. He seemed like a man who couldn't catch his breath.

"You feel that pressure in your chest, Adam? Your heart is becoming constricted. Stress will do that to you. Don't have a heart attack, okay? I don't want you to miss this. I want you to experience every second of it."

Luke stared at his prisoner and counted to ten. Adam's breath slowed down a beat.

"Good. Very good. Now tell me, what do janitors do?"

Adam shook his head.

"Ed?"

"They take out the garbage."

A stray tear rolled down Adam's cheek. His jaw clenched.

Luke smiled again. "They take out the garbage. Of course that's what janitors do. Ed and I are janitors, and we take out the garbage. Useless things. We get rid of them. You weren't transferred, my friend. You were released. As far as the FBI knows, you left their custody, and then..."

Luke raised his two empty hands, palms upward.

"Who knows?" Ed said.

"Who knows where Adam went?" Luke said, and shook his head. "Nobody knows." He paused to let that sink in. "You're already dead. That's the unpleasant fact of the matter. Ed doesn't exist. I don't exist. And neither do you. Not anymore."

Luke directed his voice to the cockpit. "Guys, how high are we?"

Jacob's eerily calm voice: "About ten thousand and climbing."

"And how far out are we?"

"Oh, we're about eight miles from shore."

"Let's go to fifteen thousand feet, ten miles out, and call it good."

"Okay."

Luke turned back to Adam. Adam's face was doing all manner of strange things now. He looked like he had almost swallowed a tennis ball, but didn't quite manage it. His eyes were two big cow eyes.

"A man like you probably doesn't have many loved ones," Luke said. "That's good. Because you're going to hit that water at terminal velocity, and your body is going to come apart like it smashed into a brick wall. There's going to be so much blood it will bring sharks from forty miles away. In a couple of days, the leftovers will wash up on the shore, but they won't be anything someone would want to bury."

Luke stood up. He grabbed Adam by the shirt and hauled the heavy man to his feet. Adam offered no resistance at all. Luke walked him over to Ed. Ed grabbed the man by the back of the shirt.

Adam was shaking now. His whole body trembled.

"Don't kill me," he said. He paused for just a second. "Please."

"Adam, you can't kill what's already dead."

Ed pushed Adam gently but firmly to the edge of the cargo door. It was a long way down. Below them, the ocean water shimmered. The direction they faced, there was no land in sight. Adam's feet were right on the threshold. His hands were tied. Ed held him by the back of the shirt. Ed leaned Adam all the way out. Ed's strong hand was the only thing keeping Adam in the chopper, and the fabric of the shirt wouldn't hold forever.

"Goodbye, Adam," Luke said.

"Wait! I know things. I can tell you."

"He's useless," Ed said. "That's what he said a minute ago."

"No! I know things. I know about the final attack."

Ed shook his head. "He's lying."

"No! Wait!"

Luke raised his hand. "Ed, hold on one second."

He got right in Adam's face. "Adam, you're a liar, and I know that. Even so, I've been kind to you. What you have in front of you is an easy way to die. It's a long fall, but you'll pass out in a few seconds. By the time you hit, you won't even know it. But if I bring you back down to the ground, and I find out you lied to me again…"

215

"I won't. I won't lie. I'll tell you everything."

"He told the FBI everything," Ed said.

Adam shook his head frantically. "No, I lied to them. I held back."

"I'm going to tell you this one last time," Luke said. "This is an easy way to die. If you lie to me, you're going to die in a very unpleasant way. I will keep you alive for a month while I kill you. By the time two days pass, you won't be begging for your life. You'll be begging me to kill you. Do you understand?

Adam did the bobblehead nod. "Yes! Yes. I understand."

"Good," Luke said. "Now tell me what you know."

CHAPTER FORTY FOUR

4:47 p.m. (7:47 p.m. Eastern Time)
Staples Center Arena, Los Angeles, California

The arena was rocking.

Nearly 20,000 people filled the stands. In a few moments, the player introductions would begin.

The man moved along a narrow tunnel beneath the arena. The ceiling, and the white cinderblock walls around him, seemed to vibrate as above his head, raucous dance music played and thousands of people stamped their feet.

BOOM! BOOM! BOOM!

The man wore a backpack that held a metal canister. Inside the canister was a mixture of water, glycol, and a very dangerous virus. That was the fog juice. A hose ran from the canister to the fog cannon in his hands. When the fog juice heated, and he opened the valve on the canister, he could spray a thick aerosol vapor into the air. The fans loved to see their favorite players run out through the fog.

He had worked here for long years. He knew this facility like he knew his own home, and he knew what the scene upstairs was like. He did not have to see it to know. He could picture it from memory.

The arena was dark. The lights were out. Soon, flashing multi-colored strobes would shine to the ceiling. A spotlight would appear. The music would play and the drums would pound. And the starting players of the opposing team would walk out into the spotlight, a haze of fog lit up in blue and green behind.

The fog would come from a large machine at the end of the court. Not this machine the man was carrying, though. This machine was a cannon. It was meant for a different kind of fog spraying.

The arena would become quiet. But there would be the swell of anticipation.

A voice would come on. "And now... your Los Angeles Lakers!"

The crowd would go berserk. The music would become louder than ever. The drums would shake the very air.

And as the players took the court, a man would appear in the darkness, away from the spotlight. He would have a fog machine strapped to his back. He would run up and down the edge of the court, firing his fog cannon.

It would seem almost normal, of course. Maybe the fog cannon was more appropriate for a rock concert, but hey, basketball was just another form of entertainment, wasn't it? And the fog was just another part of the show. It was part of the tremendous excitement. The music… the lights… the great athletes… the fog.

He nodded to himself. It would all seem perfectly normal at first, and then it would begin to seem strange.

He would spray the very rich people at courtside, who had paid thousands of dollars each for their tickets. He would spray the less rich people three and five and ten rows deep. He would spray the players and the coaches. He would spray all the VIPS and the visiting dignitaries. He would spray the courtside announcers and the food vendors alike.

And he would get sprayed a little himself too, wouldn't he?

Yes, he would. That was okay. It was good and it was right. He would die surrounded by his enemies, as he had dreamed of doing since he was a young man. Perhaps a panic would set in, and there would be a terrified stampede to exit the stadium. Or maybe everyone would remain docile, the game would begin, and only after a little while, as people became sick, would anyone realize what was happening.

The man would be interested to see.

As he reached the stairwell that lead upstairs to the arena floor, he felt a nervous tickle in his stomach. The stairwell was darkened. Shadows played on the walls.

He was the last one left. He knew that. The mission depended on him. Everything, the whole world, was counting on one solitary man. He had tried to pray about it earlier today, but he found himself without words. He asked for guidance and for courage. He asked for the strength to shoulder the burden. It was the best he could do.

Above his head, he could hear the opposing team's introductions beginning.

"… Cleveland Cavaliers!"

A roar greeted this name. The man couldn't tell if it was a roar of approval or one of derision.

A black man in a wheelchair rolled out of the darkness. He was a very big man, very muscular. He reminded the fog spraying man of people who lose the use of their legs, perhaps in a war, and then build immensely strong upper bodies and become wheelchair racers. The wheelchair man blocked the path between the fog spraying man and the staircase.

"Hey," the wheelchair-bound man said. "What are you doing here?"

"I work here," the man said. "I am wanted upstairs in just a few moments."

The black man gestured with his head. "What do you have in that tank?"

"Fog. For the pregame introductions."

"You got a virus in there? I mean, mixed in with the fog?"

"A virus?" the fog man said. "Why would I have a virus?"

"Because you're a terrorist," the black man said. "And you want to kill a lot of innocent people."

The fog man had a moment when he could not understand what the other man was saying to him. It was impossible that anyone could know what he was doing. He was simply a long-time employee of the arena. The only person who knew anything else about him was a man named...

"Adam sent me," the black man said.

The fog man's hand strayed to the trigger on the fog cannon. He removed the safety locking device. He could fire the cannon here in the stairwell. It would not be as good as firing it upstairs in the arena. It would not be nearly as good.

"Back away or I'll kill us both," he said.

"No you won't," the black man.

"Yes, I will." He didn't want to spray it here. He wanted to make his way past this big strange man and his wheelchair.

The black man shook his head. "No. I know you won't do it."

The fog man was curious enough to ask. Perhaps he could play this riddle game for thirty seconds, and somehow bluff his way past. He would still make it to his destination in time.

"How do you know that?"

"Because you'll already be dead," another voice said.

The fog man turned to his right. A blond-haired man with red, bloodshot eyes stood there. They were the kind of eyes that hadn't slept in days. The face itself betrayed no emotion, and certainly no mercy.

The man held a gun with a silencer attachment. He held it pointed directly at the fog man's face.

The fog man only had time for one thought.

He didn't think of how his finger caressed the trigger on his fog cannon.

He didn't think of the family he had left behind more than ten years ago.

He didn't think of waking up in paradise.

He thought: "No!"

*

"Would you say that was cold-blooded?" Luke said.

He stared at the body on the concrete floor of the stairwell. The smell of gunpowder rose in the confined space. Luke stepped well away from the pool of blood spreading around the ruined head, in case the man had already infected himself with the virus.

Ed sucked his teeth. "I'd say he was going to try and kill thousands of people. I'd say that failing that, he was ready to spray us both down with Ebola as a consolation prize. With those two things in mind... no, not cold-blooded. What else were you supposed to do? Arrest him?"

"I don't know, man," Luke said. "It's been a long couple of days. Sometimes I get tired of killing. Ever feel that way?"

Ed shook his head. "Luke, I get tired of innocent people dying. Like all those people in Charleston." He gestured at the man on the ground.

"This guy... nah."

Above their heads, thousands of people pounded their feet again.

BOOM, BOOM, BOOM, BOOM...

And thousands of people started screaming, not in terror—but in delight.

CHAPTER FORTY FIVE

June 14th
9:15 a.m.
Arlington National Cemetery, Arlington, Virginia

Row upon row of white gravestones, thousands of them, climbed the green hills into the distance.

Six young Army Rangers carried the casket, draped in the American flag, to the open gravesite. Luke recognized three of them—they were the remains of his B team that dropped onto Omar bin Khalid's yacht three days before. They carried their friend Charlie Something to his final resting place.

The boys looked sharp in their dress greens and their tan berets, but they also looked young. Too young. Not for the first time, Luke marveled at their youth. Their faces were hard with the pain of loss.

Just to his right, Gunner, wearing his dark blue suit, saluted the casket as it passed.

A three-man team of riflemen fired a volley into the air. Then another. Then another. Behind them, perhaps thirty yards away, a lone bugler played taps.

Fifty servicemen stood in formation near the grave. Perhaps another hundred people, most of them young, fanned out on the grass. They looked just like high school kids. Sommelier had only graduated last year.

Near the front was a row of white folding chairs. A middle-aged woman dressed in black was comforted by another woman. Near her, an honor guard made up of three Rangers, two Marines, and an Airman carefully took the flag from the casket and folded it. One of the Rangers lowered to one knee in front of the grieving woman, and presented the flag to her.

Luke and Gunner were close enough to hear what the Ranger said. In Luke's mind, it was important for Gunner to hear what was said.

"On behalf of the President of the United States," the young Ranger said, his voice breaking, "the United States Army, and a grateful nation, please accept this flag as a symbol of our appreciation for your son's honorable and faithful service."

Luke took a deep breath. He had been to too many military funerals in his time. He had been to too many funerals period. He had seen too many dead people.

When it was over, he and Gunner held hands and walked the hilly grounds. After a short time they found themselves at the John F. Kennedy gravesite. They stood for a moment at the edge of the two-hundred-year-old flagstones and watched the fire of the eternal flame.

"Who is this?" Gunner said.

"Well, this is the memorial for John F. Kennedy. His wife is also buried here, and his brothers Robert and Edward."

"John F. Kennedy was the President, wasn't he, Dad?"

"Yes, he was."

"Did you work for him like you work for the new President?"

Luke shook his head. "President Kennedy died before I was born."

Gunner seemed to think about that. A time before his dad was born? That must have been a long time ago.

Luke's eye wandered to the low granite wall at the edge of the memorial. Just above the wall, he could see the Washington Monument across the river. The wall itself had numerous inscriptions taken from Kennedy's inaugural address. Among several more famous lines from the speech, Luke kept returning to one section in particular:

LET EVERY NATION KNOW
WHETHER IT WISHES US WELL OR ILL
THAT WE SHALL PAY ANY PRICE
BEAR ANY BURDEN
MEET ANY HARDSHIP
SUPPORT ANY FRIEND
OPPOSE ANY FOE
TO ASSURE THE SURVIVAL
AND THE SUCCESS OF LIBERTY

Luke stared at those words until he felt a sharp tug on his hand.

"Dad?" Gunner said.

"Yes?"

"Do you want to go fishing with me today?"

Luke smiled.

"Yeah, monster," he said. "More than anything."

CHAPTER FORTY SIX

7:45 p.m.
The Capital Grille, Washington, DC

"How's your steak?" Ed said.

The restaurant glimmered with wealth. DC power brokers huddled up in booths along the walls. Waiters in black vests hustled to and fro. Luke was surprised to see so many people out. The city was still under heightened security. Men in hazmat suits manned the streets corners, taking the temperatures of passersby with infrared thermometers, and watched over by squads of National Guard from four states.

Life went on, he supposed.

Luke and Ed sat at a round table for four with a white tablecloth and a small lamp in the middle of it. They had a bottle of wine and two fat steaks in front of them. Luke looked up at a large photograph of Jimi Hendrix on the wall. Ed's crutches leaned against the table.

"It's good," Luke said. "Really good." He didn't have the heart to tell Ed that he was more of a ninety-nine-percent-fat-free chicken kind of guy.

"I love it here," Ed said. "It's great food."

"You eat a lot of steak?" Luke said.

Ed smiled. "You kidding? I eat steak and eggs for breakfast."

Luke took a swig of his wine. He chewed on a lump of meat and some garlic mashed potatoes. He had to admit the food was good. It was thick and heavy and good.

Ed was drinking tonight. He was talking more than Luke was accustomed to.

"How's the wife?" Ed asked.

Luke shrugged. "She let me take my son out today. That's a start."

Ed's eyes had a devilish glint. "And Trudy?"

"I called her yesterday. I told her if they really break up the Special Response Team, she can probably write her own ticket. I'll give her the highest recommendation, tell anyone and everyone there's nothing to this whole Don Morris thing."

Ed shook his head. "Not exactly what I'm talking about."

Luke didn't like where this was going.

"That other thing?" Luke said. "She told me it was a mistake. I agreed with her."

"She said she loved you. That's what I heard right before you jumped out of the chopper."

Luke nodded. "She said she meant that part. She loves me like a brother, the brother she never had."

Ed nodded. "Uh-huh." He took another sip of his wine. It looked like blood in his glass. "You think they're going to break up the Special Response Team? For real?"

"I'm not sure if I care," Luke said. "I've been talking about retiring a lot. Maybe it's time. I'm toying with teaching college."

Ed smiled. "I think you'll make a lousy college professor."

Just then, Luke's phone started to ring. It was on the table in front of him. He had it on ringer and vibrate at the same time. On each ring, the phone shook and moved a quarter of an inch along the table.

Luke looked at it. He saw the number on the screen and his gut twisted.

It was the President.

"You going to answer that?" Ed said. "Or you want me to?"

He stared across the table at Ed.

"It's her."

Ed shrugged. He shoved a thick chunk of steak into his mouth. "Who else?"

A moment passed, and it continued to buzz. What could it be now, Luke wondered? A congratulations? Another crisis?

This time, he didn't want to know. It was time to live his life again. He'd earned it.

Luke reached out and placed the phone face down on the table. Then, before it could buzz again, he powered it off.

Ed smiled back at him.

"More wine?" he asked, gesturing to the waiter.

This time, Luke smiled back.

"More wine," he replied.

TO BE PUBLISHED JUNE, 2016!

SITUATION ROOM
(A Luke Stone Thriller—Book #3)

SITUATION ROOM is book #3 in the bestselling Luke Stone thriller series, which begins with ANY MEANS NECESSARY (book #1), a free download with over 60 five star reviews!

A cyberattack on an obscure U.S. dam leaves thousands dead and the government wondering who attacked it, and why. When they realize it is just the tip of the iceberg—and that the safety of all of America is at stake—the President has no choice but to call in Luke Stone.

Head of an elite, disbanded FBI team, Luke does not want the job. But with new enemies—foreign and domestic—closing in on her from all sides, the President can only trust him. What follows is an action-packed international roller-coaster, as Luke learns that the terrorists are more sophisticated than anyone realizes, that the target is more extensive than anyone could image—and that there is very little time left to save America.

A political thriller with non-stop action, dramatic international settings, unexpected twists and heart-pounding suspense, SITUATION ROOM is book #3 in the Luke Stone series, an explosive new series that will leave you turning pages late into the night.

Book #4 in the Luke Stone series will be available soon.

BOOKS BY JACK MARS

LUKE STONE THRILLER SERIES

ANY MEANS NECESSARY (Book #1)
OATH OF OFFICE (Book #2)
SITUATION ROOM (Book #3)

Jack Mars

Jack Mars is author of the bestselling LUKE STONE thriller series, which include the suspense thrillers ANY MEANS NECESSARY (book #1), OATH OF OFFICE (book #2) and SITUATION ROOM (book #3).

Jack loves to hear from you, so please feel free to visit www.Jackmarsauthor.com to join the email list, receive a free book, receive free giveaways, connect on Facebook and Twitter, and stay in touch!

CPSIA information can be obtained at www.ICGtesting.com
Printed in the USA
BVOW05*0827091016

464554BV00014B/63/P

9 781632 916198